MW00987166

Trina Bahati

My First

Kiss

Isla Drake

Isla Drake

Copyright © 2023 by Isla Drake

All rights reserved.

No portion of this book may be reproduced in any form without written permission from the publisher or author, except as permitted by U.S. copyright law.

This one's for all the good girls.

CHAPTER 0.5

Hi! Glad you're here. There are some things to note about this book before you get started.

Possible spoilery things ahead.

This book is an adult romantic comedy set in a small town in southern Georgia. It's low angst and everyone will have a happily ever after at the end. Despite that, there are still some things in this book that may upset some readers. I've done my best to compile a detailed list of those things, so no one is blindsided.

Here it is:

Mentions of parental death

Mentions of parental abandonment

Mentions of cancer/cancer treatment

Mentions of past cheating (not between the main characters)

Single parenthood

Detailed, on-page, consensual adult content (If you know what I mean)

Dominant behavior during adult content

Edging

Foul language

Alcohol consumption

Childhood bullying/fighting

Classism

Enjoy!

CHAPTER 1

Harlow

"I'm telling you, Piper," I say, lowering my empty glass to the table. "I'm serious this time. I'm done with men. They all suck."

Piper laughs, but then she shrugs, looking at the diamond ring flashing on her left hand. "I don't know," she says. "Some of them are okay."

I roll my eyes at her because it's obvious she's been blinded by love and great sex. And maybe by that shiny diamond on her finger.

"You found the last decent man in Georgia," I say, referring to Luke Wolfe, the man who put that diamond on her finger and the smile on her face. "The rest are trash."

Piper laughs again. We both know I don't really believe all men are trash. But when you've been let down by as many men as I have in the past few years, it starts to feel like they're all the same. But I've seen the way Luke treats Piper, so I know good men are out there. It just sometimes feels like all the good guys are either taken or fictional.

Piper and Luke haven't even been dating for a year, but it's clear those two are head-over-heels in love. I wasn't surprised in the least when Piper showed up at my salon last week sporting the gorgeous ring on her left hand. I'd gushed over the rock while she'd told me the romantic story of how Luke had proposed. It really is a beautiful ring, and Luke is an amazing guy. But that isn't enough to convince me not to give up on the dating game. I'm sick of wasting my time getting to know some guy and believing he's different, only to find out I'm wrong again and he's another loser. No, thank you. I'm over it.

"You ever think that maybe you've been looking in the wrong place?" Piper's sister Layna chimes in from her seat across from me.

I scoff. "I shouldn't have to go on some kind of epic quest to find a good man. I'm not searching for lost treasure here. I'm just looking for a decent guy who won't cheat on me or steal from me. A guy who will occasionally hold open the door for me and let me use the only umbrella when it's raining. One who remembers to put the damned toilet seat down, so I don't fall in when I get up to pee in the middle of the night! It's literally the bare minimum. It's not rocket science."

We all laugh, but I'm not completely joking. My list of items for what constitutes a decent man has gotten smaller over the past few years. I don't think I'm asking for much, but it seems like I have a knack for finding losers, liars, and cheaters. The last two guys I dated both cheated on me. The guy before that stole my TV before he left. What kind of person steals someone's TV during a break-up? A loser. That's what kind. Which brings me back to being done with men.

I refill my glass from the pitcher of margaritas in the center of the table and take a large sip. I'd insisted on this girl's night out with Piper after the most recent loser broke things off via text. I'm not really all that upset over him ending things. It's not like we were soulmates or anything. But when a guy who couch-surfs his way across the county and can't keep a job dumps you, your pride takes a hit. I can't even hang on to a guy who doesn't have a place to stay or steady employment? What's wrong with me?

That's why I'd called Piper to come out with me. I hadn't wanted to be alone with my own self-pitying thoughts. It turns out that Layna had shown up for a surprise visit and the two of them had been looking for something to do. Now, we're all out at Peach Tree's most popular bar and grill, Peach Fuzz, drinking margaritas and munching on loaded fries.

"So, Layna," I say, glancing over to the woman seated across from me. "How's Atlanta?"

She shrugs and sips her drink. "Same city, different day," she says, not looking up from the tabletop.

It's easy to see that she doesn't want to talk about Atlanta. Maybe she's having issues at work. I don't know, but I'm not going to pry. I don't know her well enough to dig into her personal life. If she wanted to talk about it, she would. I turn to Piper, intending to change the subject, but I notice she's studying her sister. It's clear she has no qualms about interrogating Layna on her life because she turns to face her fully.

"Spill it," Piper says. "What happened?"

Layna rolls her eyes and shakes her head, but I notice she doesn't meet Piper's gaze. "Nothing," she says. "I just wanted to come see you."

"You came to see me 2 weeks ago," Piper says. "Not that I'm not happy you're here. I am. But that's a lot quicker than our usual time between visits. So, I ask you again: What happened?"

Layna blows out a sigh. "I quit my job," she says.

"What?!" Piper's shout draws the eyes of a few nearby patrons, but she ignores them, focusing all her attention on her sister. "You can't just quit your job."

Layna shrugs. "Well, I did."

Piper stares at Layna, her mouth opening and closing as if she can't decide what to say. Eventually, she settles on, "Why?"

Layna takes a big sip of her drink before shooting her sister a bright smile that looks anything but happy. "I realized how much I hate that job and everyone at that company. It was making me miserable. So, I made a list of pros and cons. When the cons outweighed the pros, I just said, 'fuck it,' and quit."

"A list?" Piper blinks at her sister.

Layna nods. "Yep."

Fishing around in her purse, she produces a folded sheet of notebook paper and hands it to Piper.

"Right here."

Piper takes the paper from her sister and unfolds it to read what's written on it. It takes her only a second to shoot her sister another look of disbelief.

"This isn't a list," she says. "A list has more than one thing on it."

Layna shrugs again. "Just proves I made the right choice."

I reach over and take the paper from Piper's hand to read it. Under the 'Pro' column, there's one item written in neat, swirling cursive. It just says, "pays well." The list of cons is significantly longer, filling line after line with everything from "boring" to "soul-sucking" to "too far from Piper". I can't help but smile as I hand the list back to Layna.

Everything I know about the other woman says she's not the impulsive type. Neither of the Brooks sisters are. They're both logical and methodical, thinking through a plan before acting on it. But this? This reminds me of something I would have done. Hell, I did something like this when I left Atlanta to come back to Peach Tree. While it had been a difficult transition and I know having a plan would have made my life easier, I can't help but approve of Layna's spontaneity.

"To a fresh start," I say, smiling as I raise my margarita.

Layna gives me a relieved smile while Piper casts me a disapproving frown. But she raises her glass along with us. After we all clink our glasses and take a sip, Piper turns back to her sister.

"You can stay with me and Luke until you figure out what you're going to do next," she says.

Layna starts shaking her head before Piper can finish her sentence. "Thanks for the offer, but there's no way I'm crashing the newly engaged couple's house. I'm not cock blocking you."

"You're my sister," Piper says through her laughter. "You wouldn't be crashing. Besides, I'm inviting you. That's the opposite of crashing."

"I'll stay tonight," Layna says. "But tomorrow, I'll be looking for my own place."

"Are you moving here permanently, then?" I ask.

Layna hesitates, taking a deep breath and blowing it out before speaking. "Yeah," she nods. "I am. I want to be closer to my sister. And once I sell my condo in Atlanta, I'll have more than enough money to find a place here."

"Are you serious?" Piper squeals, hugging her sister.

Layna laughs, nodding. "Yes!"

I can't help but smile at the two of them. I grew up an only child, so I never had the closeness that comes with having siblings. I always wanted it, though. Having Piper as a friend these past few months has been as close as I've ever come to having a sister.

"What about work?" Piper asks, sobering a little. "Not much call for corporate lawyers in this little town."

Layna shrugs. "I've been thinking about a career change. There's more to being a lawyer than corporate. I've got options."

I nod. "If nothing else, maybe one of my exes can hire you to defend him."

We all laugh, but I'm not entirely joking.

"I'll figure something out," Layna says once the laughter dies down. "I have time."

"You can stay with me," I say, shrugging. When she looks hesitant, I roll my eyes. "There's definitely no cock to block where I'm concerned. I've taken a vow of celibacy since the last asshole left, remember?"

The girls both laugh but I roll my eyes.

"Shut up. I'm taking a break from men. They're too much trouble and I'm sick of the bullshit. I can get myself off with far less trouble. I just need to figure out what to do with all his shit."

"What shit?" Piper asks.

I wave a dismissive hand. "Tools. I don't know. A bunch of random shit he left behind. It's all just sitting in the hallway by the front door. I haven't had time to get rid of it."

"Sell it online," Layna suggests.

Piper shrugs. "It could be worth something."

I shake my head. "That's too much effort. I'd rather just donate it."

Layna leans toward me across the table and points at me as if to emphasize her words. "You already donated your time and energy trying to domesticate that asshole. You should get paid for that. If he's not coming to get his crap, sell it."

Her vehemence makes me laugh. I don't know Layna as well as I do Piper, but I think she and I are going to get along just fine.

"Besides," Piper says, "Didn't you loan him the money to buy that stuff?"

I wince in embarrassment at the reminder that yes, I had helped him buy those tools. I feel my anger rise up all over again when I think of Derek the cheater. Who does he think he is? Why the hell shouldn't I sell his crap?

"Maybe I will sell it," I say, raising my glass to my lips for another drink. "Someone owes me for all the time I spent babysitting him."

Layna laughs. "Hopefully it wasn't all bad. Was he at least good in bed?"

I roll my eyes as I remember the few times I'd slept with him. I wasn't impressed. "Hardly," I say. "How do I say this in a diplomatic way?" I think it over for a few seconds. "He had excellent equipment, but he lacked the skill or initiative to utilize it to its full potential."

Layna shakes her head and Piper laughs. "Damn shame," Layna says. "Why do all the hot, well-hung guys act like they're too good to learn how to use their gifts?"

"You don't hear me complaining," Piper mutters from behind her margarita glass.

Her face goes red as we all erupt into laughter that goes on for far longer than it should. Piper isn't usually the one to make dirty jokes. That's usually my job. That, coupled with the alcohol probably explains why we're all laughing so hard.

"Lucky bitch," I say through my laughter.

"Am I allowed to hear the joke?" A male voice breaks in, causing us all to go quiet.

I feel an immediate thrill at the deep, familiar tone. Heat spreads through me, starting low in my belly and working its way up. I work hard to school my features into something neutral before turning to face him. Lincoln Prescott.

Linc.

Damn it. He looks hot. Of course, he does. He always looks hot. His long, dark hair is pulled back from his face in a ponytail and he's wearing a dark green T-shirt that hugs his broad shoulders along with a pair of jeans that fit him so well it should be illegal. I'm not sure how one man manages to make jeans and a t-shirt look so damned hot, but Linc somehow pulls it off.

I say a silent prayer of thanks that I put maximum effort into my hair and makeup tonight. Not that it matters, because I'm not trying to impress Linc. Or any man, for that matter. All at once, I realize that everyone is looking to me to answer Linc's question. Flustered, I shake my head and wave a hand in dismissal.

"Just an inside joke," I say, hoping the girls won't elaborate. The last thing I want is to discuss my past relationships with Linc. The very idea of it makes me slightly nauseated. I don't realize that Linc's not alone until I spot his brother, Cole standing behind him. Cole gives us all a smile of greeting.

"Ladies," he says, flashing his winning dimples for all to see. "I trust you're having a nice night out?"

Cole is the owner of the Peach Fuzz and he and Linc are best friends with Piper's fiancé. Before Piper and I became friends, I could count on one hand the number of times I'd come to this bar. But now, it seems like we're here every other week. Which means that I've run into Linc more in the past few months than I did in the 10 years since we graduated high school. It's not that I have anything against this place. It's just that I've done my best to avoid situations where I might run into people from high school, and Peach Fuzz is a prime example of one of those places.

I've known Linc since we were 10 years old, when he and his family first moved to Peach Tree. I vividly remember all the buzz surrounding a new kid at school. In a town as small as ours, it was a big deal when someone new moved to town. Linc had been my first crush. But then, he'd been the crush of all the girls in Miss Holcomb's fourth grade class. He'd been quiet and serious, especially for a ten-year-old boy. Compared to the other boys in our school, Linc had seemed so mysterious. But he'd also been kind.

He'd become popular immediately and that popularity had followed him all the way through high school. It helped that he was good at football and was ridiculously hot. He'd been prom king two years in a row, even though juniors technically weren't allowed to hold the title. As for me, I'd gone alone to prom since no one wanted to ask the dorky band nerd with the frizzy hair to be their date. By the time he left for college on a football scholarship, and I left for Atlanta, I'd known him for nearly a decade. And we'd never had a single conversation. I remember being shocked when he'd greeted me by name the first time we all hung out together at Peach Fuzz last year. Until that moment, I'd been almost convinced he didn't know my name.

Since that night, the five of us—six, if Layna was in town—have hung out more frequently. Linc doesn't usually stay as long as the others. He needs to get home to his daughter, Ella. I don't know the story there, but I know he dropped out of college when she was born and has spent the time since raising her. I don't know where the girl's mother is, but he's never mentioned her, and I don't feel comfortable asking about her. What if she died and he's spent all these years mourning her? I don't think I want to hear about the great love of Lincoln Prescott's life. And that probably makes me a horrible person, right?

Piper invites the guys to join us. I have a half a minute to hope they'll refuse before Cole smiles and accepts the invite. I do my best to pretend I'm oblivious to

Linc's closeness as he takes the empty spot beside me on the booth seat. I risk a quick glance in his direction and smile, avoiding eye contact. He's not saying much, letting the others carry the conversation. He does that a lot, it seems. I get the feeling he's the type of guy who doesn't speak to fill the silence, but instead waits until he has something worth saying. I admire that. Silence has never been my strong suit. I'm more the type of person to blurt out whatever random thought pops into my head, consequences be damned. It's been my downfall on more than one occasion, unfortunately.

Cole orders another round of drinks as everyone chats, catching up on one another's lives since we last hung out. There isn't much to report on my end unless I want to tell them about my most recent cheating ex, which I most definitely do not. Linc talks a little about his new business. He recently became a licensed contractor, and his business is growing in the area. Cole brags about his brother, but I notice that Linc still doesn't say a lot. He's so close to me that I can practically feel the heat of his large body radiating out toward me. I want to lean into it, into him. I want to climb into his lap if I'm being completely honest with myself. But I have a feeling that won't go over well, especially since he seems to be avoiding looking in my direction or speaking to me at all.

"How long are you in town, Layna?" Cole asks as he hands out a fresh round of drinks, pulling me away from my Linc obsession.

"She's moving here," Piper says, bouncing in her seat a little.

"Really?" Cole says, turning to look at Layna. "I didn't know that was your plan."

She shrugs. "It wasn't at first. It's a recent decision."

"An impulsive decision, you mean," Piper grumbles.

Layna rolls her eyes. "Maybe so, but I stand by it. It's going to be great, Pipes. Just wait."

Piper grins at her sister. "I'm happy you're going to be living closer to me. I'm just surprised at the suddenness. That's all."

"What did I miss?"

We all look up to see Luke standing next to the table, smiling down at Piper. I shoot her a look through narrowed eyes.

"Did you invite a boy to girl's night?"

Piper's face goes red, and she points at Linc and Cole accusingly. "They're here!"

"That's different," I say. "We didn't invite them. They just showed up."

"Hey," Cole says, feigning hurt. "We're right here. We can hear you."

I roll my eyes at him, making Linc laugh. The sound of that rumbling laugh hits me hard and I feel a flutter low in my belly. I suck in a slow breath to calm my suddenly racing heart. I need to get a grip. It was just a laugh. It's not like he reached up my skirt or something. Ah, shit. Now I'm thinking about him reaching up my skirt. I risk a glance at his hand resting on the leather seat between us. I picture his long, thick fingers sliding up my inner thigh, pushing my skirt up as it moves higher. My breathing becomes shallow, and I swallow hard.

Stop being a slut. Stop being a slut. Stop being a slut.

I chant the words over and over in my head until I can stop thinking filthy thoughts about the man seated beside me.

"Next round of drinks is on the guys," Layna shouts, forcefully yanking me from my dirty thoughts. "Since they crashed our girl's night out."

Luke kisses Piper's cheek. "My pleasure," he says in a voice that I'm pretty sure he meant for her ears only.

I try to ignore the slight twinge of jealousy I feel. Not that I'm into my best friend's fiancé. Jealousy is probably the wrong word. Envy might be more appropriate. I envy their relationship. I envy Piper's certainty and trust that it will last. I've never felt that. These days I'm starting to doubt I ever will. Cole says something that makes everyone at the table laugh, pulling me out of my melancholia. I hear Linc's deep, rumbling laugh from beside me and that flutter hits me again. This time though, I do my best to ignore it. Nothing good ever came from pining over Lincoln Prescott. I'm not going to start doing it again now.

By the time we all decide to call it a night and I head back to my apartment above my salon, I'm tired and ready for my pajamas. I check the time. It's barely 10pm. On a Friday night. I suddenly feel ancient. When did I become this person who's home and in her pajamas by 10:00 on a weekend?

"When you realized how much hangovers suck," I mutter to my empty bedroom as I toss my bra in the direction of the dresser.

I let out a sigh of relief at the feeling of freedom. I don't care how hot my tits look in that pushup bra; the feeling of taking it off will always outweigh the few hours of sexy cleavage and male attention. Pulling on a baggy t-shirt, I fill a glass of water in the kitchen before going to the living room to plop down on the couch. I debate turning on the television and rewatching The Office for the millionth time, but I'm not feeling it tonight. My eyes stray over to the pile of tools near the front door, and I remember Layna's advice to sell them online.

"I wonder what you're worth," I whisper.

On my phone, I do a quick search for the town's buy/sell/trade site and find it quickly. Within a few minutes, I've created an account and I'm ready to post an ad. Easy enough. I snap a few well-lit photos of the tools and start typing.

"Cheating ex-boyfriend abandoned his tools and refuses to retrieve them. His loss is your gain. I'm sure they're in new condition, as he couldn't seem to keep a job for more than a week."

Smiling, I finish up and click the button to submit the ad for approval. Hopefully someone with a sense of humor and a need for tools sees the ad and jumps on it. I'm ready to be rid of Derek the cheater, once and for all.

CHAPTER 2

Linc

Ella's already asleep when I get home from Peach Fuzz. I wave goodbye to the babysitter before making my way upstairs to check on her. Opening her door just far enough to make out her sleeping form, I smile at the sight of her. She looks so small in her too-big bed, surrounded by stuffed animals and more pillows than any kid should need. Seeing her like this almost makes me forget how loud and full of energy she can be when she's awake. Silently, I close the door and make my way down the hall to my own room to change into a pair of gym shorts.

The house is too quiet with Ella sleeping and Cole not home. It's one of those things I try not to pay attention to most of the time. But tonight, it's impossible not to notice just how empty the house is. It's also impossible not to admit to myself just how lonely I am. It's why Cole made me go out tonight. He thinks I need to get out of the house more and interact with people.

Living in such a small town means that most of the time I can predict exactly who I'll see when I go out on a Friday night. It's usually the same people I see at the grocery store or the coffee shop. Meaning, it's anyone from my graduating class who didn't move away, get arrested or die already. Some people might find that kind of life boring or too predictable, but there's something comforting about the familiarity. Though it's much harder to meet someone new when everyone has known you since you were 10 years old. Not that I'm trying to meet anyone. That's just what Cole wants.

He keeps encouraging me to make an online dating profile. Since Luke technically met his fiancé Piper on one of those sites, Cole thinks it could work for me. I keep telling him that I'm not looking for a serious relationship, but he's convinced I'd be happier as part of a couple. I'm not sure when my perpetually single little brother decided to become such a romantic, but it's downright weird.

"Ella needs a mom," he'd told me yesterday morning after Ella had climbed on the bus for school.

I rolled my eyes. "Ella is doing just fine with me and you."

"Yeah, she is," he agreed. "But we both know that she deserves more than just the two of us. Especially as she gets older. We don't know shit about being a girl, man."

Sighing, I turned to face my brother. "Don't you think I know that? I worry all the time that I'm not enough for her. That I'm not going to be able to give her everything she needs."

Cole looked immediately shamed. "That's not what I meant, Linc. You're a great dad, and you know it."

"I know you didn't mean it that way," I said. "And you're not wrong. She deserves a mom. But if or when I decide to start dating it's not going to be me shopping for a mom for Ella. That's not fair to me, Ella or to whoever the woman is. Dating when you're a parent is hard. And I haven't figured out how it all works yet. That's why I'm not looking for anything serious right now. I'm not saying never. I'm just saying not right now. I'm busy with Ella and trying to get the business up and running. It's a lot to deal with."

Cole looked like he wanted to argue the point some more, but he let it go. For the time being, at least. I know it's just a matter of time before he brings it up again. It's why I let him talk me into going out tonight. I'd hoped it would get him off my back for a while. I think back over the events of the evening as I make my way to the fridge for a beer.

Cole and I had arrived as the dinner rush was dying down, so the crowd wasn't bad. Not that it matters when we go to Peach Fuzz. Cole being the owner means we never have to worry about good service or waiting for a table. We chose to sit at the bar though, to avoid taking a table and making even more work for the servers. It had taken me exactly 5 minutes to recognize a certain laugh from across the room. My gaze zeroed in on her immediately.

Harlow St. James.

Her hair was down, falling around her face in soft blonde waves shot through with pink streaks. I hid my smile behind my beer glass as I tried not to be obvious in my ogling. I've never thought much one way or the other about bright colors in a woman's hair, but it seems to suit Harlow. There's a certain whimsy about it that works for her. Her shirt dipped low in the front, teasing a hint of cleavage while keeping everything perfectly covered. I tried to tell myself I wasn't disappointed by that. I watched her for a few seconds talking animatedly with her hands to Piper and Layna. They were about halfway into a pitcher of margaritas. It was hard to tell if it was the first pitcher of the night.

"Well, shit." Cole's words broke through my thoughts and pulled my attention away from Harlow. "Look who's here."

When I looked back to my brother, I could see that he was staring at the same table I'd just been looking at. And he was grinning.

"Did Luke say he was coming out tonight?" I asked him, thinking of Piper.

Cole just shrugged. "He didn't mention it to me. Besides, you talk to him more than I do."

It's true. Luke and I have been best friends since freshman year of college when we'd been assigned to the same dorm room. Luke and Cole had become friends almost instantly upon meeting one another a few months later when I'd dragged him home with me for Thanksgiving. Sometimes it's hard to remember that I met him first. Over the years, Cole and I kind of adopted Luke as another brother. And knowing what I know about his family, I think we were just what he needed at the time. Our friendship has evolved over the years, and now we think of Luke as family. Which means we welcomed Piper into the fold right away. Piper and Luke's relationship had gotten off to a weird start, but any idiot can see that those two were made for one another.

"It looks like it's girl's night out," Cole said.

I studied the table of women for a few more seconds while I nursed my beer. I only saw 3 glasses and no sign of any guys approaching Layna or Harlow. And no sign of my best friend.

"Let's go say hi," Cole said with a grin as he stood.

Part of me wanted to argue, but a larger part of me wanted to move closer. I didn't give myself a chance to think about why. I shot off a quick text to Luke to see if he was coming out to join his fiancé and stood. As we moved across the room, I somehow took the lead with Cole following behind me. I had no idea what to say to her—to them, I corrected in my mind. I was just going to say hello to my best friend's fiancé and her friends. That's all. We would chat for a few minutes, then Cole and I would go back to our night. But that's not what happened.

Instead, I heard Harlow laugh again. The sound hit me solidly in the gut and I stared at her for far too long before Cole nudged me from behind, reminding me that I was standing next to their table like a creepy eavesdropper. So, I made some comment about hearing their joke which had gone over like a lead balloon and made all three women stop laughing immediately. Great job, Linc. Dumbass.

Luckily Cole has always been a charmer. He spoke up and filled the silence, taking the attention off me. Piper and her sister chimed in and before I knew it, we were sitting with the ladies, ordering another round of drinks. Cole managed to squeeze himself in next to

Layna which left me sitting next to Harlow, trying not to stare at her. But damn, she looked good. Not that she doesn't always look good. Even in those silly pajamas I'd seen her in that morning all those months ago. Thinking of Harlow in pajamas led to thoughts of her in bed which led to an uncomfortable situation in my pants.

"How's the business coming along, Linc," Piper asked, pulling me out of my dirty thoughts about the woman next to me.

"Good," I managed. "It's a lot of work, but things are coming together."

Cole beamed at me. "Don't let the false modesty fool you. Linc's kicking ass and taking names."

My face went red, and I kept my gaze on the table, rather than risk meeting anyone's eyes. Luckily, the drinks showed up at that moment and I used the distraction to take the attention off me. It wasn't long before Luke joined us and evened up the numbers. We ended up sitting with Harlow and the others for more than an hour, drinking and talking and laughing. Well, the others did most of the talking and I only had to chime in here and there. I was happy to let them carry the conversation because I've never been very good in group settings. And I've always managed to get tongue-tied anytime Harlow St. James was around.

I don't know what it is about her. I've known her since I moved to this town as a kid. In a town as small as ours, it was impossible not to know everyone my age. While Harlow and I were never friends, exactly, we've always known one another. And I've never been able to string more than a few words together when she's around. After all these years, I'm sure she thinks I'm a moron. Or an asshole who just won't talk to her. I'm not sure which I'd prefer.

By the time Luke and Piper decided to call it a night, I was more than ready to head home to my nice, quiet house where I could relax and not stress over my every word. Harlow agreed that she was ready to head home as well. With their departure, I didn't see the need to stick around. Besides, the night had gotten a lot duller without Harlow there. Not that I wanted to think about the reason why. Nope. Not going there.

So, now I'm home by 10pm on a Friday night, drinking a beer alone in my living room. Pathetic. I'm 29 years old and I might as well be 75, for all the excitement in my life. Hell, I know for a fact that Mr. Perkins just turned 77 and had at least two women fighting over him on Bingo night at the senior center last weekend. Clearly, age isn't the factor here. It's me. I've been so focused on Ella and getting my business off the ground that I haven't taken the time to enjoy my life. Maybe Cole was right.

Not that it matters. I told him the truth when I said I don't have time for things like dating and going out looking for someone. I will, eventually. But right now isn't the time. I need to focus on work. Now that I have a couple of employees, it's not just about me. If I fail, they lose their livelihoods. It's a big responsibility. On that note, I pull out my laptop and pull up the local buy/sell/trade website. I need to find some decent tools for the second truck. Most of my guys have their own tools, but tools are expensive, and I don't want to force them to buy everything themselves. Besides, if I'm going to have a legitimate contractor business, I need to have everything my employees need to do their jobs.

I scroll through the listings, seeing the same items that have been posted for the last 3 days. Sighing, I change my search tag and take a sip of my beer while the screen loads with more of the same items plus a few random things that weren't in the first search. This is useless. I think I'm going to have to just give in and buy the stuff new. I know it will cost more that way, but at least I'll get quality items. I refresh the screen one more time, on the off chance that something new will pop up, but I'm not holding out much hope. I suppose I could expand my search parameters if I'm willing to drive further to pick up the tools. But I don't want to drive an hour each way only to find out the tools are no good. I'm about to give up and close my laptop when a new listing pops up on the screen. The headline grabs my attention immediately and I nearly spit my beer out.

"Cheating ex abandoned his tools. His loss is your gain!"

I can't click on the listing fast enough. I scroll through the pictures first, noting that there's a circular saw that looks brand-new and an impact drill that I know costs a pretty penny at the big box hardware store. There are other quality items too. There's a leather tool belt that looks like it's never been worn. I scroll back up to read the listing, my eyes growing wide.

"Cheating ex refuses to retrieve his tools. Everything is practically new as he couldn't maintain a job for more than a week during our entire relationship. And yes, that lack of staying power trickled over into ALL other aspects of his life, if you know what I mean.

If you're wondering if this is legit, I have the original purchase receipts for everything, since he used my credit card to buy them a week before he ghosted me. Since he couldn't be bothered to take them with him, I've decided to try and recoup my losses. I can't get back the three months I spent trying to domesticate a cheater, but I can try and get back some of my money. So, if you want high-quality tools at a decent price, please make me an offer."

I read over the listing again and scroll through the images. I mentally catalogue all the items and what they would cost brand-new. Whoever this woman is, she spent a lot of money on these tools. And he'd cheated on her if what she says is true. Ouch. That's rough.

I've never understood cheating. If you want to be with someone else, why string someone along? Be honest and let them go before it comes to that. This guy sounds like a piece of shit. She's probably better off without him. And why am I reading into some stranger's love life after reading 2 paragraphs on the internet? *Because I'm alone on a Friday night?* Pathetic. But I can't let what might be a great deal slip through my fingers.

I click the button to message the seller, asking if I can meet her to look at the tools. With any luck, she'll sell them to me at a great price and I'll be one step closer to fully equipping the second truck with the tools it needs. I'm about to shut the laptop and go to bed when a notification pops up in the lower right corner. She responded already. That was fast.

"I can meet you tomorrow evening. Is 5pm okay?"

I can't prevent the smile that spreads across my face. This might just be my lucky night after all. I message her back to confirm the time. We arrange to meet at a neutral, public location. Smart. No one wants to invite strangers to their home. She wants to meet across the street from the police station. I give her props for that. If I were a criminal intent on robbing her, I'd certainly think twice about doing it in front of the police station. By the time we finish making the plan, I'm tired and ready for bed. It's been a long day and I have a full day of work tomorrow.

CHAPTER 3

Linc

The next morning is chaotic. I don't always work on Saturdays. In fact, I usually don't. I prefer to spend my weekends with Ella since she's out of school. But I'm close to a deadline on a job and we need everyone to pitch in and get it finished on time. I won't ask my guys to do something I'm not willing to do myself. So, if they're missing out on family time on a Saturday, so am I. Which means I need to take Ella to my parents' house for the day. She loves spending time with her grandparents, but she hates it when I work on the weekends. And she's not a morning person. Luckily, I've perfected this morning routine with her since she started school.

She needs to be woken up in stages if I want to avoid a meltdown. It's an artform that I'm quite proud of mastering. I go into her room and sit on the edge of her bed.

"Time to wake up, sweet girl," I say in a soft voice.

She makes a little grumbling sound and burrows into her pillow. Smiling, I stroke a hand over her hair.

"Sleeping Beauty," I whisper. "Time to wake up."

She mumbles something I can't quite make out, but her eyes don't open.

"What's that? I didn't hear you."

"Cinderella," she mumbles sleepily.

I smile. Ella. Cinderella. She's been obsessed with the princess since she was old enough to make a connection between the two names.

"But Cinderella wasn't a sleepy head like you," I say. I glance around the bedroom at the toys scattered around. "And her room was probably cleaner."

"The mice helped," Ella says, her eyes finally opening a crack to peer at me.

"Well, we don't have mice."

"Maybe we should get some."

I laugh. "You know real mice don't help you clean, right? They just poop everywhere and eat your food."

"Says you," she grumbles.

I rub her back and lean over to kiss her head. "Come on, kiddo. Time to get up and get ready for Mimi's house."

She groans. "I don't want you to go to work today, Daddy."

The words pierce my heart and send a wave of guilt through me. "I know. But they need me today. I promise I'm not working tomorrow. And next weekend is all you and me. No work."

She eyes me. "You pinky promise?" She holds up her tiny finger, making me grin.

"Pinky promise," I say, linking my pinky with hers. "Now, get ready."

She sighs dramatically as if I'm asking her to go off to war instead of to brush her teeth. "Fine," she says. "But I want pizza for dinner."

"Deal," I say.

"Extra cheese?"

I eye her for a moment. "You drive a hard bargain, but okay. Extra cheese."

She smiles at me and shakes her head. "You gotta learn to bargain better."

I laugh. "Joke's on you because I wanted pizza anyway. And this means I don't have to cook. So, who's the real winner here?"

She shrugs. "I guess we both are."

By the time Ella has gotten dressed and I've tamed her wild curls into something manageable, we have just enough time for a quick breakfast before we need to be on the road. Still, I know I'm going to be pushing it to make it to the job site on time. During the week, Cole is usually home to help me with the morning routine. He even volunteers to drive Ella to school some days, which makes those mornings much easier. But I woke up to a text from him saying he wasn't coming home last night and not to worry. Of course, he talked me into going out with him and he's the one who ended up getting lucky. Typical.

Actually, that's not true. Cole used to be that guy, but over the past year or so, he's changed. He's stopped staying out late and hooking up with random women. Which makes me wonder who he changed his mind for last night. I make a mental note to ask him about it later. Or tease him mercilessly. Or both. I pull into my parents' driveway and grab Ella's backpack, trying to hurry her along without making it seem like I'm hurrying her along. But she doesn't drag her feet this morning, thankfully. My mom is standing at the front door waiting with her arms open wide for Ella's hug. I smile at the sight.

I love how much my parents love their granddaughter. I mean, all grandparents are supposed to love their grandkids, but I know that's not always the case. Hell, my own grandparents don't really have much to do with Cole and me. They'd moved to south Florida after their kids had moved out and we rarely made the trip down to visit them when I was growing up. They never come to visit us in Georgia. I think they've met Ella twice in the eight years since she was born. And I know for a fact that my grandma didn't approve of my fathering a baby without having a wife. I overheard her once when she was on the phone with my dad. I don't think Cole or I missed out on anything where our grandparents are concerned. But Ella never has to feel that way about her grandparents. From the second she was born, my parents were absolutely in love with her. Can't say I blame them. I'd been a goner from the moment I saw her.

I met Ella's mom Meghan at a party after a football game during my sophomore year of college. We had a few hot weeks spent either in her dorm room or mine, in the library once, and several times in the back of my car. I wouldn't call what we had a relationship, exactly. We were both in it for the sex and we both knew that going in. We always used protection, but I guess nothing is 100% effective.

When Meghan told me she was pregnant, I remember feeling like my whole world was crashing down around me. I could see the future I'd planned for and dreamed of fading away and being replaced by a completely different one. One where I was someone's dad. A dad when I was still a kid myself? I wasn't sure how it would work. I wasn't sure if I'd be able to do it. So, I went to my parents for advice. I didn't know how they would react or what they would think of me. But they just hugged me. Mom cried. And Dad told me that it was time for me to stop being a kid. One way or another, I was going to have to be an adult and make adult decisions. So, when Meghan decided to have the baby, I stepped up. I promised her that I'd be the best father possible to our child, no matter what happened between the two of us.

We made it work for a while. I finished my sophomore year of college and never went back to school. Instead, I got a job working for a construction company and busted my ass to take care of my daughter. Meghan and I didn't last long as a couple after Ella's birth. Not that we'd had much of a relationship to start with. When she came to me and told me she wasn't cut out to be a mom and that she didn't want to do it anymore, I was shocked. I didn't understand how she could look at our daughter and not feel what I felt. I couldn't wrap my head around it. But I kept my anger to myself. It wouldn't help anything and anyway, I didn't want Ella to have a mom who resented her existence. So, when Meghan offered to terminate her parental rights and move back to Washington to be near her family, I agreed.

If I thought being a parent was hard before, it was nothing compared to life as a single dad. Working, diaper changes, teething, tantrums, babyproofing; it was all so hard and so foreign. Luckily, I had plenty of help from my parents and even Cole. To my surprise, my little brother stepped into the role of doting uncle with ease and enthusiasm. He came home from college every chance he could to spend time with Ella and me. When he eventually dropped out of college, I was so pissed at him. It's still the biggest argument my brother and I have ever had. But there wasn't any reasoning with him once he set his mind to something.

He decided that college wasn't for him. He wanted to settle down in Peach Tree and open his own bar and restaurant. It took a few years, but he'd eventually done it with Peach Fuzz. I helped with the renovations to the old, run-down building and Cole supplied the vision for what he wanted it to be. Now, the restaurant is more successful than even he'd anticipated. I'm proud of my little brother for all that he's accomplished.

I don't remember when he decided to move in with me. I just remember him staying over more and more and how convenient it was to have him around all the time. I finally started to feel like I had breathing room. Being Ella's dad had become my only identity for those early years and while I don't regret any of the time I spent devoted to her, it was nice to have a second person in the house to take some of the responsibility from me. Now, Cole's been living with me for almost 5 years, and I don't know if he's ever planning to leave. Not that I want him to. But eventually, he's going to want his own space, or he's going to find someone to settle down with. For now, though, I'm happy with the arrangement we have.

By the time I hug Ella and my mom goodbye, I know I need to hurry if I want to make it to the job site on time. I hate arriving after my employees get there. It sets a bad example. I want them to know I'm going to work just as hard as they do, if not harder. Showing up when they've already been working for half an hour doesn't really do that. I wish I had time to stop for coffee, but I'll definitely be late if I do that. Maybe I can text Cole and have him bring some by later. That is, if he's crawled out of whichever bed he ended up in last night. I shake my head as I pull out onto the highway. My baby brother might have grown up, but he's still got some of that wildness in him.

CHAPTER 4

Harlow

Saturdays are usually the busiest day for me at the shop. Most people have trouble getting time off work during the week for a hair appointment. So, Saturdays are usually booked for at least a month in advance. Today is no different. It's another reason I called it an early night last night. There's nothing worse than the chemical smell of hair color when you're hungover. Believe me, I know.

So, I'd gone home and taken Layna and Piper's advice and posted Derek's tools for sale. Well, technically they're my tools since I bought them. I need to stop thinking of them as his. I paid for them and they're in my house. So, they're mine. I still can't believe I worded that ad the way I did. I'd been going for funny and eye-catching. I guess it worked.

I've had so many comments and messages that I turned off the notifications for it. I agreed to meet with the first person who messaged me later today. If they don't end up buying, I'll reach out to the next person. But I don't have time to field dozens of messages from people. I have two more highlights and a haircut today. Then I need to clean up before meeting the buyer at the police station. No way was I giving my address to a stranger.

I manage a few minutes to eat my lunch before Miss Dottie comes in for her appointment. I've been styling Miss Dottie's hair for the past 3 years, ever since she got a bad color job at a chain salon in Savannah. She has a standing appointment with me every 8 weeks and she's never late. Being in Miss Dottie's good graces is one of the things that can make or break a business in Peach Tree. She's kind of the unofficial queen of this town. I do my best to stay on her good side.

I listen to Miss Dottie as she fills me in on the gossip in town. I swear, the woman must have secret spies because she knows more about the scandals in this town than I thought possible. I don't even know how a town this small could have this much drama. It turns out that Mr. Harris, who owns the hardware store, has been having an affair with his wife's sister, Stella who manages the post office. It's why everyone's mail has been running late for the past month. And apparently when Mrs. Harris found out about her sister and her husband, she cleaned out his bank account and took a vacation to the Bahamas. And the rumors are that she didn't come back alone.

Miss Dottie also tells me how her niece who works at the grocery store saw Lydia Paulsen buying out the Little Debbie cakes. Which means she's stressed about something. She only ever eats processed sugar when she feels like eating her feelings. Catching a glimpse of my reflection in the mirror, I take in my curves and round ass. Part of me wishes I was more like Lydia. But then I shrug. I like food and I see nothing wrong with that. Besides, I like my curves too. And so do most of the guys I've dated. I refuse to feel shame for my body. Women have enough pressure already.

I learn all this while I apply color to Miss Dottie's hair. I can't wait to tell Piper all the gossip later. She loves to hear all the juicy news from around town. Especially since neither of us really knows the people involved very well. It's almost like watching a soap opera, except we get Miss Dottie's commentary along with it. By the time I lead her over to the sink to rinse her hair, my mind is full of so much new gossip that I don't know where to start when I talk to Piper later.

I turn on the water and adjust it to a comfortably warm temperature before instructing Miss Dottie to lean back. The water sputters a little before coming back to its full stream and I begin to rinse the color from her hair. I take my time, adding a light scalp massage to the hair-washing. I can see Miss Dottie relaxing into it, enjoying the experience of being pampered. I smile as I lather the shampoo into her short curls, working it through to the ends. I've just finished rinsing the conditioner out of her hair when the water sputters again and I hear a gurgling sound. I reach over to turn off the water, but then a loud groan comes from under the sink. Before I can make heads or tails of the sound, a geyser of water erupts from under the sink, straight up into the air.

I freeze as I watch the torrent of water rain down onto Miss Dottie. She lets out a loud scream of shock at the icy water. Because of course it's cold. I remain frozen for another second before springing into action and pulling Miss Dottie up out of her chair. I motion her toward the front of the shop, away from the torrential downpour taking place near the shampoo bowls.

What the fuck is happening right now? More importantly, how do I make it stop? There must be a cut-off valve, right? I'm sure it's under the sink. I eye the spray of water. Of course, it is. Where else would it be? Knowing I don't have a choice, I dart over to the sink and drop to my knees ignoring the way I just went from dry and warm to soaking wet and freezing in a second. How much water is pouring out of this pipe right now? Holy shit. This is bad.

I fumble around under the sink, feeling blindly for the valve to turn off the flow of water. Unfortunately, the spray of water in my face is impairing my vision. I can hear Miss Dottie talking behind me, but I can't make out what she's saying over the sound of the water. It doesn't matter, though. I already know what the next bit of gossip in this town will be. Me.

Shit, shit, shit.

I keep the profanity in my head because I don't need to give Miss Dottie more ammunition for the gossip canon. Blindly, I feel for the valve that will shut off the water. It takes me a few seconds of being blasted by cold water before I finally feel the metal valve in my hand. I turn it as quickly as I can, but nothing happens. Water continues to pump from what I can now see is a broken pipe. Feeling around some more, I feel another valve. I must have turned off the hot water and it's clearly the cold water that's currently trying to drown me. I turn the second valve off and feel immediate relief when the flow of water slows and eventually stops.

The silence in the shop is broken only by the drip, drip, drip of water coming from literally everywhere. I sit on the wet floor and work to catch my breath. I don't turn to look at Miss Dottie. I don't know if I'm quite ready to face her judgment. She's mostly a nice woman, but I've never been on her bad side before. I don't know what that entails, but I'm sure I want no part of it.

Once the water is shut off, I know there's no way I'll be able to remain open for the rest of the day. There's no way I can even finish Dottie's hair. I can't work while walking around in 2 inches of standing water. Plus, Dottie and I both look like drowned rats. Unfortunately, the only towels I have in the shop are small towels used specifically for hair. Not that a towel is doing to fix this mess.

I manage to dry Dottie off as best I can, thanking whatever divine intervention let me finish rinsing the conditioner from her hair before all hell broke loose. At least it's clean and not full of products. She lets me comb out her damp hair and scrunch it with the towel and assures me she's going straight home. Her clothes are wet, and I hate seeing her leaving here with her hair like this, but there's nothing else I can do. I wave away her offer to pay for today's services. The last thing I'm going to do is take her money after what just happened.

Once she's gone, I lock the front door and flip the sign over to 'closed'. Then I call my two afternoon clients to cancel their appointments. I try not to think about the lost revenue those clients would have brought in. The thing about hair is that most people don't want to wait. If they can find someone else to do it while they're waiting for you, they often will. Especially if you haven't already earned their loyalty. I have no idea if I've just lost their future business or not, but I can't think about that right now. I turn to survey the room and wince. How the hell am I going to clean this up?

Like most people my age, when I have a problem I don't know how to solve, I head to the internet for advice. Most of the suggestions say to use a wet/dry vacuum and a rubber squeegee to get rid of the water. Great idea. Except I don't own either of those things. Though I know she's working at her shop, I call the only person I know to ask for help. Piper answers on the first ring.

"Hello?"

"Do you own a shop vac and a squeegee?"

"Um...why?"

I sigh. "Do you?"

"No. Why do you need a shop vac and a squeegee?"

I hesitate, though I don't know why. This is Piper. My closest friend. She's not going to judge me. She'll probably want to drop everything to come help. That's probably the reason I hesitate if I'm being honest with myself. I don't want to pull her away from her work. I don't want to be a burden. I lift one foot and watch the water run out of my shoe and splash onto the floor. I can't fix this alone.

"The shop is flooded, and I need to get the water out," I say in a miserable voice.

"I'm coming over right now," Piper says before the call ends abruptly.

I don't know why I'm hit with a sense of relief that Piper is coming to help. I don't know what she'll be able to do that I can't. But it feels nice to know I'm not alone in this mess. Even if it is my mess. I work to move things off the floor and out of the path of the water while I wait for her to arrive. Luckily the floors are sealed tile, which means they won't be damaged by the water. But it does make them awfully slippery. I need to be careful not to fall and break something. The last thing I need is to be out of work from a broken arm along with a ruined shop.

The knock on the front door grabs my attention a short time later. Piper must have had to run to get here so fast. I turn and see Piper and Luke standing outside the door. I sigh, knowing I don't have a choice. I hadn't wanted more witnesses to my humiliation, but Luke loves Piper and he's a good guy. Plus, I need all the help I can get to clean this mess. When I open the door to let them in, they both eye me warily before peering around at the flooded shop. Luke lets out a low whistle.

"You weren't kidding," Piper says. "It's flooded."

I nod. "Yep."

"What happened?" Luke asks, looking around.

"Pipe burst," I say.

"Holy shit," Piper says. "Was anyone hurt?"

I shake my head. "Thankfully no. I'd just finished rinsing the conditioner from Miss Dottie's hair when it happened. She got drenched, but no injuries."

Piper and Luke both stare at me, wide-eyed. I know what they're thinking. Of all the people to have in my chair when disaster strikes, it would have to be her.

"I know," I say with a sigh. "Believe me."

"This is bad," Piper whispers.

Luke nods. "At least no one was hurt. That's the important thing. We can fix everything else."

I don't know why, but his reassuring words and calm tone make my eyes prick and my throat feel tight. Clearing my throat, I turn away from them and pretend to look at the mess while I blink a few times to clear my eyes.

"Right," I say, once I'm sure my voice won't break. "How do we clean it up?"

I turn to look back at Piper and Luke, but Luke stepped back outside while I was turned away. I can see him outside on the sidewalk, pacing in front of the salon with his phone to his ear as he talks. Piper gestures toward him.

"He's calling in reinforcements," she says.

I have no idea what that means, but I can't afford to be picky right now. I need help. Luke returns and gives me a quick nod.

"I've got a shop vac on the way," he says. "In the meantime, let's try to move what we can out of the flood zone."

I don't ask where the vacuum is coming from. I'm just happy to have someone taking charge. I've always been self-reliant, and I've never liked needing anyone's help. But having Piper and Luke show up for me and immediately spring into action is more of a comfort than I expected. The three of us get to work clearing out anything that can be moved out of the water. As I'm rolling up the small rug that now weighs a ton, I hear the bell above the front door ring. I look up from my place on the wet floor and freeze when I see the last person I expect standing in the doorway.

Before I can ask him what he's doing here, Linc sloshes through the water and takes the rug from me, making it look practically weightless as he carries it outside. Stunned by his sudden presence—and the way his ass looks in those jeans—it takes me a second to find my voice. By the time I do, he's walking back inside, dragging a giant vacuum behind him. Luke follows him back out and returns with a couple of squeegees on long poles.

"Thought those could help," Linc says, nodding toward the squeegees.

"These are great, man," Luke says. "We'll have this place cleaned up in no time."

The two men finish moving furniture and soaked rugs out of the space while Piper and I use the squeegees to push the water out the front door and into the street. It doesn't take long before most of the water is cleared away. I'm starting to feel more optimistic about the situation as the afternoon wears on.

"Thanks for coming," I say to Linc as he's unrolling the cord to the vacuum. "I hope I didn't ruin your Saturday afternoon."

For some reason, even saying those few words to him has me flustered. But I couldn't let him keep working to save my business without telling him how grateful I am. He smiles down at me and, *holy shit*. All my thoughts scatter and all I can think is how hot he is. My stomach does a flip and I feel myself leaning toward him without meaning to.

"I'm happy I could help," he says. "And you didn't ruin my day. I just finished up a job nearby."

I nod. "Regardless. Thank you."

"Anytime," he says, somehow short-circuiting my brain with one simple word.

Before I can do something foolish, like kiss this unsuspecting man, I turn and busy myself with the vacuum. I stretch the cord over to the outlet and plug it in. As I do, there's a loud pop and a jolt of pain shoots up my arm. Then all the lights in the shop die.

"Shit! Fuck! Ow!" I shout, shaking my hand.

The pain from the shock is gone, but the memory of it makes me keep shaking my hand for a few seconds. I look down at it, expecting to see burn marks, but there's nothing.

"Are you okay?" Piper asks, hurrying toward me.

"I'm fine," I say through gritted teeth.

"What happened?" Linc asks, suddenly standing so close to me that I can make out the gold flecks in his dark eyes.

His fingers are digging into my upper arms. When had he reached out to grab me? I don't remember. One second, I'd been cursing and the next, Linc had grabbed me. I try not to focus on the feel of his large hands wrapped around my arms or just how close he's standing right now. And I'm definitely not trying to breathe in the scent of him so I can dwell on it later when I'm alone. Self-care Saturday is sounding damned good right now.

"Harlow?" Linc says, giving me a little shake.

I'm glad he did because I think I was ridiculously close to burying my face in his chest and sniffing him for all

I'm worth. Shaking off those thoughts, I focus on the present.

"Damned thing shocked me," I say looking toward the outlet where I'd just attempted to plug in the vacuum.

Linc doesn't look away from my face. It's as if he's studying me to make sure I'm okay. To be honest, I'm more surprised by my reaction to his nearness than the shock of the outlet.

"Are you sure you're okay?" Piper asks, clearly worried.

I drag my gaze away from Linc's to give her what I hope is a reassuring smile.

"I'm fine. I promise. It scared me more than anything."

Linc releases my arms only to take my hand in both of his. My heart jumps into my throat at the feel of his big hands enveloping mine. *Don't freak out,* I tell myself. *He's just making sure you're okay. That's all.* But I can't help but glue my eyes to our joined hands to try and memorize the sight. He inspects my hand as if looking for a wound. I try not to think about the way his skin feels against mine or the way I don't want him to stop touching me. My heart is pounding so loud I'm surprised the others don't hear it. When Linc doesn't find a wound, he seems satisfied and releases me. I look up at him to find that his expression has shifted from concern to something else.

"When's the last time someone took a look at the wiring in this building?"

I almost don't recognize Linc's voice. It's hard and angry. The smile from a few moments before is gone and the dim light from the front windows makes his dark eyes look almost sinister. His jaw is clenched, and I can see a muscle ticking there. He's waiting for me to answer his question. I try to think back.

"Um," I say. "I'm not sure. There haven't been any problems before now. I guess when I bought the place. There was an inspection."

Linc's eyes darken even further. "Who did the inspection?"

I shrug. "I don't know. The guy the realtor recommended."

Linc closes his eyes and pulls in a deep breath before slowly exhaling. I've never seen him like this. He looks pissed off, but I don't understand why.

"Was it Todd Ralston?" he asks.

"Yes!" I say, pointing at him. "That was his name. Why?"

"Because Todd Ralston was arrested for fraud last year," he says. "It turns out he wasn't a licensed contractor and never has been. He'd take people's money, do a half-assed inspection, and throw out a couple of easy fixes to make it look convincing. He passed a lot of buildings that weren't even up to code."

A sinking feeling spreads in my gut. "What are you saying?"

He turns his dark eyes on me. "I'm saying that this old building of yours might need more than a couple of new pipes."

CHAPTER 5

Linc

Harlow hasn't said much since I told her that her inspection was most likely bogus. She looks worried and a little pissed off, but that's to be expected when you find out your livelihood might be on the line because of someone else's greed. I keep hearing her shout of pain and that pop that I'd known immediately was the sound of electricity arcing. For a split second, I'd imagined the worst. I'd pictured her small frame falling to the floor, lifeless. It had been enough to make my own heart stutter.

I try not to think about the fear that shot through me at the possibility of something bad happening to Harlow. Instead, I focus on the anger I feel at her shoddy realtor who didn't do his homework and find a licensed inspector. Not to mention Ralston himself. The piece of shit. He's lucky he's already in jail. I'd love to get my hands on him. Faulty wiring can start fires or electrocute people. His shitty work could get someone killed. Harlow's lucky this place hasn't caught fire while she was asleep upstairs.

That brings me right back to my fear over Harlow being shocked by that outlet. Which just puts me into a shitty mood. I was at work earlier when Luke called to ask if I had a spare wet/dry vac. When he told me the reason he needed it, I'd left right away. But I hadn't lied to Harlow. I'd been mostly finished with the job when I left. Still, I'd planned to drop off the vacuum and go back to check on any last-minute issues before calling it a day. I'd hoped to have time to clean up a bit before meeting the seller about those tools. But I'd taken one look at the mess in Harlow's shop and seen the worry in her eyes and decided to stay. It had nothing to do with the way her wet shirt had been clinging to her body. Nothing at all.

The cleanup had looked worse than it was. It hadn't taken long for the four of us to clear out the bulk of the water and the water-logged items. I think most of it is salvageable. The floors are quality, sealed tile so they'll survive. But I have a feeling those pipes are as old as the building itself. And I have real concerns about the wiring now. I try not to let my concern show as I search for the fuse box. It doesn't take long for me to assess the situation.

"I hate to say it, but we have to go soon if we're going to make dinner with Art," Luke says, coming up behind me with Piper at his side.

"I can skip dinner and help Harlow get this place cleaned up," Piper says.

"You've both done more than enough," Harlow says. "I already pulled you away from the shop for the afternoon. I refuse to let you miss dinner. Go. I'll be fine."

"Where are you staying tonight?" Piper asks, her voice skeptical.

"Upstairs. In my apartment."

"No, you're not," I say, the words spilling out before I can stop them. "You have no electricity."

Harlow just shrugs. "So? It'll be like camping. I'll open some windows. I have flashlights. I can sleep without power for one night."

"You can stay with us," Piper suggests.

"You've already got Layna in your guest bedroom," Harlow points out. "And she was supposed to be staying with me anyway, remember?"

Harlow scowls at the mess of dirty, wet footprints spread across the pretty, white tile and fans herself with her hand. Since the power went out, taking the air conditioning with it, the air in here has gotten a little stagnant. Georgia in April means humid air, surprise thunderstorms and mosquitos. I can't let her stay here with no electricity.

"You're welcome to stay with us for as long as you need," Luke says. "Besides, we'll be home late tonight anyway. You and Layna will practically have the house to yourselves."

"I need to finish cleaning this mess," Harlow says. "There are still a few hours of daylight left."

"And then you'll come stay with us?" Piper asks.

I can see Harlow wavering. I know I should stay out of it. I barely know Harlow. She's barely an acquaintance, even if we did sort of grow up together. But I can't stand to see the defeated look in her eyes or the sad slump of her shoulders. She's always so optimistic. Seeing her so down has me wanting to fix this for her.

"I can fix it."

All eyes turn to me, surprising me until I realize that I'm the one who just spoke. Harlow immediately begins to shake her head, but I ignore her protests.

"I have most of what I need in the truck," I say, walking back toward the front door. "I might need to make a trip to the hardware store before they close."

I don't realize Harlow is following me until I reach my truck and lower the tailgate.

"Linc, wait," she says, stilling me with her hand on my arm. "You don't need to do this. I know you're busy."

I shrug. "I don't mind. I just need to call my mom and see if she can keep Ella a little longer."

Harlow looks stricken. "No," she says, shaking her head. "I'm keeping you from your daughter. That's not okay. You should go. I'll stay with Piper tonight and figure something out tomorrow."

I sigh and narrow my eyes at her. "And how do you plan to get it fixed tomorrow? You need electricity to run the vacuums and fans that you'll need to dry this place out before mold sets in. Do you have an electrician on speed-dial?"

She huffs out a sigh. "No."

"And you know they'll charge a premium for it being a weekend," I say. "And it being such short notice will automatically make it an emergency call which will cost even more."

Harlow's shoulders sag.

"I can fix it," I say gently. "Just let me help you."

I don't know why I'm being so insistent that she take my help. It's not like we're close friends. And I can tell she hates the idea of needing help almost as much as she hates the idea of accepting it. But I can't stand the idea of her losing her business or having to spend even more money to fix a problem that I know I can help with.

"Okay," she says with a small nod. When she raises her head to meet my gaze, the sadness is hidden behind a determined expression. I almost smile at the sight. But then she speaks.

"But I'm paying you."

I shake my head as I begin pulling items from the back of my truck. "No need. I'm just helping out a friend."

When she doesn't respond, I finally turn to see her watching me, a strange expression on her face.

"Why?" she asks. "You don't really even know me."

I want to laugh at the question because it's ridiculous. Of course, I know her. I've known her since we were ten years old. But it's true that we've never been friends. Not really. Not until her best friend started a fake relationship with mine last year. And I still don't know her as well as I'd like to if I'm being honest. But that doesn't mean that I haven't paid attention. I know her favorite soda and how she takes her coffee. I know that she played in marching band in high school and looked cute as fuck in that uniform. I know she prefers salty snacks to sweet ones and French fries are her weakness. I also know she'd think I was crazy if I said any of that out loud. So, I don't.

"Can't I just do something nice?" I ask, frustration making my voice come out far harsher than I mean for it to.

I want to call back the words immediately or apologize to her. Instead, I busy myself with pulling the items I need from the back of the truck and when I turn around, Harlow has gone back inside. I tell myself that's for the best. I probably should have made up some nice explanation for my behavior instead of snapping at her. I wish I could go back in time and keep my mouth shut. I've spent months keeping quiet when I'm around her. I don't know why I picked today to start talking.

"Idiot," I mutter as I turn to head back into the shop.

Luke and Piper leave a few minutes later and I spend the next hour replacing blown fuses and some of the wires in the fuse box in silence. By the time 5pm rolls around, I've got the shop lights on as well as the air conditioner. I warn Harlow not to use the washer or dryer until she can get an electrician in to look at the wiring in depth. I know I could do it myself, but I'm not sure how long it would take and I'm not sure Harlow would even welcome my help. Maybe I should come back tomorrow and see what I can do.

"Shit!" Harlow shouts from the front of the shop where she's been busy cleaning up the rest of the water.

I rush out there, hoping she's okay and no other disasters have befallen this old building. "What happened?" I ask.

"I forgot about a meeting I had," she says, looking at her watch. "I was supposed to be there at 5:00."

Her words spur a memory and I sigh, closing my eyes. "Damn it," I whisper.

"What?"

"I was supposed to meet someone to look at some tools this afternoon," I say. "I got caught up and completely forgot."

Harlow goes still, staring at me for several long seconds before closing her eyes and letting out a soft laugh. "Of course," she mutters. "Why the hell not?"

"What?"

She opens her eyes and gives me a curious look. "Cheating ex abandoned his tools. Sound familiar?"

Unsure what she's talking about, I just look at her. "Huh?"

She rolls her eyes. "Follow me," she says, turning to walk out the front door of the shop.

I follow her, still confused as to what she's talking about. When we go out to her car and she opens the back, understanding dawns. In the back of her SUV are a bunch of nearly new tools that look identical to the ones in the ad I responded to last night. I look at them for a few moments before turning to face Harlow. She smiles at me.

"This saves me a trip to the police station, I guess."

"I guess so," I say. "What are the odds?"

She just looks at me. "In a town this small? Better than you think."

"True enough."

I look through the tools, lifting some items and turning them over. Some still have the tags attached to them from the store where they were purchased. She hadn't been exaggerating in her sales ad. They really are practically new.

"How much do you want for all of it?" I ask, turning back to Harlow.

She shrugs. "I'm not expecting to get back what I paid for them. They've just been sitting by my front door for weeks now. Make me an offer."

I turn back to the pile of tools and do some mental math. My guess is the tools cost her a good amount when she bought them new. That impact driver alone is worth $200. And everything is basically untouched. I think about the shop and all the repairs she's going to need to pay for. I know how much a plumber will quote her to replace those pipes. And that's just to fix the known issues. I've never seen a plumbing job that didn't introduce at least three new problems when I've gone to fix it. That's not to mention the electrical issues. The old building probably needs all new wiring. I know what I'd quote for a job like that.

"I'll give you $850 for everything," I say, tossing out a number that's well over what I calculated for their worth.

Her mouth drops open in surprise and she shakes her head. "That's ridiculous," she sputters.

I know it is, but I can't take it back now. "That's what they're worth," I say, trying to sound like the expert I am.

"No way," she says, crossing her arms over her chest. "I didn't even pay that much."

I shrug. "You must have gotten them on sale."

"You're crazy if you think I'm letting you pay that much," she says, her eyes flashing angrily. "I don't need pity money."

What? Whoa. She thinks I'm doing this out of pity? That's not the reason. I'm doing it because—well, shit. I don't know why I'm doing it. I just want to help her. And I don't ever want her to think I'm taking advantage of her. Especially after learning that she was one of Ralston's victims. And that her ex was stupid enough to cheat on her. That's something I truly don't understand.

I hold up my hands. "Wait a minute," I say. "That's not what this is."

She raises one brow in challenge. Why is that such a turn-on? It's not. It isn't. *Look away!*

"What is it, then? Why offer me such a high price for tools that we both know aren't worth that?"

I sigh. She has a point.

"Fine," I say. "Instead of the cash, what if I work for them?"

She looks instantly suspicious. "What do you mean?"

"I can fix your plumbing problem."

Unsurprisingly, Harlow shakes her head immediately and begins to argue.

"No, Linc," she says. "You've done enough by getting my electricity working again."

"You know it still needs more work, right?" I ask her. "You might need the whole building rewired." I don't want to worry her more, but I want to be honest with her about what's happening.

She sighs. "I know. But you've done enough already. You've spent your entire afternoon here with me when I know you'd rather spend it doing something else."

I try not to let the guilt of missing this time with Ella eat at me, but it's there all the same. I know she understands that sometimes I need to work on the weekends, but it's hard not to feel awful about working instead of spending my free time with her. I tell myself I'll make it up to her next weekend.

"It's not a big deal," I say.

"Yes, it is," she says. "I know you usually spend the weekends with Ella. Instead, you've spent hours here at my shop, cleaning up my messes. You should go home. Be with your daughter while there's still a little bit of the weekend left."

I study her, wondering how she figured out exactly what I'd been thinking. I can see the guilt and worry in her eyes, and I hate it.

"Don't worry about that," I tell her. "Ella understands that sometimes I have to work weekends."

She shakes her head. "Don't let me be the reason a little girl misses out on spending time with her only parent."

As soon as the words are out, she looks like she wants to call them back. She snaps her mouth shut as her eyes go wide.

"Shit. I'm sorry," she says, clearly flustered. "I didn't mean that. I don't know your situation."

"It's okay," I say, cutting her off. She looks like she's worried I'll be angry, but I'm not. There's no way she can know the truth about my past with Ella's mom. It's not as if I advertise it.

"It's been years since Ella's mom had any kind of contact with me," I say. "And even longer since she tried to be a mom to Ella. She left when Ella was a baby, and I didn't try hard to convince her to stay. I didn't want Ella to have a resentful parent. You're right. I am her only parent. And I do try to spend as much of my free time with her as possible, especially on the weekends. I don't want her to feel like she's not important to me. But trust me when I tell you that I have talked to her about this, and she understands. She's a good kid and I'm raising her to help others when they need it.

"Also yes, I'm a single parent. But I'm not the only family Ella has. Cole lives with us. He's with her almost as much as I am. And my parents live 10 minutes away. Ella has plenty of people who love her and help take care of her."

I smile. "Hell, lately she's been wanting to hang out with Piper more than she does me. I think she likes having a girl around."

Harlow smiles. "Piper loves her, too. She told me."

I nod. "So, you see? I'm not neglecting her by helping you get your shop up and running."

"I never thought that," she says softly. "You're a good dad."

I don't know how to respond to that, so I don't say anything. The silence between us lingers for several seconds until Harlow finally nods as though coming to a decision. There's still a hint of worry in her eyes though.

"How much to fix it?" she asks. "Properly, I mean."

I smile. "As if I could do it any other way?"

She grins. "That's not what I meant, and you know it."

"I know," I say. "I already told you. I'll take the tools in exchange for fixing your plumbing issues."

Harlow immediately shakes her head. "Absolutely not," she says. "I won't let you work for less than you deserve. I'll pay what you would charge anyone else."

I sigh. I'd had a feeling she would argue. She seems to enjoy arguing with me. Plus, she's not the type of woman to take the easy way out. She's busted her ass to get where she is now. I can respect it. Hell, it's kind of hot. But this is different. She's a friend. I would do the same for Piper or Luke. The idea of charging her for my time seems ludicrous. I smile at her, planning to explain my thought process.

"It's a fair trade," I say. "Besides I don't charge my friends for my time."

"Shitty way to run a business," she says in a dry tone that makes me laugh.

"That's what I've been doing wrong," I say as though the idea is brand new to me. "Listen, Harlow, I know you don't know much about what I do. Just like I don't know much about what you do. But trust me when I tell you that the work you need isn't all that hard. It's a little time-consuming. Which means that any other contractor would come in here and quote you some ridiculously high price to fix your broken pipe. All because he'd be able to work the time aspect to his advantage. The parts themselves aren't all that expensive."

She bristles. "I can buy them myself. I don't need charity."

I keep my voice easy. "That's not what this is. Much as I'd love to be able to do it all for free, you were right before. I have a business to run. And a child to support. Offering my own free labor is one thing. That's just my body and my time." I ignore the way those words sound and keep going, hoping Harlow didn't notice me stumbling over my words. "If I paid for the supplies, I'd have to cut back on John's hours. And I know he needs the money. Then I'd also have to work those hours myself to make sure my contracts get completed. I'm not an idiot, Harlow. This isn't charity. You didn't let me finish."

I can see a muscle ticking in her jaw. She crosses her arms over her chest and looks at me expectantly, waiting for me to continue. The sight is almost enough to make me smile, but I can guess how she'd take that. Instead, I keep my expression neutral.

"I'll do the repairs in the evenings after I finish work for the day. That way it won't cut into my business since you seem concerned about that. And I won't charge you for my time, because I'm not an asshole who takes advantage of his friends. But if you trade me the tools for my time, that leaves me with the money I would have spent to buy those tools. If it's just repairing broken pipes, that's not all that expensive. I promise, it won't break the bank. And I can use my contractor discount to get the best deals on quality materials." I pause. "Do we have a deal?"

Harlow still looks like she wants to argue, but I can tell she knows she doesn't have a valid argument. This is the best deal she's going to get in this town, and I don't think she can afford to pay an exorbitant amount to have the repairs done. Part of me wonders why I'm so set on being the one to fix this problem for her. I don't have a real answer for that. I can claim I'm helping a friend, but until recently I hadn't spoken to her since high school. It's only because her friend started dating my friend that we interacted at all. She's more of an acquaintance than a close friend. So, why am I being so insistent? Before I can delve into the inner workings of my own mind, Harlow speaks.

"You're right," she says. I can tell the words don't taste good on the way out. I manage to keep my smile contained. "I do need help. I can't do the work on my own. I wouldn't know the first thing about plumbing or electrical work. YouTube probably has some great tutorials, but I want everything up to code and I don't trust myself to do the job of a professional. And no, I probably can't afford your hourly rate. Or that of another contractor."

I can see how much that admittance costs her. Harlow isn't the type of woman who likes to admit she can't do something. And she's certainly not the type of woman to ask for help. In her roundabout way, this is her asking.

"I accept your offer," she says. Before I can say anything, she adds, "On one condition."

I huff out a laugh. I should have known she'd have something to add. "Which is?"

"I want to help," she says. "I want to learn. At least the basics. I don't want to be helpless if something like this happens again."

I grin at her, shaking my head. "Harlow, you've never been helpless a day in your life."

She narrows her eyes at me. "I'm going to choose to take that as a compliment."

I shrug. "If you want."

Now she's outright glaring at me. I can't help the smile that spreads across my face. Teasing her is a lot more fun than my usual haggling with clients. I can tell she wants to say something snarky, but I hold up a hand to stall her.

"Fine," I say. "I'll teach you. But you know it's going to take longer than if I just do it myself?"

She nods. "Maybe a little. But I'm a quick learner."

I shake my head, wondering how the hell I ended up here, agreeing to spend hours working with the woman I used to spend hours obsessing over back when we were kids.

"I'm sure you are," I say, pretending to be unaffected by our new agreement.

"So, we have a deal?" she asks, her tone all business.

I hold out a hand. "We have a deal."

She hesitates for a split second before reaching out to shake my hand. The instant I feel her smaller hand in mind, a little thrill runs through me, shooting up from the place our hands are touching. I glance down at our joined hands, half-convinced I'll see a bolt of lightning there. But there's nothing. After a quick shake of her hand, I reluctantly release her. I regret it almost immediately, missing the feel of her soft skin against my calloused hand.

Harlow shoves her hands into her pockets and takes a step back from me. Clearing her throat, she nods once.

"Okay," she says, her voice a little tight. "When do you want to start?"

I swallow, hoping my voice comes out steady. What the hell is wrong with me? How does shaking a woman's hand turn me into a mindless idiot? I clear my own throat.

"You were right before. I need to get home to Ella tonight. But I can stop by in the morning to get started on a list of supplies. We can discuss the details tomorrow," I say. "Is 9:00 okay?"

She nods. "Works for me."

"It's a date," I say, unthinking. Before the words are fully out of my mouth, I want to recall them. But it's too late. She's looking at me with a weird expression and I can feel my face heating. I open my mouth, unsure what I plan to say, but Harlow beats me to it.

She grins at me. "Not my usual first date, but points for originality."

The playful statement is enough to break whatever weird tension seems to have popped up between us since that handshake and we both laugh. I dip my head in a nod.

"I'll see you tomorrow."

She smiles. "See you."

CHAPTER 6

Harlow

What in the actual fuck was that?

It's the one thought running through my brain over and over. Linc left almost 20 minutes ago, and my heart is still beating too fast. There's also this weird rolling sensation in my belly like the first dip on a roller coaster every time I remember that handshake. A handshake, for god's sake. What the hell is wrong with me? It's not like I'm twelve and hoping he'll ask me to the middle school dance. Been there, done that. I'm almost 30 years old now. And nowhere near that innocent. So, why did that brief touch send me into a tailspin?

Because it's Linc, I tell myself. It's the one guy you've always wished would notice you. Today's conversation was probably the longest I've ever had with him, just the two of us. We've hung out in group settings with his brother and Piper and Luke. Layna has even joined us on occasion. But it's always been at Peach Fuzz. Always in a crowded room with dozens of other people. Not once, in all the years I've known Linc, have we spent any time alone together. The second Luke and Piper left us, it was like the air had become charged with electricity. Had Linc felt that too? Or am I a crazy person who's just imagining something that doesn't exist after almost 2 decades of obsessing over the same boy?

"Get it together, Harlow," I mutter to the empty shop.

Great. Now I'm talking to myself. I need to stop obsessing over Lincoln Prescott. There's never been anything between us and there never will be. He's just being a nice guy. He's always been that way, always ready to lend a helping hand. I'd be stupid to try and read anything more into that.

I look around at the empty salon. While the water might be gone, the floors are a mess of dirty footprints. With a sigh, I get to work mopping them. By the time I'm finished, it's fully dark outside. My back and shoulders are sore and there's a dull headache forming behind my eyes. But I feel better now that everything is clean. I turn to look at the two sinks, taking in the broken pipe beneath one of them. Technically, I can work with one sink for a while. It's not the end of the world.

I try to ignore the small voice telling me that this is just the beginning. This building is old and has needed major updates since well before I bought it. The broken pipe is probably just the first of many things that might go wrong. Not to mention the wiring. I'd had so many plans for this space when I'd first bought it. I'd planned to update the sinks and the chairs. Not to mention the cabinets. The only thing I've managed in the past few years is new paint. I thought I'd have more time before I'd be forced to make the improvements. I know what

Linc and I discussed, but I wonder if I should just face the fact that this place needs more than I've been giving it.

I know what's in my savings account, down to the cent. I've been saving since I purchased the building 4 years ago. I'd planned to use it to buy a house, but now I wonder if that's going to be possible. I reach for my phone and pull up the listing for the house I've had my eye on for years. It's a bit too large for one person, but I know in my heart it's supposed to be mine. It's also slightly out of my price range, hence the years of saving. I scroll through the listing photos, feeling a pang of regret for what I know I need to do. What good is buying a house if my business falls apart around me? My focus needs to be on getting this place in shape. Then I can worry about how to buy my dream house. I just hope the house doesn't sell again before I can find a way to buy it.

Closing the tab, I pull up the wish list I made for the salon when I bought it 4 years ago. I've updated it regularly each time I've found something that's perfect for the space. I have the exact sinks and faucets I want, along with the chairs. I know what each item costs and there's a running total at the bottom of the list. I know exactly what it will take to buy the items I need. What I don't know is how much I'll need to spend to have them installed. But I know someone who does.

CHAPTER 7

Harlow

I wake up early the next morning after a fitful night's sleep. After Linc left last night, I'd spent nearly 2 hours scrubbing the floors in the shop and airing out anything that had gotten wet. Luckily, nothing seems to be permanently damaged besides the pipes themselves. Along with whatever is happening with the wiring in the building.

I try not to think about everything that's wrong and focus on getting ready for Linc's arrival. Now that I've decided to renovate the building, I need to find a way to talk to Linc about it. I want to see if hiring his company is an option. I know he's been busy lately. He's even had to hire more people onto his crew. He may not have time to fit my shop into his schedule. But I trust him to do a good job and to give me a fair price. I don't delve too deeply into my reasons for trusting Linc when technically, I barely know him. It has nothing to do with my silly childhood crush. That would be ridiculous.

By the time Linc arrives, promptly at 9am, I'm a walking ball of nerves. I don't know if it's the thought of seeing him again, one-on-one; or if it's the worry over what this endeavor will cost me. Either way, I have knots in my stomach as I watch him walking toward my front door from his truck. He's wearing a pair of light wash jeans that fit him entirely too well and a dark gray Henley that shows off his muscled forearms. His long hair is pulled back off his face and my hands practically itch to touch it. A shiver runs through me, and I swear I feel myself grow wet just from looking at him. This is going to be a long morning. Doing my best to ignore the flutters in my belly—and lower—I paste on a smile and open the door to let Linc inside.

"Good morning," I say. "I hope I'm not messing up your Sunday?"

He shakes his head. "This shouldn't take too long. Ella and I have plans to have lunch and ice cream later. But she's with Cole now."

I nod. "Ice cream is always a good call."

He grins, setting off more of those stupid flutters inside me. "Ella thinks it was her idea and that she's pulling one over on me," he says as he walks toward the sink in the back. "But the joke is on her because I've been craving one of those massive sundaes from Judy's all week."

I laugh. "They make the best sundaes in town."

"Damned right, they do," Linc says with a nod. "Alright, let's take a look at what I'm working with." He walks toward the back of the salon where the two sinks are located, talking as he goes.

"With any luck, it'll just be some pipes and fittings. Shouldn't be too much trouble."

I take a deep breath, working up the nerve to ask him what it will cost to replace both sinks and install two new chairs. And whether he can recommend an electrician I can trust to look at the wiring. I don't want to hire just anyone, and I know Linc only works with reputable people. Judging by how angry he'd been yesterday when he found out I'd been one of Todd Ralston's victims, I feel like I can trust his word when it comes to finding a dependable electrician.

I follow him to the sink where he bends down to inspect the broken pipes. His jeans stretch tight over his ass as he does, and I can't help but look. It should be illegal for a man to look that good in a pair of jeans. I know I shouldn't ogle him, but I'm only human. I can't seem to help myself where Linc is concerned. I wonder how I'm supposed to work with him and learn anything without being distracted the entire time by how much I want to kiss him. Or grab his ass.

"These pipes are pretty old," Linc says, oblivious to my pervy thoughts. "It would be good to replace them all if you're okay with that. It'll take a little longer, but the cost shouldn't be too much higher."

I nod, even though he's looking at the pipe, rather than at me. "Right," I say. "And what if we did more?"

He turns to look at me, brows raised. "Like what?"

"What if we replaced both sinks and chairs and replaced all the pipes?"

Linc's eyes go wide, and he looks thoughtful. "Well, it'll take a little longer, but not by much. Replacing the pipes will be the most labor-intensive part. But I'm sure you know the sinks and chairs will be the most expensive element."

I nod, feeling nauseated at the idea of how much money I'm about to spend. But I already did the math last night and I know I can afford it. I just need to be frugal with some of my other expenses. And I need to get clients back into the shop as soon as possible.

"I can run the shop with one working sink for now while we wait for the new sinks and chairs to come in. The ones I want will need to be ordered."

"If you're going to replace them, you might as well get what you want."

I almost laugh. "Believe me, I've been shopping for new sinks since I bought the place," I say. "I know exactly what I want."

He nods. "If you're going to operate with one sink, I guess you don't need me poking around here until the new ones show up."

I balk at the idea that he won't be working here every day, but I can't argue his point. If he's not going to do any plumbing work right now, he doesn't need to be here. But I still need to talk to him about the electrical work.

"Actually," I say. "I was hoping you could help me find an electrician to thoroughly check the wiring."

"That's a good idea," he says. "I don't like the idea of you in this old building with what might be faulty wiring."

Is he worried about me? I ignore the warm feeling spreading through me at the idea. He's just being kind. Knowing the type of man Linc is, he'd probably worry about anyone in my situation. It's not personal. He's just being a nice guy.

"Exactly." I nod. "But I want to make sure that whoever I hire won't rip me off or lie to me. I've had enough of that already."

His jaw clenches and his eyes narrow as he pulls in a breath. He's no doubt thinking about Todd Ralston, the con artist. After a few seconds of silence, he nods.

"I know someone," he says. "He won't charge you just to come look at it and he won't bullshit you. He's honest and does good work. And he's a licensed electrician who specializes in older buildings."

I feel a spark of optimism. Things just might be looking up. If this person Linc knows can give me a good deal, maybe I won't have to use all my savings on the renovations. My dream house might still be within reach, after all.

"Really?" I ask, excitement coloring my voice. "Do you have his contact info?"

Linc grins. "As a matter of fact, I do."

I pull my phone out of my back pocket. "What his name?"

"I actually have his number, if you'd rather I just give you that?" Linc says.

I nod as I unlock my phone and pull up the keypad. "That would be great. Thank you so much."

Linc recites a stream of numbers from memory, and I type them into my phone and save the number under "Electrician". Pocketing the phone, I smile up at Linc.

"Thank you," I say. "I really appreciate your help on this. If I can get a good price on the electrical repairs, it'll be a lifesaver."

Linc returns the smile with one of his own. "It's my pleasure."

Something about the way those three words roll off his tongue has my breath catching in my throat. Had he meant that to sound so sexy? Probably not. Get a grip. It's a common expression. Like saying, 'You're welcome' or 'No problem'. I'm sure he didn't mean it to sound sexual. Even if it did make me want to see what else might be *his pleasure.* And now I'm fantasizing about a man who's just here to do me a favor. Am I really that desperate?

I shy away from the answer to that question. I'm not desperate, exactly. It's just that this is Linc. And I've spent more time alone with him in the last 24 hours than I have in the last 20 years. Of course, my mind is going to wander a bit. I'm a living, breathing woman with two working eyes. And he's gorgeous. Can I help it if everything he says sounds sexual?

Yes, you pervert. He's not trying to be sexual.

Shaking off my dirty thoughts, I nod. "I'll give him a call later today. Oh. Or maybe I should wait until tomorrow. It being Sunday, and all."

Linc shakes his head as he makes a few notes in a small pocket notebook. He carries a tiny notebook. Of course, he does. Why is that hot? Right. Because I'm a pervert who finds everything he does hot.

"He'll answer," Linc says, pocketing the notebook. "Give him a call."

"Okay. I will."

"Good." He gestures toward the sink. "I might be able to get a discount on the new sinks and chairs. Can you show me what you want?"

I grin, excited by the prospect of shopping, even if I hate the idea of how much it's going to cost. I reach for my phone again and pull up the link I bookmarked last night.

"I've got it narrowed down to these two," I say, swiping back and forth between two web pages. The two sinks are the same price, but I can't decide which one I like better. They're both gorgeous and functional. Linc studies the two sinks for several long moments. I don't know why, but I'd expected him to be dismissive about my choice. Most men zone out when I talk about my work. But Linc leans in close to see the screen, his face inches from mine. I go still, even as my heart hammers in my chest. He's so close, I know I could easily kiss him if I turned just a little.

"What about the chairs?" he asks, startling me from my thoughts. I clear my throat and toggle over to another web page and show him the chair I decided on.

"This one is the perfect height and reclines to the perfect angle," I say, hoping my voice doesn't sound shaky. "Plus, all the reviews seem to be positive."

He nods before reaching over to swipe the screen back to the sinks. Pointing, he says, "That one looks more comfortable. See the shape of the front of the bowl? It's more ergonomic for your clients' head to rest on. It'll also work better with the chair you want."

I blink at the phone screen. I hadn't thought of that. I'm sort of surprised that Linc did. He's right, though. The chairs I picked won't work with one of the sinks. I guess my decision is made.

"Huh. You're right," I say, turning to face him. He's still dangerously close as he grins at me.

"It happens on occasion."

That grin is dangerous to my health, so I try not to stare at it too long. Clearing my throat, I gesture toward my phone.

"Do you want me to text you the links?"

"Email them to the official company email," he says. "Helps with the paperwork later."

I nod. "Right."

Linc tells me the email address and I send him the links. Now that I've made the decision to replace the sinks and chairs, I feel less stressed about the whole endeavor. I've never been what I would call impulsive. I usually worry over a major decision for a while before making it. But once my mind is made up, I always feel better and I tend to act on it quickly. I know this project is going to be expensive but knowing that Linc is going to try and get me better deals makes me feel less stressed over the financial aspect.

"Thank you, again," I say. "I know you didn't really sign on for replacing sinks. I can pay you for the difference. I doubt those tools are going to cover it."

He waves a hand, dismissing my words. "Don't worry about it."

I narrow my eyes at him. "I'll say it again. That's a shitty way to run a business."

Linc barks out a laugh, catching me off-guard. What I said wasn't that funny. And it's not the first time he's heard me say it.

He shakes his head, still smiling. "Let me worry about that, Harlow. For now, let's focus on getting your new items ordered and on their way. Then we can worry about everything else."

I nod, once again feeling a sense of peace settle over me at his calm, no-nonsense words. I'm so used to always being the one who needs to fix what's broken that it feels strange to have someone else helping me. Not just helping but taking control of the situation. It should feel strange, but instead it's comforting. I'm not used to having someone else take charge of the messes·in my life. I'm not quite sure how to feel about it.

CHAPTER 8

Linc

I've barely left Harlow's place before my cellphone rings. Grinning, I press the button on my truck's steering wheel to answer the call.

"Prescott Construction. How can I help you?" I say, the words sounding obnoxiously cheery and upbeat.

There's a brief hesitation from the caller before I hear Harlow's voice. "Hi. I'm calling to see about a quote for some electrical work."

Keeping that annoyingly obnoxious customer service voice going, I say, "Absolutely, ma'am. You've called the right place!" It's hard to contain my laughter.

There's another long pause before Harlow speaks again. "Linc?"

My grin stretches wider, but I manage not to laugh. "Yes? Who is this?"

"Damn it, Linc," Harlow says. "I thought you were giving me the number of an electrician."

Now, I do laugh. "I did. Me."

I hear her sigh. "But you let me think it was someone you know."

I turn the truck toward my street. "I mean, who knows me better than me?"

There's a sound that might just be a growl of frustration and I almost laugh again. Teasing Harlow is more fun than I imagined it could be. But she's definitely getting irritated now.

"Look," I say, adopting a conciliatory tone. "I wasn't lying. I'm a licensed electrician and I specialize in older buildings. Plus, I won't give you a bad deal or lie to you. I do solid work and I already have knowledge of the problem. Which saves time, right?"

I can practically hear the wheels turning in her head. For whatever reason, Harlow doesn't seem eager to work with me. I'm not sure why. I've never done or said anything rude to her. Unless she's taken my near silence during our many group outings to mean that I'm an asshole rather than just awkwardly shy. I frown at that. Maybe she does think I'm a jerk.

"I promise, I'm a decent guy," I say, feeling the need to defend myself. "I won't screw you over."

She mutters something I can't quite make out.

"What?"

"Nothing," she says on a sigh. "When do you want to come take a look at the wiring?"

I smile. Victory. "Already did. Yesterday. I know what needs to be replaced and what needs to be repaired. I have a rough idea of what it will cost. I just need to check on a couple things before I can give you an official estimate."

There's another brief pause. "Wow," she says. "Okay. Um, I'm afraid to ask, but can you give me a rough idea of what it's going to cost? I won't hold you to a price until you give your official estimate, obviously. But just so I have an idea of what I'm going to be paying."

I want to refuse her request. It's on the tip of my tongue to do so. I'd never give anyone else an unofficial price quote. It's too easy to miscalculate and then the customer always gets angry when the cost ends up higher than the unofficial price I'd given. I learned that the hard way. But this is Harlow. I know how hard she's worked to build her business and to keep it going. Besides, after Ella went to bed last night, I spent two hours working on a quote for her. I didn't know if she'd decide to make the electrical repairs or not, but if she did, I wanted her to be armed with the knowledge of exactly what needed to be fixed and what it might cost. I don't want someone to take advantage of her again.

With a sigh, I break my own rule and give her the number I'd calculated the night before. She doesn't need to know that I subtracted my own normal hourly rate from the estimate. The sum is still a significant one. Besides, I know she'll just argue about it if she knows. She's silent for a few moments before speaking. Her voice is different than before. She sounds resigned and maybe a little sad.

"How long will it take?"

I want to say something that will reassure her. I know how much an unexpected expense like this can affect a small business. But I also know that Harlow is a woman who appreciates honesty above all else. I won't sugarcoat things just to make her feel better. It would only piss her off.

"My work schedule is booked through the end of the month," I say. "But if I come by in the evenings for a couple hours, I think I can have it finished in two weeks or so. The good thing is that the apartment was wired for electricity well after the original salon, so I don't need to do any repairs up there."

She sighs. "It's just my business that needs all the help."

"Unfortunately, yes. But try not to worry. You have one sink that's up and running right now. I'll try to do the electrical work in stages, so you won't be down for long, and you'll still be able to run your business in the meantime. It's going to be okay. Trust me."

I don't know why I added that last part. Why should she trust me? She barely knows me. But I don't want to be lumped in with the likes of Todd Ralston or her cheating ex. I get the feeling Harlow hasn't had a lot of people in her life she could trust. For some reason, I want to be one of them.

"Okay," she says. "You're hired."

I smile as I pull into my driveway. "Thank you for your business."

"Does this make me your boss now?" Harlow asks.

I blink at the teasing tone. Before I can think through my response, the words are out. "Do you like to be in charge, then?"

There's a moment of hesitation before she speaks again. "Not always."

I'm not sure what we're even talking about now. Is this still about business? It doesn't feel like it. And when had the shift occurred? It feels like I'm flirting with Harlow and she's flirting back.

"Care to elaborate?" I ask.

The silence stretches out between us for several seconds before Harlow answers.

"I should go. We'll talk soon."

Disappointed that she's ending our conversation, I almost sigh. But I switch my voice back to professional mode instead. "Right. I'll come by tomorrow with the contract and get started."

"Sounds great. Thanks, Linc."

We end the call, but I remain sitting in my truck in my driveway for several minutes, replaying the conversation in my head. Why had I asked her that? It just came out. I hadn't planned the words. But she'd kept it going. Right? Had I offended her? I hope not. Her voice had been teasing when she'd asked if she was my boss now. But maybe that had just been normal teasing and I'd just read something into it that didn't exist. I lower my forehead to the steering wheel with a sigh. Why do I have to be so awkward around her? The next couple of weeks should be interesting.

CHAPTER 9

Harlow

I stare at the phone in my hand for several minutes after ending the call with Linc. What the hell was that? Had I just been flirting with him? Had he flirted back? Why did I make that boss comment? I'd just meant it as a teasing sort of question, but then his voice had shifted, and I'd had all sorts of inappropriate thoughts about being bossed around. By Linc.

I shift a little in my chair as I feel a little thrill run through me at the idea. I allow myself a moment to picture what that would look like. Linc, in control. Telling me what to do. Telling me how to please him. A little sigh escapes me, and I can feel myself grow wet just thinking about it. What the hell is wrong with me? Two encounters with the man and I'm picturing him naked like some sort of sex fiend. I need help.

My phone buzzes in my hand, pulling me from my thoughts. It's Piper. I texted her last night to tell her that Linc had agreed to help with the repairs and was coming by this morning to assess the situation. I hadn't given her all the details of our conversation yesterday, though. I'm sure she's dying to know everything.

Piper: I just saw Linc leave. What's the verdict?

I start to type out a response and then delete it. Nothing I can say in a text will adequately explain. Besides, I could use some coffee.

Me: I'm coming to the shop.

Piper: Ooh, that bad? Your latte will be ready when you get here.

I smile as I grab my keys and shut off the lights in the shop. Piper knows me well. We've grown close since she moved here nearly a year ago. Before she moved to Peach Tree, I didn't have any close friends I could confide in. I've grown used to her presence in my life in a short time. I like knowing I have someone nearby to celebrate my wins with or to commiserate when life punches me in the tit. I'm glad she's sticking around. I know I have Luke to thank for that. He helped make her shop a success when this town wouldn't give her much of a chance. Granted, she'd also fallen hard for the guy in the process, but I don't blame her for that. Luke Wolfe is one of the hottest guys in this town.

That thought brings me back to the actual hottest guy in town, Linc. At least, in my opinion. Luke has that golden boy thing going for him, which is nice if you're into that. But Linc? I let out a little involuntary sigh as I lock the front door. The long, dark hair? The beard? The callouses on his hands that I'd felt for just a few seconds yesterday? Not to mention those thickly muscled arms peeking out from his shirt sleeves. Add in the quiet, brooding personality and he's the perfect male specimen. My stomach flips again and I feel another rush of heat to my core. Just thinking about that man is enough to turn me into a raging ball of sexual tension. I don't know how I'm going to get through working with him every day. Why had I thought that was a good idea?

My thoughts ramble in circles as I make the short walk to Piping Hot Brews, the coffee shop that Piper owns. It's an adorable shop filled with lots of comfortable chairs and bookshelves. It's the perfect place to come and enjoy a cup of coffee and a good book. And there's no place like it in town. Once the people here finally gave Piper and her coffee shop a chance, Piping Hot started thriving. Now, I see the white cups with the shop's logo on them all over town. I'm happy for my friend's success, especially since it means she's going to stay in Peach Tree. I've gotten spoiled having a friend living and working just down the street. I don't want to go back to being alone here.

The tinkling bell on Piping Hot's front door pulls me out of my musings and I see Piper smiling at me from behind the counter, a steaming cup in her hand. I flash her a wide grin and make my way over to take the cup from her. Inhaling deeply, I savor the scent of the coffee.

"You are a true hero among women," I say, raising the cup to my lips for a sip.

Piper rolls her eyes, but she's smiling. "Wait until you taste my blueberry coffee cake."

She hands me a small plate with a thick slice of cake along with a fork.

"Oh, my god. You're amazing," I gush. "Tell me, did it hurt?"

When she just looks at me blankly, I say, "When you fell from heaven?"

She rolls her eyes again. "Shut up and stop stalling," she says, pointing toward the back corner of the shop where a small sofa sits empty. "Come sit with me and tell me what's happening with the shop. What did Linc say?"

At the mention of his name, I feel that stupid fluttery sensation again, but I keep my focus on the coffee and pastry in my hand and hope Piper doesn't notice. We make our way over to the couch and sit. I make a show of getting comfortable, taking my time. Piper just watches me, waiting patiently. I take a big bite of the coffee cake and take my time chewing, not just to stall for time but also because it's the best damned coffee cake I've ever eaten.

"Holy shit," I say, trying not to spray crumbs as I talk with my mouth full. "This is fucking delicious!"

Piper laughs and hands me a napkin. "Thanks," she says. "Luke said the same thing, but I wondered if he was just biased."

I shrug. "He's definitely biased. We both are. But that doesn't mean this cake isn't amazing. Because it is." I shovel another forkful of the moist, crumbly cake into my mouth, savoring it.

Piper waits patiently, watching while I eat every last crumb of the cake before setting the plate down on the table with a sigh and picking up my coffee cup.

"You good?" she asks.

I nod. "Yep."

When several seconds go by and I don't say anything more, Piper sighs. "Will you just tell me already? How bad is it?"

I keep my gaze on my cup. "Bad."

Piper reaches out and puts a hand on my arm. "Can Linc fix it?"

I nod. "Yeah, but I need to replace both sinks and some of the plumbing. While I'm at it, I'm going to replace the chairs too. No sense in doing it half-assed. The wiring in the shop is in bad shape too, but I don't need to rewire the whole building. Just the shop itself. Which will still probably cost most of my savings."

She looks stricken. "But that means—"

"I know," I say, stopping her before she can say it for me. "Buying back my mom's house is on hold. It's just going to take longer. That's all."

Piper doesn't say anything. She just nods and gives my arm a squeeze. "You'll get there," she says. "I know it."

I'd gotten drunk with Piper one night several months ago and confided in her about all the things that had gone wrong after my mom's death. She'd hugged me and we'd commiserated over our respective losses. In my case, I'd been all alone when I lost my mom. But Piper had had her older sister to look after her. Granted, I'd been an adult when my mom had died, but that hadn't made the loss any easier.

When I'd told her about having to sell the house that my mom had worked her ass off to buy to pay off hospital bills, Piper had nearly cried with me. I've spent the six years since I sold it saving and waiting for it to go back onto the market. Piper is the one who let me know about the listing she'd stumbled across last week. I know she feels my disappointment as strongly as I do right now. But I need to make a choice. As much as I want to own my mom's house, I need my business to survive more.

I give her a small smile that isn't convincing in the least. "Yeah," I say. "Eventually."

Piper doesn't say anything. She just gives my arm another squeeze. I love that about her. She always respects my silence when it's clear I'm not ready to talk about something. She gets me.

I sip from my cup. "But that's not all of it," I say. "The price Linc quoted me for the plumbing doesn't even include labor. That's just for the supplies and new fixtures."

Piper's mouth drops open. "How much is he charging you for labor?"

"That's just it," I say. "He won't give me a real quote. He says he isn't letting me pay him for his time or his work. Just the parts."

Piper smiles. "Well, that's great. He's such a nice guy."

I nod. "Yep. Nice guy."

Piper's eyes narrow. "There's something else?"

I shrug. "Sort of. Not really. He agreed to show me how to do the repairs. In case I ever have this kind of issue again."

Piper laughs. "No offense, but that sounds like the least fun thing I can think of."

I laugh with her. "You're probably right," I say. "But I can't afford to have something like this happen again and be helpless to do anything about it."

"You? Helpless? Ha!"

Piper's amusement annoys me for some reason. It reminds me of what Linc said yesterday about me never having been helpless before. I've worked hard to project that sort of confidence and capability. Fake it 'til you make it. If my closest friend believes it, I guess it's working. But it doesn't mean it doesn't sting a little for them not to see the truth. Immediately, I tell myself that it's not fair to be hurt by that. I'm showing them what I want them to see. It's not their fault if I'm a good liar. Shaking off the thought, I bring myself back to the current conversation.

"You know what I mean," I say. "I need to be able to fix things myself."

"I get it," Piper says softly. "If anyone can, it's you."

I smile at her. "Thanks."

"Before I forget," Piper says, "Layna said she'll just stay with us for now. Until everything is settled with your place or she finds her own place. Whichever happens first."

I wince, guilt washing over me. "Shit. I almost forgot. She can still stay with me if she wants. I promise the place is not the death trap Linc previously suspected."

Piper shrugs. "She's fine. Besides, something's off with her lately and I kind of want to keep her around so maybe she'll tell me what's wrong."

I nod. "I get that. For what it's worth, she seems pretty happy with her decision to move here."

"I'm happy she's here," Piper says. "Truly. Having my sister here makes it feel like I have everything I want. But I want to know that it's what she wants and that she's not just doing it for me. I don't want her to ruin her career over her quarter-life crisis."

I smile. "Do you think that's what she's going through?"

Piper sighs. "I don't know. But I plan to find out. Enough of me, though. Back to you. What's got you so flustered when it comes to this repair job?"

My gaze shoots to hers. "What?"

"Is it just the money? Or is it something else?" she asks. "Because something has you acting a little off."

I shake my head in denial. "I don't know what you mean. I'm just worried about the salon and the money."

"Linc said he can fix it," she says. "Luke says he's a good guy, and I trust Luke."

I nod, fighting against that fluttery feeling at the mention of Linc's name.

"Hmm," Piper says, a knowing tone in her voice.

I narrow my eyes at her. "Hmm? What, hmm?"

She points a finger at me. "You get weird whenever I say Linc's name."

I open my mouth to argue, but my face betrays me when a blush creeps up my cheeks.

Piper makes a startled sound and her mouth drops open. "Holy shit! I'm right, aren't I?"

I shake my head. "Shut up!" I whisper, looking around as if someone might overhear us, though no one is looking in our direction.

She looks absolutely delighted by this new revelation. "Did something happen?" she asks in an excited whisper. "Did he kiss you? Are you two secretly a thing? Why didn't you tell me?"

I shove her arm lightly. "No!" I say, suddenly annoyed by the line of questioning. "Stop it. There's nothing between me and Linc."

Piper eyes me for a moment, clearly trying to piece together this new puzzle. I can feel those stupid butterflies in my belly going nuts again.

"Were you guys ever a thing?" she asks in a quiet voice. "Like, back in high school?"

My face goes hot, and I feel like the air has been sucked out of the room. I manage a laugh that I hope sounds dismissive, but I'm pretty sure it just sounds like I'm choking.

"Me and Linc?" I scoff. "No. Definitely not."

Piper just looks at me, not saying a word. But I know her. She's waiting for me to crack, to spill the tea. The problem is that there's never been any tea to spill where Linc is concerned. There's only ever been my crush on him and his absolute indifference to me. I've never told another soul about that crush, either. It's always just been this secret that I've kept, barely able to acknowledge it even to myself. I always thought I'd get over it eventually. Now, here I am almost 20 years into this crush and I'm starting to wonder if this is just my life. Am I always going to wonder what it would be like to kiss Lincoln Prescott?

I look up to find Piper watching me, waiting for me to speak. I feel the butterflies in my stomach having a full-blown riot as they do anytime I've thought of anyone finding out how I feel about Linc. But it might be nice to share this secret with someone. It might be good to get it out. And this is Piper. She's my best friend. I trust her not to say a word. Besides, I think she already suspects something is up, especially since I can't seem to be myself around him. I sigh.

"Linc and I have never been a thing," I say, letting the truth of how I feel about that fact color my tone.

Piper's eyes widen slightly, but her voice is soft when she speaks. "But you want to be?"

My heart pounds harder and I suck in a shaky breath. Then, I say aloud the one thing I've sworn to never tell a soul. "Yes," I whisper. "I've had a crush on him since we were ten."

I bury my face in my hands, trying to hide the blush I can feel heating my cheeks.

"Holy shit," Piper says. "Have you tried telling him?"

My gaze shoots to her, eyes wide, and I know she can read the horror on my face as I shake my head. "What? No! Absolutely not!"

Piper just looks confused. "Why not?"

"Are you insane? I know you're still kind of new here but let me explain. I was a band geek. The geekiest of band geeks. Invisible. Linc was a football god. Everyone knew him. He was a legend in this town. There was no way he even knew who I was in high school, and we graduated in a class of like, 200 kids."

Piper rolls her eyes. "High school was a long time ago, Harlow."

"I'm not that old," I say defensively, making her laugh.

"That's not what I meant, and you know it," she says. "And stop trying to change the subject. Why did you never make a move on him? Did you ever think that maybe Linc feels the same way?"

I scoff. "Definitely not. And if he did, he's had, like 20 years to tell me."

Piper's voice is gentle. "Maybe he thinks the same thing about you."

I ignore the sharp spike of hope that zings through me at her words. It's nothing I didn't daydream about all through junior high school. And high school. And maybe for the first year after I left Peach Tree.

"Men can be oblivious," Piper says. "Besides, he's been busy raising Ella these past 8 years. That's not a bad excuse for not noticing the hot girl next door who's been crushing on him."

I roll my eyes. "Shut up," I mutter. "Don't make me regret telling you."

Piper shrugs. "Maybe this is the perfect opportunity for you to shoot your shot."

I shake my head, wishing I'd just sent her a text and avoided this conversation altogether.

"I can't," I say.

"Why not?" she asks.

Rolling my eyes, I set my coffee cup on the table, and I shift to face her. "Because you're my best friend. My only friend in this whole town. And I've lived here for most of my life, so that should tell you something. And you're marrying Linc's best friend."

When Piper just looks at me without saying anything, I sigh. "If he turned me down, I'd have to live with seeing him every time I go to Peach Fuzz, and every time I hang out with you and Luke. And in a town this small, every time I go to the freaking grocery store. No, thank you."

She looks at me for a moment before responding. "So, you're a chicken shit?"

I reach for my coffee cup. "Basically."

She waits until I've taken a sip and settled back against the couch again. "Don't use our friendship as a reason not to go after what you want," she says softly. "If he's worth 20 years of infatuation, maybe you should see if he's worth more. Just a suggestion."

I sigh. "You're not an excuse. I love our friendship, Piper. And no, I don't think my crush on Linc would mess that up. The truth is, I don't think I could take it if I finally told him, and he turned me down. It's easier to live with the wanting."

I hate myself for the catch in my voice and the burning in my eyes. I haven't cried in years, and certainly not over a boy. Piper's arms come around me and she pulls me against her for a sideways hug.

"I get it," she says. "I respect whatever decision you make. But just know that I think he'd be lucky to have you."

I smile, reaching up to put a hand on her arm that's wrapped around me.

"Thanks."

Piper releases me. She's quiet for a moment before she says, "What are you going to do about the house?" Her voice is gentle, as if she's worried I might break.

I force a smile. "The same thing I've been doing for the past six years. The timeline might have changed, but my goals haven't. First off, I need to prove to my clients that I can still do the work they expect, even with this setback. I'm sure Dottie has been busy letting everyone in town know about what happened."

Piper winces. "Actually, she was here this morning."

My stomach drops, though I shouldn't be surprised. "What did she say?"

"Nothing directly to me," Piper says. "But I overheard her talking to a group of ladies from the church and telling them that your shop is practically destroyed and that you might not be able to reopen."

"What?!" I practically shout the word before remembering I'm in public. I get an odd look from the new barista at the counter, but Piper gives the kid a smile and a wave to let him know everything is okay and he turns back to stocking the shelf.

"Seriously?" I groan. "I knew she was a gossip, but now she's just making up lies."

"More like exaggerating the truth," Piper says, earning a glare from me.

"Whose side are you on?"

Her eyes go wide. "Yours. Obviously. But you know this town better than I do. They love a juicy story."

I sigh, rolling my eyes. "One broken pipe isn't a juicy story," I mutter.

Piper nudges me with her elbow. "But the hot guy coming to fix your broken pipe is."

I feel my face heating against my will. "Shut up."

She grins at me and waggles her eyebrows. "Is he going to come lay some pipe, Harlow?"

"Shut up."

"What kind of tool is he working with?"

"Shut up."

"I love a man who's good with his hands."

"I'm telling Luke about this."

Piper just laughs. "You will not. It's against girl code. Besides, I can admire an attractive man when I see one."

She's right and she knows it. I won't tell Luke about her teasing. Because then he might ask why we were discussing Linc in the first place and then another person would know about my stupid crush.

"I hate you," I mutter.

Piper waves away my words. "Nah. You love me. Can't live without me."

I glare at her through narrowed eyes. She's right, but I won't give her the satisfaction of admitting it.

"Hmm. Whatever you choose to believe."

CHAPTER 10

Harlow

I spend most of Sunday afternoon doing damage control. I start by calling my clients for the coming week and reassuring them that the shop will be open for business and confirming that they'll still be coming in for their scheduled appointments. Luckily, no one cancels. That's a surprise that I'm grateful for. Something is finally going my way.

Then, I call Dottie and apologize again for what happened and offer her a free haircut next time she comes for her appointment. I assure her that the shop is back in working order and that it will be like new the next time she sees it. I make sure to talk a big game in hopes that she'll spread the word around town. There's no guarantee she will, but I need all the help I can get. I even drop Linc's name, letting her know that he's the contractor.

Linc's popularity is a holdover from his days as a high school football star. It doesn't hurt that he grew up to be one of the nicest guys in town. Not to mention the hottest. Needless to say, the ladies of Peach Tree are fans of Linc Prescott. I'm hoping to use that popularity to my advantage. Everyone in town knows Linc's business does quality work. The knowledge that he has a hand in fixing my salon should help my own credibility. By the time I end my call with Dottie, I feel marginally better about the whole situation. I do feel a little guilty using his name like that, but I tell myself it's for a good cause. And I doubt Linc would be bothered by it. In fact, he'd probably laugh about it.

By the time Monday morning rolls around, I'm too busy pretending everything is perfect to worry about being nervous. I talk up the planned renovations with my clients, making it seem like they'd already been in the works before Saturday's disaster. When my last client finally leaves in the afternoon, I'm exhausted. I feel like I've run a marathon after being on my feet all day and my face hurts from all the fake smiling.

I'm sweeping the floor when I hear a knock and turn to see Linc standing on the other side of the glass door. He gives me a little wave and a smile as I walk over and unlock the door to let him in.

"Sorry," I say. "I guess I should have left it unlocked. Habit."

He shakes his head. "It's a good habit to have. Even in a town this small, you should lock your doors."

"You can never be too careful," I say, wincing inwardly at the awkwardness of the conversation. When did things between us get so awkward?

Linc motions toward the back of the building. "I'm going to go get started, if that's okay."

"Of course."

He walks past me, and I can't help but follow his progress with my eyes. Damn, the man looks good in those jeans. They fit snug across his ass, and I can't help but imagine what it would feel like in my hands. Great. He's been here for all of 5 minutes and I'm already ogling him and thinking dirty thoughts about his body. How the hell I'm going to last through 2 weeks or more of this, I don't know. Especially since I asked him to show me how to fix it. What was I thinking?

"Harlow?" Linc calls from the back room.

"Yeah?"

"Didn't you want me to teach you?"

Shit.

"Yeah," I call out. "I'll be right there. Just give me a minute to finish sweeping."

"No problem."

I finish sweeping the floor in record time despite my nerves urging me to stall. I remind myself that I asked Linc to teach me. Which means I can't back out now. And I need to stop acting like a weirdo around him. He's just a guy I went to high school with. Right. Like that line is going to work. After taking a few deep breaths to steady myself, I head toward the back of the salon where I see that Linc is already pulling items out of the bag he carried in earlier. He glances up when he sees me and smiles. I ignore the way that smile hits me right in the nether region and attempt a smile in return.

"What's first on the agenda?" I ask.

Linc gestures toward the panel on the wall that I know houses the electrical breakers for the building. "I figured I'd replace some of the breakers for now, so you'll be able to wash clothes. I know a salon uses a lot of towels. Plus, those cape things." He waves his hand around his chest in a vague motion.

I'm oddly touched by the fact that he considered the needs of my salon. Most men wouldn't have thought about the laundry a salon produces. It's not one of those details they usually notice.

I smile. "Thanks. That's nice of you to think of it. Luckily, I just washed all the linen on Friday before all this happened. So, there's not much laundry from the salon." I grimace. "But my own clothes are definitely piling up. Sundays are usually my laundry days."

He grins. "I know the feeling. If I don't stay on top of mine and Ella's laundry, it turns into a nightmare." He gestures toward the electrical panel. "I've been looking at your wiring and I don't know that we'll need to replace all of it down here. I'll need to do a better inspection to know for sure. But this panel isn't up to code. I think they just added whatever they wanted as the need arose instead of properly configuring the breakers."

I nod as if I'm familiar with everything he's saying. As if I don't have a ton of questions already. What's wrong with the panel? How can he tell it's not up to code? How long will it take to fix? Will I be without electricity for days? As if he can sense my confusion and worry, Linc reaches out a hand and touches my shoulder.

"I told you to trust me, remember?" he says, voice gentle. "I've got this. I promise."

I nod, feeling immediately better at his calm reassurance. "Okay," I say, injecting confidence into the single word. "What's first?"

Linc's smile is brilliant and lasts for just a second before his face takes on a serious expression. He nods toward the panel.

"First thing you need to understand," he says, his tone filled with authority. "That thing right there can kill you if you're not careful."

I nod, remembering the little shock I'd felt the other day. "I don't want a repeat."

"I'm serious," he says, his voice hard and commanding. "You need to do everything I tell you or I won't teach you."

His dark eyes are laser-focused on mine. I couldn't look away if I wanted to. There's an intensity to his gaze that I don't think I've ever seen before. It sends a liquid heat through me to pool low in my gut. I'm locked in place, unable to move or turn away. I somehow manage a small nod.

"I understand," I say, my voice barely above a whisper.

"Good," he says, his gaze immediately softening into his normal, laid-back expression.

He turns back to the electrical panel and begins to explain things to me. I listen as best I can, but I can't get over what just happened. The command in his voice, the implication that I'd be disappointing him if I did anything other than what he instructed. Not to mention the way it had made me feel. Like I wanted his approval? Like I needed it. Since when do I obey a man telling me what to do? And since when do I like it?

Since it's him, I think.

I force myself to focus on Linc's instruction, ignoring the way the deep rumble of his voice makes me want to hear that commanding tone again. I push out all thoughts of his strong hands on me, his arms wrapped around me, his mouth on mine. I absolutely do not daydream about what his ass might feel like in my hands.

He shows me how to make sure the current is turned off to the breaker before starting any work on it. Then he shows me how to test to see if a breaker is bad. It's all tedious and it would be downright boring if not for the man teaching me. He'd been right before, though. He could do this in half the time if he weren't teaching me. I should let him off the hook. It would save a lot of time. But I find that the more I'm around him, the more I like being in his presence.

He has a calm and patient demeanor that puts me at ease, even when I'm worried about my salon or trying not to be turned on by his mere presence. So, I stay. And I let him show me how to strip and splice wires and how to exchange a bad breaker for a new one. We've only been working for an hour or so before we're interrupted by Linc's phone ringing. He stops to look at the screen and frowns before answering.

"Cole, what's up? Is everything okay?"

I try not to watch him while he's on the phone, but I'm nosy. Besides, the room is small, and he doesn't leave it to find a more private area for his conversation. It's impossible not to hear.

"Is she okay?"

I feel a stab of worry. Is he talking about Ella? Did something happen? But Linc doesn't look as concerned as I think most parents would be if their kid was hurt. Not that I have a lot of experience in that department. My own father was gone before I turned 2 and my mother worked so much that she was rarely home to notice me. Linc is nodding now.

"No, I know," he says. "It's totally fine. You're needed at the restaurant. Just bring her by Harlow's place. We're close to wrapping up for the night anyway."

I feel a little pang at the thought that my time with Linc is nearly over for the day. It feels like he only just got here. But something obviously happened that requires Cole to go into work on his night off. Which means Ella needs her dad at home. I try to get Linc's attention to tell him that he can go ahead and go home if he needs to, but he ignores me. He ends the call with his brother and turns to look at me with a sheepish smile.

"That was Cole," he says.

"I figured."

"One of the bartenders twisted her ankle and needs to go get it checked out, so he needs to go fill in for her," he says.

I wince. "Is she okay?"

Linc nods. "He sounded like it's probably not serious. But she's getting x-rays as a precaution."

I nod. "Good idea. So, do you need to go?"

"Not just yet," he says, turning back to the panel. "Cole's bringing Ella here. He picked her up after school today because I was still working. But it won't take me long to finish what I'm doing. I hope that's okay?"

I blink. "Of course, it is. This is a kid friendly salon."

He laughs. "I didn't mean it like that. I just know that some people get irritated when kids are underfoot. Especially at a place of business."

I shrug. "This isn't that kind of business. And I'm not that kind of person. I love kids. I can't wait to meet her."

I don't know where all this is coming from. I mean, I do love kids. Even though technically the only kids I know are the ones who come to me with their parents for a haircut. Most of them behave well and get a lollipop at the end. But I haven't spent any prolonged time with a kid since I was a kid myself. I'm not sure I liked many of them back then. I'm suddenly a little nervous about meeting Linc's daughter. What if she's awful? What if she hates me? What if she hates me and that makes Linc decide he hates me too? Why do I suddenly feel the intense need to be liked by an eight-year-old?

Linc smiles, oblivious to my inner turmoil. "She's going to love you."

I manage to nod. "I hope so."

CHAPTER 11

Linc

Harlow walks to the front of the store to unlock the door before returning to help me work. Less than 10 minutes later, we hear the front door open, and Cole calls my name.

"Back here," I call out.

I'm leaning over my tool box, searching for my wire stripper when I hear footsteps.

"Daddy!"

Ella's voice calls out from behind me a second before she throws her arms around my neck, squeezing for all she's worth. I can't help but laugh as I pull her around for a hug. I give her an extra squeeze that makes her giggle before setting her on her feet. I take in her wild curls and the smudge of what looks like chocolate on her shirt.

"Did you have fun with Uncle Cole today?"

Her eyes light up and she nods. "Yep! We threw axes and had ice cream and Uncle Cole let me drive—"

"He did what?" I interrupt, looking around for my brother.

Cole is laughing from the doorway. "Way to sell me out, kid. And after I let you win."

"You didn't let me win," Ella says, sticking her tongue out at Cole. "I'm just better than you."

He rolls his eyes. "Please." Turning to me, he grins. "We went to the arcade. She's not bad at driving games. Though I wouldn't let her drive your truck just yet. She crashed like six times."

"Only four," Ella says.

Laughing, I rise to my feet, keeping a hand on Ella's shoulder. I gesture toward Harlow. "Ella, this is Harlow. She's friends with Piper. She owns this beauty shop."

Ella smiles up at Harlow. I risk a glance at her and see that she's smiling down at my daughter. I can see a hint of amusement in her blue eyes.

"It's so nice to meet you, Ella," she says.

"Are you marrying my dad?"

Harlow's expression goes from smiling to shock in an instant. Her wide eyes shoot back and forth between me and Ella. She opens her mouth to respond, but nothing comes out.

Marry? Who said anything about getting married? We're not even dating. I hear Cole's laughter from beside me and turn to see Ella grinning up at him. He reaches out a hand and she slaps it with her smaller one.

I shoot my brother a glare as Ella giggles up at him. "Seriously?"

Cole shrugs. "I couldn't resist." He looks over at Harlow. "Sorry," he says, but he looks more amused than apologetic. "I can't pass up a chance to make this guy uncomfortable."

Harlow seems to have recovered from the shock of Ella's question. She narrows her eyes at my brother. "Hmm," she says. "I'll think of a suitable act of revenge."

Cole looks delighted by the prospect and shoots her a grin. "Do your worst."

"Careful what you wish for," Harlow says in a sing-song voice.

Something sharp lances through me as I watch their brief interaction. Is Cole flirting? With Harlow? I've witnessed my brother flirt with women enough times that I should be able to recognize it. But why would he flirt with Harlow? He knows how I feel—felt, I correct—about her. That's all in the past. Surely, he wouldn't try to flirt with her now, would he? I mean, she's gorgeous. That's obvious to anyone with eyes. And single. As is Cole.

Before I can stop it, an image of the two of them together flashes into my head and it feels like someone punched me in the gut. I shake off the image as quickly as possible, but I can't quite forget it. What the hell is wrong with me? Why should I care if they are flirting? Harlow can flirt with whomever she wants. They're both adults.

"Don't you have to go?" I ask, my voice sounding harsher than I intended in the silence of the room.

Both their gazes shoot to me. Harlow looks confused, but Cole is grinning even wider now.

"Yeah," he says before turning back to Harlow. "I'd love to stay longer and catch up, Harlow. But duty calls." He lets out a sigh of regret.

Is it just me or is he being even flirtier now? Is he leaning in toward her? What the hell? Unable to look at them, I busy myself searching for the wire stripper.

Cole says something that makes Harlow laugh and makes me grit my teeth. Then he ruffles Ella's hair and waves at me before turning to go. I watch Harlow to see if she watches him leave, but she turns to Ella instead.

"Want to check out the spinning chairs?" she asks in a conspiratorial tone.

Ella's eyes light up. "How fast do they spin?"

Harlow nods toward the chair. "Depends on how fast someone can push you." She leads the way to one of the two chairs in the front room.

"I like your hair," Ella tells her as she climbs into the chair.

Harlow smiles, running a hand through her blonde and pink locks. "Thank you. But I like yours better. I always wished I had curly hair."

Ella gives her a wide smile, clearly pleased by the compliment. "You should do purple next," Ella says. "It's my favorite color."

"Mine, too," Harlow says. "I like to switch it up sometimes, though."

I watch the two of them for a few seconds as they spin in the chairs and talk about hair. Something about the scene makes my breath catch in my throat. It's the first time I've heard Ella talk about her hair at all, except when she gets irritated with her untamable curls. But right now, she's so animated discussing it with Harlow. I wonder if she's never cared about her hair before because she's been surrounded by men for most of her life. Or maybe it's just because Harlow is a hairdresser.

Maybe she's just old enough to care about it now. I'm overthinking this. It seems to be a theme for me lately.

Shaking off my rambling thoughts, I pull my focus back to the work at hand. I need to finish replacing this last breaker so Harlow can safely wash and dry her laundry. Plus, it's getting later, and I need to get Ella home for dinner and a bath. She's got school tomorrow.

It takes me another 10 minutes to finish with the breaker. I test the appliances to make sure they work okay and don't cause the breaker to trip before gathering up my tools and joining Harlow and Ella in the main room of the salon. Ella is still seated in one of the chairs with Harlow standing behind her, arranging her hair with tiny clips. Ella's attention is focused on her reflection in the mirror and Harlow is focused on what she's doing. Neither of them notices me as I watch them from the doorway.

Seeing the excitement on my daughter's face makes me smile even as it sends a stab of guilt through me. She's clearly been missing out on having a woman around. Weekly visits with my mom aren't quite cutting it. My mom means well, but I can't remember her ever having long hair. I don't know if she knows the first thing about how to style Ella's curls. And all my google searches haven't helped me in the least.

Harlow glances toward the mirror and her eyes go to my reflection. She looks a little nervous, but she shoots me a smile. "What do you think, Dad?"

I walk further into the room. "Ella, you look beautiful," I say.

Ella bounces in her seat, a big smile on her face. "Harlow made me pretty!"

"I did not!" Harlow says with a smile. "You were already pretty. I just styled your hair. That's all."

Ella can't seem to take her eyes off her own reflection in the mirror. I can't blame her. It's the best her hair has looked in a long time.

"Thank you," I say softly, holding Harlow's gaze in the mirror.

She goes still, her blue eyes locked on mine. Finally, she nods. "It's no trouble."

"Ella, what do you say to Miss Harlow?" I say, finally dragging my eyes away from the woman in the mirror.

Ella turns back to look at Harlow, the smile still firmly planted on her face. "Thank you! Thank you! Thank you!" she shouts.

Harlow laughs, shaking her head. "You are so welcome, Ella. You come back any time and I'll fix your hair however you like."

Ella's eyes go wide. "Really?"

Harlow nods.

"Can I get purple?"

Harlow's mouth drops open and she looks at me. "Um. That's up to your dad, sweetie."

Ella turns to me. "Daddy? Can I?"

"We'll discuss it," I say. "Maybe when you're a bit older."

"That's what you say to everything," Ella whines.

I glance at Harlow who's wearing a pleading expression. *Sorry*, she mouths silently.

I smile to let her know I'm not upset with her.

"Ella, your hair color is so pretty the way it is," Harlow says.

"It's brown," Ella mutters as if she's talking about something on the bottom of her shoe.

"It's such a pretty brown," Harlow says, touching Ella's hair. "See this? This is a natural highlight. It's got gold and auburn. No hair is ever just one color."

"It's not purple, though," Ella says with a sigh.

Harlow laughs. "No, but then no one is born with purple hair. Do you know how old I was before I colored my hair for the first time?"

Ella shakes her head.

"I was eighteen years old," Harlow says. "I was already in college. And you know what? I didn't even like the way it turned out."

"Really?" Ella asks. "What happened?"

Harlow sighs. "It turned orange. A really ugly orange color that I couldn't fix for two weeks."

Ella's eyes go wide, and she looks at Harlow as if trying to picture her with orange hair. I admit, I'm trying to do the same.

"Sometimes it's a good thing to wait until you're older to make big hair decisions," Harlow says.

Ella nods, her eyes still wide.

"Time to go, kiddo," I say. "Go wait for me by the front door."

Ella scrambles off the chair and walks around to where Harlow is standing. She hesitates for only a moment before throwing her arms around her in a hug. Harlow looks startled but recovers quickly, hugging her back.

"Bye, sweetie," Harlow says.

"Bye!" Ella calls as she skips toward the front door, leaving us in semi-privacy.

I stand there for a few seconds, trying to figure out what to say. Eventually I settle on the reason I came here today.

"The washer and dryer are up and running," I say. "You shouldn't have any issues using them. But if something goes wrong, let me know and I'll fix it."

She nods. "Thanks, Linc. And thank you for teaching me today. I really appreciate it."

I grin. "It's no trouble. Like you said, you're a fast learner."

She smiles. "I'm an overachiever."

"You always were the teacher's pet," I tease.

Her mouth drops open. "I was not! I just liked making good grades."

I laugh. "You were always at the top of the class."

She shrugs and I can't help but think how cute she looks. "Jealous?"

"Maybe, a little," I admit.

"Daddy?" Ella calls from the door. "I thought we were going?"

"Just a sec," I say. Turning back to Harlow, I smile. "Thanks for fixing her hair. I don't think I've ever seen her that excited about her hair before."

Harlow smiles. "It was my pleasure," she says.

An idea occurs to me, and I speak before I can consider if it's a good one or not. "Do you think you could teach me? How to do her hair, I mean?"

Harlow's expression shifts slightly. She's still smiling but there's something different in her eyes when she looks at me.

"That's really sweet of you," she says.

I shrug. "She's my daughter and I don't know how to style her hair. You do. It seems like common sense to ask for help."

A small laugh escapes her. "You'd be surprised how many parents don't take the time to learn anything about their kids."

Something about the way she says it makes me wonder if she's talking about her own upbringing. I know she was raised by a single mother who worked two jobs. I don't remember ever hearing about her father. She grew up in a big house that had once belonged to her grandparents. After her mom died of cancer, the house had gone on the market. I'd always assumed Harlow sold it since it was far too large for one person. Besides, it needed a lot of work from what I can remember.

"Not all parents are able to be what their kids need," I say, trying to be tactful. "I wonder all the time if I'm enough for her. I don't think the worry ever really goes away."

Harlow looks over at Ella where she's bouncing in place near the door. "I don't know," she says. "I think you're doing a good job."

"Thanks," I say, touched by the compliment. "I'll see you tomorrow?"

She nods. "See you tomorrow."

I turn to leave, taking Ella's hand in mine as we walk to my truck in the low evening light.

CHAPTER 12

Harlow

"How's the salon coming?" Layna asks, reaching over to snag a chip from the bowl in the center of the table.

We're out to lunch at one of Peach Tree's only Mexican restaurants. Piper and I try to meet up for lunch every couple of weeks. Now that Layna is living in Peach Tree, she's taken to joining us. That suits me just fine. I enjoy Layna's company. She's smart and snarky and fits in perfectly. When I'd first met her, I'd worried that maybe she was overbearing or uptight, but that's not the case at all. Since she's moved to town, I've seen a different side of her. Piper seems concerned about the shift in her sister's personality, but I don't see a problem.

"Not bad," I say. "The new sinks arrived yesterday. Linc and I are going to try to install one of them tomorrow after he finishes work."

"What's that been like?" Piper asks. "Working with Linc, I mean."

I shrug, focusing on the menu in my hands. "Fine."

"Fine?" Piper asks. "That's all you have to say? Fine?"

"That man is fine, though," Layna says, making me laugh. She's not wrong.

"You two have been working together for hours each day for the past week," Piper says. "And all I get is 'fine.' That's unacceptable. I want all the dirty details."

I roll my eyes. "There are no dirty details. We're just working. He's showing me how to make repairs. I'm learning a lot. He's a patient teacher."

"Hmm," Layna says. "I wish my teachers had looked like him."

"Me, too," Piper says.

"Need I remind you that you're marrying his best friend?" I ask her.

Piper shrugs as she reaches for a chip and scoops up some salsa. "Doesn't mean I can't appreciate the fact that he's hot. Don't worry. I'm more than happy with my man. You can have Linc."

Layna's gaze shoots to mine and I feel my face heat. "Have Linc?" she asks. "What's that mean?"

Piper closes her eyes for a moment before turning her apologetic gaze my way.

"Oh, come on," Layna says. "A blind person could see you're into him."

My eyes go wide. "What?"

She shrugs. "Obviously not Linc, though. He seems totally oblivious."

My heart pounds as I think over all my interactions with Linc over the last week. Have I been that obvious? Have I not hidden my attraction as well as I hoped? It's true I've been checking him out every chance I get, but that's just because the man is so fun to look at. There shouldn't be anything sexy about jeans and a t-shirt, but somehow Linc makes it sexy. There's something about the way his shoulders fill out those shirts and the way his forearms move when he's tightening a bolt or even just pushing his hair out of his eyes. Shit. Now I'm wondering just how obvious I've been while staring at him.

"Stop looking so freaked out," Layna says. "He doesn't have a clue. I'm just really observant."

I sigh, my shoulders drooping in defeat.

"So," Layna says. "What are you going to do about it?"

"What do you mean? Nothing."

Layna's brows lower in confusion. "What do *you* mean, nothing? You need to make a move, girl."

"That's what I said," Piper says. "She wouldn't listen to me either."

"You guys don't get it," I say. "You don't live in the same tiny town you grew up in filled with the same people who knew you when you were a frizzy-haired nobody in high school. Linc doesn't see me that way. I don't think he ever can."

"I don't think you're giving him enough credit," Piper says gently. "And I know for a fact you're not giving yourself enough credit. You're amazing. You're gorgeous. You own a successful business. And he'd be lucky to have you."

I shake my head, waving away her words. I've never been very comfortable with compliments. It's hard for me to know how to respond, so I normally try to block them out or ignore them. But this is Piper. She won't let me get away with that.

"Seriously, Harlow," she says. "Why can't you understand that you're a fucking catch? Just because those other losers didn't recognize it doesn't make it less true. So, stop doubting that someone like Linc would want you. He'd be lucky to have you."

"Damned right, he would," Layna says.

I laugh. "You two are ridiculous."

"But you love us," Piper says.

I nod. "I do. Thank you for hyping me up. I'm not sure how much good it will do. I'm still too chicken shit to make a move on him."

"Why?" Layna asks.

I shrug. "I just wish I knew whether or not he was interested in me."

Piper rolls her eyes. "There's only one way to know for sure. Either ask him or make a move."

"Shit, or get off the toilet," Layna says, making me laugh.

"I hate that expression," I say, tossing a chip at her.

Laughing, she catches it and tosses it onto the table. "I stand by it."

I shake my head. "Enough about me and my problems. What about you, Layna? Any luck on the job front?"

She shrugs. "I've sent my resume to a few places. I haven't heard back yet. I'm not desperate yet. I still have some savings. And I close on the sale of the condo next week, so that will give me more of a cushion. The right job will come along. I just need to be patient."

Piper shakes her head. "I can't believe you're the same person who freaked out when I quit my job to come to Peach Tree and run a coffee shop. Didn't you say that it's important to always have a backup plan?"

Layna shrugs. "Plans change. And backup plans can too. Life is short and you can't sit back wondering what might have been. Sometimes you need to take a chance on something new."

I find myself agreeing with the sentiment, even if I can't quite find it in me to take a chance of my own when it comes to Linc. Piper looks like she wants to make another comment, but the server arrives with our meals. For the next half hour, we're all too distracted by delicious food to talk about anything more important than whether we should order fried ice cream for dessert. But when we're leaving the restaurant, Piper stops me with a hand on my arm.

"You should think about what I said, Harlow," she says. "You deserve to be happy. Don't be afraid to go for what you want."

I smile, knowing she means well even if she doesn't understand. I know I've come a long way from the girl I was in high school, but that doesn't mean that people in this town see me that way. And part of me will always be that poor kid with the absent parent who dreamed of being cool enough, rich enough, pretty enough, to be noticed by someone like Linc. But I don't say any of that. Instead, I just smile.

"Thanks, Piper," I say. "I'll think about it."

CHAPTER 13

Linc

"When we get there, you have to be really good, okay?" I say, glancing at Ella in the rearview mirror.

"I know," she says, making it clear that this isn't the first time she's heard me say this.

"I know you know," I say, smiling. "But I'm really close to finishing up at Harlow's salon and I don't want it to take even longer. So, I'm going to set you up a place to work on your homework while Miss Harlow and I finish up some work, okay?"

"Okay," she says, clearly finished with this conversation.

I hadn't planned on bringing her with me today, but Cole had something come up at work and my parents are unavailable on Thursdays, so it was either this or cancel for the day. I'd considered it, but when I'd called Harlow to tell her she'd insisted that Ella was welcome to come hang out while we work. I'd been relieved, not only because I want to finish the repairs on Harlow's salon, but also because I've gotten used to seeing Harlow each evening after work. I've started looking forward to it.

That's because you like her, idiot. I shake my head as I park my truck in front of the salon. I've been trying not to think about Harlow that way, even though I can't help but acknowledge how attractive I find her. That's not weird. I'm a single man. It's totally normal to notice a pretty woman, right? Of course, it is. It's nothing more than that.

Ella and I climb out of the truck and I reach in to grab her backpack. Harlow greets us at the front door with a smile for Ella that hits me like a punch to the gut. Had I thought she was pretty? She's fucking gorgeous. That smile lights up her face and makes me wish it was directed at me.

"Hey, Ella," she says. "Come on in."

Ella smiles up at Harlow and I can see that same curiosity in her gaze that I'd seen the last time she was here in the salon. Since that day, she mentions Harlow constantly and talks about her hair and all the ways she wants to style it. Not that I understand a lot of what she's saying. But I've been writing down the things she says so I can ask Harlow about them when I see her. She's been amazing at explaining things to me and even sending me hair videos online so I can learn. I've mostly been practicing on my own hair, but that's a pain in the ass. I want to surprise Ella with one of the fancy French braids she's been wanting to wear. I still need some more practice before I'm ready.

Harlow leads Ella to a desk in the back where she can sit and work on her spelling homework. I follow behind and help Ella get set up with all her stuff. Once I'm sure she's settled and working on her school work, I turn to Harlow and smile.

"Thanks," I say.

She shrugs. "It's really not a big deal. Ella's welcome here whenever you need to bring her."

I can see that she's being sincere. She's not just saying it to be nice or so I won't feel bad about bringing my daughter to work.

"Still," I say. "It means a lot to me."

She shrugs and looks away, clearly uncomfortable with my gratitude. I let it go and direct her over to the new sink we're planning to finish installing tonight. Like the other nights we've worked together, it isn't long before we settle into an easy rhythm, working side by side. Harlow is good with her hands, and I'd be lying if I said I didn't like watching her work. She's small but capable and there's something about seeing her master a skill that I taught her that sends a little thrill through me. It's also more than a little sexy to watch. Not that it matters. I'm here to do a job, not ogle Harlow.

After a half-hour of working quietly on her homework, Ella calls me over to check her progress. I go over her work, pointing out a misspelled word for her to correct. She grumbles but erases it and writes it correctly this time.

"Perfect," I say, smiling.

Ella looks up at me with a smile that melts my heart a little. Leaning down, I kiss the top of her head. "Work on your math next," I say. "Let me know if you need help."

Math isn't her favorite subject. I know she'd make me help her with every problem if I stayed here with her. Which is why I'm leaving her to work on it independently. She's smart and she knows how to solve problems. She just hates math and will try to get out of doing the work if she can.

"Is she okay?" Harlow asks when I rejoin her.

I nod. "She's good. Thanks."

"Does she want a snack? I can grab her something from upstairs."

I shake my head as I look at my watch. "If she eats a snack now, she won't eat dinner."

Harlow winces. "I'm keeping you two from dinner, aren't I?"

I shake my head. "We still have some time. Cole has been cooking for us since I started work here. I feel a little guilty about that."

"You guys should go," she says. "Things have been running smoothly so far with one sink. One more day won't make much difference. Go. Take Ella home and feed her a balanced meal."

She smiles as she says it, but I still don't like the idea of leaving a job unfinished or falling behind schedule.

"Harlow can eat dinner at our house!" Ella says from beside me. I turn to look at her. I hadn't realized she'd walked up beside me while I was talking to Harlow. I open my mouth to respond, but Harlow speaks before I can.

"That's really sweet of you, Ella," she says. "But I'm not sure tonight is a good night for that."

She looks to me as if unsure if she said the right thing.

"Please," Ella says. "My dad is the best cook. You'll love it."

Harlow opens her mouth—probably to refuse again—but something makes me speak up.

"We'd love to have you," I say. "I don't know if I'm the best cook, but I do okay."

Harlow's wide-eyed gaze shoots to mine and I wonder if I've made a mistake. I should have let her refuse. It's clear she was going to say no. But now Ella and I have both ganged up on her and she has no choice but to say yes. What was I thinking? I hadn't been. I'd just suddenly pictured Harlow seated at the table in my small kitchen, eating something I cooked and smiling at me. And I'd wanted it to be real.

"You don't have to—" I begin.

"I'd love to," she says, speaking over me.

"Yay!" Ella shouts, bouncing up and down beside me.

Harlow smiles down at her, unable to resist her excitement.

"How about you come by in an hour?" I ask.

"Sounds good. That will give me time to clean up a bit."

"I'll see you then."

CHAPTER 14

Linc

"Cole?" I call out as I hurry into the house, Ella on my heels. I scan the entryway for anything that might be deemed messy.

I hadn't expected Cole to be here when I arrived home, but his car is in the driveway. He must have finished whatever he'd needed to do at work and come home early. I'm surprised he didn't text me to see if I needed him to get Ella. He normally would. But it's not like Ella is his daughter. It's not his responsibility to babysit her whenever I need him to. But I don't have time to think about that right now. Harlow is coming over. To my house. For dinner. *Shit.* Ella kicks off her shoes and tosses her pink backpack to the floor. I grab her before she can run off.

"Nope," I say, pointing to the shoes and backpack.

She deflates slightly, but she's still grinning as she pushes the shoes into the small cubby under the bench. Then, she hangs her backpack neatly on the hook I installed specifically for her. The hook she never uses, opting instead to toss her backpack to the floor every day. Normally, I don't make a big deal of it, but today is different. Due to Ella's insistence, we have a guest coming for dinner. My stomach clenches tight with nerves that I try to ignore. I make my way into the living room, straightening the throw pillows on the couch.

"Cole!" I call again, making my way into the kitchen.

Luckily the kitchen is practically spotless. Cole must have cleaned up the breakfast dishes while we were gone. I thank my lucky stars for that small miracle.

"Cole!" I practically bark his name this time.

He walks into the kitchen, looking slightly flustered. "Why are you screaming like a maniac?"

He looks like he just got home from a workout. His skin is flushed and he's wearing gym shorts and no shirt. He looks a little sweaty. I'm guessing he was about to get into the shower. Not that I have time to question where he's been or what he's been doing. I move to the refrigerator to start pulling out ingredients.

"Someone's coming for dinner," I say, not looking up from what I'm doing.

"Who?" Cole asks, coming up beside me to snag a bottle of water from the refrigerator door.

I don't answer right away, not ready for the interrogation I'm sure to get once he finds out that the dinner guest is Harlow. I move a gallon of milk aside and spot the leftover roast chicken from last night. Bingo! I can use it to make a pot pie. Does Harlow eat chicken? Shit. I think I remember her eating chicken wings at Peach Fuzz with Piper once. I shrug, pulling the chicken out of the fridge to set it on the counter. I'm making a mental list of ingredients when I feel a solid thump on my shoulder. I turn to find my brother glaring at me.

"Earth to Lincoln," he says, raising his brows.

"What?" I ask, confused.

"I asked who's coming to dinner," he repeats.

"Oh," I say, dropping my gaze back to the interior of the refrigerator. "Harlow," I mutter in a low voice.

"What's that?" Cole asks. "I couldn't hear you with your face stuffed into the fridge."

He tugs on my shoulder, and I turn to face him. His eyes hold a hint of amusement mixed with curiosity. "Who did you say?"

I sigh. "Harlow," I say, trying to maintain an air of nonchalance. But Cole's eyes light up immediately.

"Holy shit." Cole says, eyeing me.

"Shut up," I say, pushing him away and closing the fridge door. I turn to make my way upstairs to change clothes, but of course, Cole follows me.

"Dude," he says, a hint of awe in his voice. "It's finally happening."

I sigh as I make my way up the stairs, Cole on my heels. "Nothing is happening. Ella invited her and she couldn't tell her no."

Cole scoffs. "Details," he says dismissively. "It's happening. You finally have a date with Harlow."

"It's not a date," I say, ignoring the way his words make my heart speed up.

"Close enough," he says.

At the top of the stairs, I turn to face my brother. "It's not a date. If anything, it's a pity acceptance on her part. You've met your niece. You've seen her be convincing. Harlow never stood a chance."

Cole considers this for a moment and gives a nod. "Okay, maybe you're right about that part." Then he lights up. "But this is your chance, bro."

I roll my eyes, turning toward my bedroom at the end of the hall. "My chance for what?"

"To woo her," Cole says, making me laugh at his old-fashioned statement.

"Woo?" I ask. "Who the fuck says woo?"

He shrugs, still following me. "I do. And this is your chance to woo."

"You're an idiot," I say, ignoring the sliver of optimism his words make me feel. "And you need a shower," I say, wrinkling my nose. "You stink."

Cole glances down at his bare chest and tips his head in acknowledgment. "You're right," he says. "But so am I." He points a finger in my face. "Think about it."

"Yeah, yeah," I say, closing the door in his face.

Once I'm closed inside the safety of my bedroom, I let out a sigh. I try not to take anything Cole said seriously. I regret ever telling him about my crush on Harlow. Former crush, I mentally correct. Past tense. That was high school, for fuck's sake. Whatever silly, childhood infatuation I'd had with her is long dead. She's a friend. Nothing more. And tonight isn't a date, no matter what Cole wants to believe. Ella blindsided both of us with her spontaneous invitation. In the truck on the way home, I'd scolded her for it, making sure she understood that she can't just randomly invite people over to our house without talking to me first. She'd been suitably chastised, but I know she's still excited about Harlow coming over.

Much as I want to be upset with her, I can't be. She craves female interaction, I think. I'd always assumed having her grandmother in her life would be enough to soothe that need, but maybe I've been wrong. Maybe Cole was right, and I need to start thinking about dating. That thought brings me back full circle to Cole's words. *You finally have a date with Harlow.* Except this isn't a date. She only accepted Ella's invitation so she wouldn't hurt a little girl's feelings. This isn't about me at all. Why does that bother me so much?

Just for a second, I let my mind wander to the possibility of a real date with Harlow. What would that look like? I'd pick her up in my truck and take her to a nice restaurant. Maybe in Savannah, near the riverfront. We could walk along the cobblestone street afterward and admire the view of the river. I'd reach out and hold her hand. Maybe end the night with a kiss. The mere idea of it sets my heart racing and my dick jumps to attention. Shit. What the hell was that?

Why am I thinking about Harlow that way? She's my friend. That's all. She's a client, too. I can't start down the road of picturing myself with her that way. It will only make things awkward. Besides, I don't want her that way. Do I? I picture Harlow in my mind, remembering the curve of her smile and the way she laughs with her whole body. The lack of filter she seems to have when she talks and the way she talks with her hands. If she's happy, it's obvious for the world to see. Same with if she's upset. I love that about her. My mouth quirks up in a smile as the truth hits me like a sledgehammer blow. Cole is right. My crush on Harlow St. James never really went away. I still want her. And I have no fucking clue what to do about that.

I try to push the thought out of my mind while I shower and get ready. Harlow will be here in less than an hour, and I need to get started on dinner. I don't have time to delve into whatever I may or may not feel for her. I make my way down to the kitchen and find Cole already there, his hands covered in chicken as he debones the roasted chicken.

"Pot pie, right?" he asks.

I nod as I pull out a pan and start melting butter on the stove. "How'd you know?"

He laughs. "You're predictable. It was either this or chicken noodle soup and I know you don't like soup when it's hot out."

I shake my head at his observation. "Maybe I need to get some new recipes."

"Nah," he says, sliding the bowl of chicken toward me. "Don't mess with the classics. Besides, your chicken pot pie is delicious. Good enough to woo Harlow."

I feel the tips of my ears turning red. I keep my focus on the butter melting in the pan before me and don't risk turning to look at my brother. When Cole finishes washing his hands, he moves to start dicing an onion.

"She doesn't have any allergies, does she?" he asks.

"I don't think so," I say.

"I hope not," Cole says. "Can't fall in love after an anaphylactic episode."

I clench my jaw against the need to reply. I know it will only encourage him. That's what little brothers do. They love to press buttons. If Cole finds out that this is a button that he can press, he'll keep doing it. It's best to ignore him and he'll eventually get bored and drop it. I hope.

"What, no snappy comeback?" he says, still chopping. "No argument? You're no fun."

I keep my mouth shut, stirring the melted butter.

"Oh, shit," Cole says, wonder in his tone.

I risk a glance over and see him staring at me, eyes wide and a grin on his face. "What?"

"You *do* still like her." He says, pointing a finger at me.

My face gets hot, and I reach over to take the chopped onions from him. "Shut up."

"You do!" he shouts. "I mean, I knew you had a crush on her back in high school, but that was, like 10 years ago, man."

I dump the onions into the melted butter with more force than necessary. "I do not have a crush on her. Drop it."

Cole just laughs. "This is going to be so much fun."

I turn to face my brother. "Cole, I swear on everything, if you make tonight awkward, I'm going to smother you with a pillow in your sleep."

He just laughs again, patting me on the shoulder. "Mom would be mad if you did. Besides, I don't think you'll need my help making things awkward. You'll do a fine job of that all on your own."

"I hate you," I mutter, trying to ignore the nerves in my belly.

"No, you don't," he says with utter confidence. "You love me."

I work on sauteing the onions and try to block out Cole's taunts. Great. The one person I know who's horrible at keeping secrets knows that I like Harlow. It's just a matter of time before it gets out and the whole town knows. I might as well tell Miss Dottie or hang a sign on the giant, peach-shaped water tower. My stomach clenches painfully at that thought of Harlow finding out. The last thing I need is for her to feel sorry for me. Or worse, give me that 'we can be friends' speech. Not that I wouldn't respect her wishes if she did. It would just be incredibly awkward every time we ran into each other. And I'd have to avoid outings where she might be there. I sigh as I add the chicken to the pan. I'm inventing scenarios that don't exist. I need to focus on one thing at a time. Right now, that means dinner. I turn to face my brother.

"Cole, I need you to behave tonight," I say.

He rolls his eyes. "I always do."

"I'm serious," I say. "Harlow and I are just friends, so please don't do anything to make her uncomfortable."

He grins. "It's you I want to make uncomfortable."

I don't smile. "I'm serious. You don't think teasing me about liking her would make her uncomfortable, too?"

"Ha!" Cole says. "So, you admit you like her?"

I roll my eyes. "It doesn't matter because we're just friends. Besides, I don't want Ella to hear your teasing and think there's something happening that isn't. She might want a mom, but I won't get her hopes up like that."

Cole's smile fades and he looks serious for the first time since I came home. He nods. "You're right," he says. "I won't do that to Ella or to Harlow."

Relieved, I smile. "Thank you."

"Good thing they're not here yet," he says, grinning again. "So, I can enjoy messing with you a little longer."

I turn back to the stove. "I really do hate you."

Harlow arrives just as I'm finishing up dinner. I swallow down my nerves and greet her at the door with a smile. She looks beautiful, as always. She's changed from the clothes she was wearing earlier into a black, sleeveless top that dips low in the back and a pair of jeans that hug her curves just right. It's a casual outfit, but it still manages to be eye-catching. Though I have a feeling Harlow would be attractive even if she were wearing a burlap sack.

"Thank you for the invitation," she says.

"Of course. I'm happy you came."

I wince inwardly. Why does everything I say sound stilted and awkward? I wish I had some of Cole's smoothness or Luke's charm. Instead, I'm just awkward and shy and I can't seem to get out of my own head long enough to have a conversation. It's no wonder I haven't had a date in almost a year.

Harlow wrinkles her nose. "This is awkward, isn't it?"

I let out a laugh, relieved that she said what I was just thinking. "A little."

"Whew," she says. "I thought it was just me."

"It's definitely not you," I say, still laughing. "The awkwardness is all me."

She laughs. "Not true. I'm plenty awkward all on my own. Trust me. Besides, it's just dinner. It doesn't need to be awkward if we don't make it awkward."

I nod. "You're right. Speaking of dinner."

The oven timer begins beeping, signaling that it's time for me to take the food out of the oven. I gesture toward the kitchen.

"Come on," I say. "Let me take care of that and I'll grab you something to drink. Ella and Cole should be down soon."

I lead the way toward the kitchen with Harlow following behind me. I take several deep breaths on the short walk through the house. *Get your shit together,* I tell myself. *You invited her for dinner. Deal with it. Stop acting like a fucking idiot and channel your inner charm.*

When we enter the kitchen, I head straight for the oven to silence the timer. I check on the pot pie and see that it needs maybe another 10 minutes. After resetting the timer, I head directly to the fridge.

"Iced tea? Wine? Water?" I say, giving her a smile.

"Wine, please," she says, her words overlapping mine.

I laugh. "Excellent choice."

I fill two glasses and hand one to Harlow. "I'm sorry if Ella put you on the spot with the dinner invitation today," I say. "She can be impulsive sometimes."

Harlow just smiles at me over the rim of her wineglass. "She's eight. I'd be shocked if she weren't impulsive. Besides." She shrugs. "We can all be a little impulsive, right?"

I'm sure she didn't mean for that to sound as flirty as it did. She's not flirting with me, right? I mean, there have been times when I've thought she might be, but I feel like I'd know for sure if she were. Then again, I'm out of practice when it comes to being flirted with. I wish there was a way to know for certain without ruining the way things are now. Before I can think of a way to respond, I hear the stomping of feet on the stairs.

Smiling, I say, "Brace yourself."

Harlow looks slightly concerned, but more amused than anything as Ella comes running into the kitchen and skids to a stop in front of her.

"You're here!" she shouts.

"Inside voice, El," I say.

She gives me a cursory glance before turning back to Harlow. "You're here," she says in a slightly lower octave.

Harlow nods. "Of course. I told you I was coming for dinner, right?"

Ella nods. "Right."

"So, here I am."

Ella's practically vibrating with energy. I'm glad she already did her homework because getting her to settle long enough to focus on spelling words would probably be impossible tonight.

"Hey, El. Why don't you set the table for four people?" I call out as I go to check on the food.

Ella nods, excited to be able to help. "Okay!"

Harlow watches as Ella races around the kitchen, gathering silverware and the plates I'd set out on the counter earlier.

"I think you made her week by agreeing to come to dinner," I say, smiling.

Harlow smiles as she watches Ella move around the table. "I'm glad I came," she says softly.

"Me too," I say, ignoring the odd look she gives me as I do.

Instead, I turn back to the oven and make a show of checking on our dinner even though I just checked it

30 seconds ago. The truth is, admitting that I'm happy she came to dinner tonight feels a little too close to admitting how I feel about her. And since I've only recently figured that out for myself, I'm not quite ready to share the news yet. Before I can say anything too embarrassing, Cole walks into the kitchen, hair still damp from his shower. He ignores me and walks straight over to Harlow with a grin. What is he up to?

"Harlow," he says in a warm voice. "It's so good to see you."

"Hey, Cole," she says. "Not working tonight?"

He shakes his head. "Nope. So I get to hang out with you two tonight." He smiles over at me. "Isn't that fun?"

I glare at my brother, knowing he's going to find some way to torture me tonight. When Harlow turns a confused look on me, I drop the scowl and smile at her.

"Can't wait." I make sure the sarcasm isn't hidden in my words.

To my surprise, dinner isn't awkward at all. As concerned as I'd been about Cole and his big mouth, having him here helped dispel some of the awkwardness. The glass of wine also didn't hurt. Cole keeps the conversation going, asking Harlow about her salon and the repairs we've been making. I love watching her face light up when she talks about her work. It's so clear that she loves what she does. It makes me feel that much better to be helping her.

Plus, she seems to love my cooking. She raved about dinner so much I was starting to think she just did it to make me feel good. But she did eat two helpings, so maybe she really did love it. When we finish eating, Cole starts cleaning up the dinner dishes.

"I've got this," he says when Harlow offers to help him. "You two go relax in the living room. Let me clean up."

Harlow hesitates, looking to me for what to do. I nod and gesture toward the living room. "Take a seat. I'll grab us another glass of wine?"

She nods. "I'd like that."

I quickly refill our glasses while steadfastly ignoring my brother who's making kissing noises over near the sink. I shoot him a death glare before turning to leave the kitchen. When I enter the living room, I find Harlow standing near one wall as she looks at the framed photos there. She turns to smile at me as I approach.

"Thanks," she says, taking the glass of wine. She gestures toward one of the photos. "Where was that taken?"

I look at the photo she indicated. It's of me and Ella when she was 4 years old. We're at the beach and she's passed out on my shoulder while I sit in a beach chair under an umbrella. Cole had snapped the photo with his phone when I wasn't paying attention. I don't even really remember that moment. It's one of dozens of similar moments we've had over the years.

I smile. "That was taken during a beach vacation Cole and I took Ella on one year. It was really just for a weekend. I don't think I could afford much more back then. Ella loved the beach, but the sun and the waves wore her out within an hour or two and she ended up falling asleep on me."

"It's a great picture," she says softly. "The way you're looking at Ella while she sleeps is my favorite part. If love could be photographed, it's in that photo."

I turn to look at her, surprised that she somehow put into words my own thoughts. "I never realized that, but I think it's why I love that picture too," I say.

She smiles and takes a sip of wine as we make our way over to the couch to sit. I take the seat next to her, but I leave a few inches between us so we're not too close.

"Well, anyone can see how much you love her," Harlow says. "You're a good dad, Linc. I just hate that my salon is keeping you away from your daughter every evening."

"Stop," I say. "You're not keeping me from anything. If working on the salon was a burden, I'd tell you. But Ella isn't being neglected. I see her every night before bed and every morning before school. And I try to make up for lost time on my days off. Stop thinking you're a problem. I want to help."

"Why?" she asks. "Why do you want to help me, I mean. And don't say you're just helping a friend. I know you're a nice guy, but it's not like we've ever been that close. You barely know me."

I sigh, suddenly annoyed by her saying that again. She thinks I barely know her. Of course, she thinks that. It's not like we ran in the same circles in high school. And we haven't exactly hung out since graduating nearly a decade ago. It's only been since she and Piper became friends that I've started seeing her with any regularity. But the idea that she thinks I don't know her irks me. I know more about her than she thinks. I realize that I want to prove her wrong. Before I can consider the consequences, I speak.

"You were first chair clarinet in marching band our senior year," I say, keeping my gaze on her. "You were at every one of our football games, rain or shine. You came to prom by yourself, which I thought was really brave, though it surprised me. Your volcano won second place in the fifth-grade science fair and your mom grew the biggest roses in the county. She used to enter them in the county fair, and she won every year."

Harlow goes still, eyes wide. But I'm not quite finished.

"You hate salt and vinegar chips, but love dill pickles on your burger. You don't eat ketchup on your fries, and you prefer bourbon over tequila. You were the smartest girl in our graduating class. You should have been valedictorian, but you kept to yourself and never went out of your way to be noticed. Which is a damned shame because I've always thought you deserved better than this town gave you. You love it when it rains, but not when it storms. You're a cat person. Which I don't understand, by the way. Dogs are far superior. And you drink strawberry milkshakes whenever you have a really bad day. We may not talk all that much, Harlow. But I do know you."

I close my mouth, surprised by my own outburst. I hope I didn't just reveal how much I've been paying attention to her over the past twenty years. I don't need her to analyze my words and figure out just how long I've been crushing on her. Not that it matters. She's just a friend. Besides, I've got a business to run and a daughter to raise. I don't have time to have a crush on anyone.

Harlow is looking at me, her eyes wide. "Linc," she whispers. "I—"

"Daddy!"

I pull my gaze away from Harlow to look over at Ella where she's standing near the doorway to the living room in her nightgown. I clear my throat.

"What is it, El?" I ask, grateful for the interruption.

She walks over to me, holding a hairbrush. I smile and gesture for her to come over and climb into my lap like she does every night when it's time to brush her hair. She walks across the room and stops in front of me. But instead of climbing into my lap, she turns to look at Harlow.

"Can you do it?" she asks, her voice full of hope.

Harlow hesitates for only a second before a brilliant smile lights up her face.

"Of course, I can," she says.

Without missing a beat, Ella climbs up and sits on Harlow's lap. I can tell Harlow wasn't expecting that, but she doesn't make a comment. She catches my eye and smiles at my questioning expression. I'm trying to ask her if she's okay with this, but she seems to understand and gives me a little nod before reaching a hand out to take the brush Ella offers her.

"You know," Harlow says as she begins to work the brush through Ella's hair. "Curly hair is a lot different from straight hair."

"Yeah, it's a pain," Ella says, making us laugh.

"It can be," Harlow says, smiling. "But if you learn how to give it what it needs, it can be easy."

Ella shifts to try and look at Harlow. "What does it need?"

Harlow points her finger for Ella to turn back around. She works the brush through Ella's hair as she speaks.

"Well, all hair is different. But usually, for curly hair, it needs a gentle touch and lots of moisture."

"Like water?" Ella asks.

"Not just water," Harlow says. "There's more to hair than just washing it."

I feel like an idiot as I listen to Harlow explain about the different types of curly hair to my daughter. I had no idea that I might need to do things differently for her hair than mine. Is this why we can't ever seem to tame the frizz? I clearly need to talk to the expert if I'm ever going to get Ella to be happy and comfortable with her hair. It's been an ongoing battle for the last year. By the time Harlow is finished brushing Ella's hair, I can tell that Ella is on the verge of falling asleep in her lap. I need to get her into her bed before that happens.

"Hey sleepyhead," I say, reaching out to squeeze her shoulder lightly. "Time for bed."

She makes a half-hearted attempt at an argument, but it's spoiled by the massive yawn that follows her grumbling. She reaches for me, and I scoop her into my arms and stand. Ella immediately lays her head on my shoulder.

"Say goodnight to Harlow," I say, rubbing her back gently.

"Goodnight," Ella murmurs.

"Goodnight, sweetie," Harlow says with a smile.

"I'll be right back," I say in a low voice as I turn toward the stairs.

Ella is nearly asleep by the time I get her upstairs and into her bed. I tuck her in and make sure she has her favorite stuffed dinosaur in her arms.

"Goodnight, El," I whisper. "Love you."

"Love you, Daddy," she says in a sleepy whisper.

Those words never fail to make my heart squeeze in my chest. I smile as I tiptoe out of the room, leaving the door open so the hallway light can filter in. I take a moment to think over the events of the evening. Had I ruined everything with what I'd said earlier? Harlow had been about to speak when Ella had surprised us with her appearance. What had she been about to say? Should I bring it up? It might be better if she does. Maybe I should see if she mentions it. Do I even want her to?

If she asks me why I know all those things about her, I don't know that I'll be able to lie to her. But I can't just blurt out that I've had a crush on her since high school that I'm afraid never really went away. She'll think I'm insane. Or a creepy stalker. No. I'll just go back downstairs and pretend like nothing happened. That's the best move.

Resolved, I make my way back downstairs. As I approach the living room, I hear talking. Then I hear Harlow's soft laugh followed by my brother's deeper one. I guess Cole is finished with the dishes. That's probably a good thing. Harlow isn't likely to bring up my outburst with my brother here. And I'm less likely to do something stupid, like tell her how beautiful she is and how much I'd like to kiss her. I plaster a smile on my face and enter the living room to see Cole sitting next to Harlow on the couch. He's sitting awfully close to her. Much closer than I'd been sitting earlier. The smile threatens to turn to a scowl at the sight, but I manage to keep it in place.

"That was fast," I say, making them both turn to look at me.

Grinning, Cole just nods, making no move to widen the distance between himself and Harlow. Harlow shifts to look at me.

"Your brother was just telling me a story about your college days," she says, her voice teasing.

I shake my head. "Don't believe anything he says. He's a liar."

Cole's mouth drops open in mock outrage. "I'm not a liar. I just embellish a little."

I roll my eyes. "The truth doesn't need to be embellished."

"Sure, it does," he argues. "Otherwise, the stories are all the same."

Harlow laughs. "Is it true you got stranded in a girl's dorm without your pants?"

I turn to glare at Cole. "Really?"

He smiles back at me with a shrug. "What? It was hilarious."

Harlow is looking at me expectantly, waiting for me to tell the story. I sigh. "Fine," I say. "I'll tell the story, but only because he lies." I point at my brother.

"Embellishes," he corrects.

Ignoring him, I turn to Harlow. "And it wasn't the girls' dorm. It was a sorority house."

"I'm not sure that makes it better," Harlow says, giggling.

I dip my head to acknowledge that she has a point. "You're probably right," I say. "But it wasn't my fault."

Harlow looks amused. "I can't wait to hear this."

"I need to make one thing clear, first," I say. "This story doesn't paint me in the best light, but I swear to you that

I am and always have been a gentleman. And Ella can never hear this story. Got it?"

Harlow looks like she's trying to hold in a laugh, but she nods and brings her hand up to her chest, tracing an X over her heart.

"Cross my heart," she says.

I let out a sigh. "I can't believe I'm telling this story. Here goes. In freshman year of college, I was dating this sorority girl named Kylie. It wasn't serious, for either of us. We were just having fun. One night after a home game, there's this party at one of the frat houses. She meets me there and we hang out, have a great time. Then she invites me back to her room at the sorority house. But guys aren't allowed in the sorority house, right? But Kylie assures me that no one is home because all of her sisters are at the party."

"Uh oh," Harlow says. "I think I see where this is going."

I shake my head. "I doubt it. So, I'm an 18-year-old guy, right? I'm not exactly letting my brain do most of my thinking. So, I obviously agree. We go to her house, and it's dark and quiet. Clearly, no one is home. Perfect, right? We go to her room, and we're...um...enjoying ourselves."

I feel my face start to heat as I realize I'm talking about sex. With Harlow. I hesitate, trying to figure out the best way to tell the story without getting too detailed.

"But before he can actually hit a home run, so to speak," Cole breaks in. "They hear someone in the house."

"Oh, shit," Harlow says, giggling. "Were you naked?"

I feel the tips of my ears turn hot and shake my head. "I still had my underwear on," I say. "But she was naked."

I glance at Harlow, trying to gauge her reaction to the story so far. She doesn't seem uncomfortable; just amused. So, I keep going.

"When Kylie hears someone in the house, it's like someone pulls a fire alarm," I say. "She jumps up, totally naked and shoves me toward the window. The fucking window. Why not the bathroom, I'll never know. She's telling me I have to leave before the house mom finds me in her room. I'm trying to gather up my clothes that are scattered all over the room, but the light's off and I can't see shit."

Harlow is shaking with laughter.

"Kylie shoves a pair of jeans at me and pushes me out the window into a very unforgiving hedge. I'm lucky I didn't end up with a branch up my ass. I hide in the bushes for a few minutes thinking that maybe Kylie will come back and let me in so we can finish what we started. But she doesn't. The house goes totally silent. I don't want to risk knocking on the window and getting her into trouble, so I say screw it and decide to just go home."

"Aw," Harlow coos. "You really were a gentleman."

"He still is," Cole says.

I nod in his direction. "Thank you. Anyway, that's when I go to put the jeans on, and I realize that they're not mine. They're Kylie's."

"No!" Harlow shouts, still laughing.

"Yep," I say, nodding. "And since I was about a foot taller and a hundred pounds heavier than her, there was no way I could wear them."

Harlow's hands are covering her face and she's shaking with laughter. "What did you do?" she manages to say.

I shrug. "I didn't have much choice. I put on my shoes and started jogging."

"You did not!" Harlow says.

"I did. I acted like I was just out for a late-night run."

"In your underwear?"

I nod. "Yep."

She narrows her eyes at me in thought. "What kind of underwear? Please don't say they were briefs."

I open my mouth in mock outrage. "Excuse me, but are you trying to find out what kind of underwear I wear?"

She smirks at me. "I was trying to find out what kind of underwear you wore ten years ago, if you must know."

"They were boxer briefs, actually," I say.

"So, all the bits were covered," she says. "A shame."

I eye her for a moment. Is she teasing me or flirting? And where is Cole? He seems to have slipped out of the room sometime during my story. I didn't even notice him leaving.

"What does that mean?" I ask.

She shrugs. "Just that you could have made some girl's night by giving her a glimpse of the goodies."

I shake my head. "Did I forget to mention that it was early November? And we were in the middle of a cold snap? It was 42 degrees. And while yes, all the bits were covered, those boxer briefs didn't leave much to the imagination."

Harlow's biting her lip to keep from laughing, but I can see the amusement in her eyes. "So, there was some shrinkage? Did you run into anyone you knew?"

I roll my eyes upward. "I don't know why I'm telling you this story," I say with a sigh.

"Because it's hilarious and you like making me laugh?" she suggests, grinning widely.

I look over at her and take in her blue eyes sparkling with amusement and the smile at my expense that she can't quite hide. I nod.

"Yeah," I say softly. "I like making you laugh."

My eyes linger on her mouth, and I allow myself the briefest of seconds to imagine what it would be like to lean over and kiss her. Something in my chest constricts and I shake away the image as quickly as it comes. I clear my throat and blink a few times.

"But to answer your question," I say. "Thankfully, no one I knew saw me running across campus in my underwear. Until I got back to my dorm, that is."

"Oh, no," Harlow says. "Who was it?"

I grin. "Luckily, it was just Luke. He was my roommate, remember? He didn't let me live that down for a long time. And it's his fault that Cole knows about it at all. He told him one night when we were all drinking. No honor."

Harlow laughs. "He's your brother," she says. "If anyone has the right to know embarrassing stories, it's your siblings."

"I guess," I say. "Didn't give him the right to tell you about it."

She shrugs. "To be fair, you're the one who told me." She nudges me with her elbow.

I narrow my eyes at her, but she's not wrong. Cole might have brought it up, but I'm the one who told the whole embarrassing tale.

"I'm glad you told me," she says. "I like thinking of young Linc off at college and making questionable choices. You're so serious all the time."

"Not all the time," I argue.

"It's not a bad thing," she says. "I like that you take your responsibilities seriously. It's admirable. Not everyone is like that. Believe me. I know."

It hits me that she's probably talking about her cheating, piece of shit ex. The guy whose tools I now own. I hate that she's thinking of him at all. Or of any man who might have let her down in the past.

"Harlow," I say, reaching toward her just as she moves to stand.

"I should really get going," she says. "It's getting late, and we both work tomorrow."

I feel a sharp stab of disappointment at her words, but I tamp it down and nod. "I'll walk you out."

"Thanks for dinner," she says. "The food was great and Ella's amazing."

I smile, even though I want to beg her not to go just yet. "Thanks," I say. "I think she's great, too. But I'm biased."

She shrugs. "Parents are supposed to be."

We stop at the front door, and she reaches for the knob. "I'll see you tomorrow?" she asks.

I nod. "Of course."

"Goodnight, Linc."

Harlow places a hand on my chest and leans up on her tiptoes to plant a soft kiss on my cheek. It's quick, and over before I can even react to the feel of her lips on my skin. Then, she walks out the door before I can reply.

"Goodnight," I whisper, bringing my hand up to touch the place she just kissed.

Chapter 15

Harlow

"Pick up, pick up, pick up," I mutter as the ringing phone echoes over my car's speakers.

"Hello?"

I sigh in relief when I hear Piper's voice.

"Good, you're awake. I need to talk to you."

"It's like 8:45," Piper says. "I'm not that old."

I shrug, though she can't see it. "You wake up at the ass crack of dawn. How do I know when you go to bed?

"Is everything okay?" Piper asks. "You're rambling."

I sigh. "I just left Linc's house."

"Oh, my god!" Piper shrieks. "Did it finally happen?"

"What? No. Nothing happened."

"Oh." Piper sounds disappointed. "Then why the phone call and the rambling?"

"Because he said some things that made me wonder about stuff. And then he *looked* at me. And I think he wanted to kiss me. And then I kissed him on the cheek, but I really wanted to kiss him on the lips. But then I was scared and I ran away and now I'm driving home, and I needed to talk to someone about it. And since you're my best friend, I called you."

"Whoa," Piper says when I stop to catch my breath. "That's a lot of words. Where are you now?"

"In my car."

"No shit," she says. "Come to my house. We'll have a glass of wine, and you can tell me everything."

A feeling of relief washes over me. "Really?"

"Don't be stupid," Piper says. "Just get your ass over here. I'll have the wine ready."

"Thanks, Piper."

I pull into Piper's driveway ten minutes later, parking my car behind Luke's black luxury sedan. It's still a little strange to think of someone with Luke's family background living in Peach Tree. But after getting to know Luke, I know he's nothing like the rich family he comes from. He may have been born into money, but he's one of the most down-to-earth people I've ever met. And he clearly loves my best friend and makes her happy, which is all that matters to me.

Piper greets me at the door before I can knock. She puts an arm around my shoulders and leads me back into her living room. Two glasses of wine are waiting on the coffee table, and I grab one as soon as I'm settled on the couch. Piper waits until I take my first sip to start the interrogation.

"Okay, tell me what happened," she says. "Slower, this time. Start at the beginning. Why were you at Linc's house?"

"We had dinner," I say.

"Like a date?" Piper's eyes light up with excitement.

I shake my head. "Not a date. Ella invited me. She kind of insisted. And I felt bad disappointing a kid, even though I wasn't sure if Linc actually wanted me there. But then he smiled at me and said he'd love for me to come for dinner. So, I said yes."

She smiles. "Is Ella playing matchmaker?"

I shake my head. "I don't think so. I think she just likes having me around. She's only got guys in that house. We talk about hair and clothes. She even had me brush her hair tonight instead of Linc." I smile, feeling my heart catch at the memory of her climbing into my lap. "She's so sweet, Piper."

Piper smiles. "She's such a great kid. Luke and I adore her."

"Me, too," I say.

"What did Linc say?" Piper asks, confusing me with the change in topic.

"Huh?"

"On the phone earlier," she says. "You said Linc said some things that made you wonder. What did he say."

"Oh. Right."

I take a sip of wine as the memory of his words washes over me. How does he know all those things about me? We barely knew one another in high school. And why did he tell me all of it tonight? I'm so confused. But that's why I'm here, right? To get Piper's opinion. I shift on the couch to face her more fully.

"We were talking after dinner. It was just the two of us in the living room. We were talking about him and Ella and I said I felt bad about keeping him away from her in the evenings. He insisted he wanted to help. Then I asked him why he's doing all this. Why he's helping me when he barely knows me. He got this look on his face. He looked almost angry, Piper." I shake my head.

"Then he just started listing off all these things that he knows about me. My favorite foods and stuff from high school. Random things going all the way back to 5th grade. How I hate thunderstorms but love the rain. How my mom used to grow roses." I trail off, my throat growing tight at the memory of his words. I turn to look at Piper.

"Why does he know all those things? Why does he remember?"

Piper's eyes are wide as she takes a large sip of wine. "Wow," she says after lowering her glass. "What happened after he said all that?"

I shake my head. "Nothing," I say. "I was going to ask him how he knows all that stuff, why he knows all that stuff. But then Ella came in and asked me to brush her hair. The moment was gone."

"Wow," Piper says again. "No man pays that much attention to someone without a reason. What if I was right before and he's been crushing on you for all these years too?"

I smash down the tiny sliver of hope that tries to rise up inside me and shake my head.

"Not a chance," I say. "He's probably just a really observant person. You've seen him when we're out at Peach Fuzz. He's always so quiet. Listening and paying attention to everyone else. He probably just has a good memory for details."

"Those are some pretty specific details," Piper says. "I didn't know you hate thunderstorms."

I roll my eyes. "That's because you've been distracted by Luke Wolfe."

"I heard that," Luke calls from the kitchen.

I turn wide eyes to Piper. "Has he been in there the whole time?" I hiss.

She shakes her head. "No, he was finishing up some work in his office."

"I swear, I wasn't eavesdropping," Luke says, walking over to give Piper a quick kiss. "But you know she's probably going to tell me everything later, right?"

Piper smacks him lightly in the stomach. "Not if she doesn't want me to."

I roll my eyes. "I know couples tell each other everything. I figured Luke would hear it all eventually."

Piper looks only a tiny bit guilty. "Sorry," she says.

I shrug. "Don't be. Maybe a man's opinion is what I need."

Luke starts shaking his head and backing away, but Piper grabs his arm and holds tight before he can make an escape. Her eyes are alight with purpose.

"That's a great idea!"

"It sounds like a terrible idea to me," Luke grumbles. But he doesn't move to leave. Instead, he lowers himself to sit on the arm of the couch next to Piper.

"Let's hear it," he says with a sigh.

Piper smiles up at him before turning to me. "Tell him what Linc said. All of it."

I repeat the story for Luke, telling him all the things Linc remembered about me.

"So, what do you think?" Piper asks. "Is that a weird coincidence? Or is it something else?"

Luke rubs the back of his neck, not meeting either of our gazes.

"Well?" I ask. "What does it mean?"

He finally sighs. "I can't speak for Linc," he says. "But as a guy, I can honestly say that we don't typically memorize someone's favorite things unless that someone is important to us." He looks at me. "Why don't you just ask him?"

I roll my eyes as Piper shakes her head. "She can't just ask him."

Luke throws his hands up. "Why the hell not? Be direct. Guys like direct."

"Like you were so direct with me?" Piper mutters.

Luke grins down at her. "Oh, you were direct with me, though. Remember?"

The low, teasing tone in his voice makes me feel like I'm intruding on their private moment.

"I remember," Piper says, pulling him down for a kiss.

I wait patiently for them to finish before pointedly clearing my throat. "Back to my problem, please?"

Luke smiles over at me. "Sorry," he says, looking smug rather than apologetic.

"No, you aren't," I tease.

He grins. "I'm really not."

Piper rolls her eyes at him, but she's smiling too. "Let's focus on Harlow and Linc, please."

"Right," Luke nods. "I still think the best option is to ask him about it. But I can understand why you don't want to." He gives me a thoughtful look. "I do have a question, though."

"Okay."

"Why does it matter?"

I shrug, my gaze going to the glass in my hands. "I'm just curious. That's all."

"Bullshit."

"Luke!" Piper protests.

He shrugs. "Tell me why it matters so much so I can give adequate advice. From the male perspective."

I look at Piper who gives a little shrug as if to say, 'It's your call.'

"I didn't tell him anything," she says.

I close my eyes and blow out a sigh. "Fine. I've had a crush on Linc since we were ten. Happy?"

Luke is quiet for several long seconds before he starts to laugh. Piper swats at him.

"Don't laugh," she hisses.

I glare at Luke, more than a little annoyed by his reaction. "Why is that funny?"

He shakes his head and pulls in a breath. "Because Linc had a thing for you back in high school."

My mouth drops open in shock. I shake my head. "He did not." I lower my wine glass to the coffee table since I'm close to losing feeling in my extremities and I'd rather not ruin Piper's couch.

Luke just nods. "He did."

"There's no way," I insist, shaking my head. "He never even talked to me. We never hung out. How could he have a crush on me?"

Luke shrugs. "I don't know about all of that. I didn't know him then. I just remember Cole teasing him about it once back in college and he admitted it, but he said it was just a high school crush. It wasn't until I met you that night at Peach Fuzz and saw how weird he was acting that I put it together that you were the girl they were talking about."

Of course. Just a high school crush. Because normal people move on from their high school crushes after nearly a decade passes. Unlike me, still pining away for a guy who moved on years ago.

"Maybe he still has a thing for you," Luke says with a shrug. "I think the best option is to just ask him. Be direct. If he says it's all in the past, you can let it go."

Piper nods. "That's a good idea. You don't have to tell him you like him. Just play it by ear."

"You can start by just asking him why he knows all that stuff about you," Luke says. "If he brings up the crush, you can go from there. See if it leads to more."

"You should flirt with him and see what happens," a voice calls from the kitchen entryway.

We all look over to see Layna standing there, glass of wine in her hand. She shrugs. "What? If he flirts back, there's your answer. If he gets all weird, you'll know to back off."

I cover my face with my hands and groan. How did I end up here? I kept this secret for nearly 20 years and now it seems like everyone knows that I have a thing for Linc. All I need now is for Miss Dottie to get wind of it.

"This is stupid," I say, picking up my wineglass and draining the rest of it.

"Or you could kiss him," Layna says. "Be bold."

I look at her like she's lost her mind. "Don't let the pink hair fool you," I say. "I'm not as bold as I look. Not when it comes to him."

Layna shrugs. "Why not?"

"This is a small town," I say. "Everyone knows everyone else. I'd be humiliated if he turned me down. I can't just kiss him."

"Okay, fine," Layna says. "If you say so. But what about some light flirting? See if he gets the hint. Let him know you're interested in a subtle way."

I think about her advice for a moment, trying to decide if I can go through with it. Can I subtly flirt with Linc without being completely awkward? I'm not sure. But I know I can't ask him outright if he's into me. And there's no way I can bring up high school crushes without letting it slip that my crush on him is still alive and well. I don't realize that my foot is tapping maniacally until I feel Piper's hand on my knee.

"Breathe," she says gently. "You got this."

I still my movements and nod, sucking in a long, slow breath. "You're right," I say. "I can do this."

I look around at the others, taking in Piper's encouraging smile, Luke's resigned frown and Layna's delighted grin.

"Hell yeah, you can," Layna says. "He won't know what hit him."

Luke shakes his head. "Not sure why you asked my advice if you weren't going to take it," he grumbles.

Piper pats his knee. "There, there, honey."

He shoots her a glare that's ruined when he adds a wink.

"You two are nauseating," Layna says, but her lips are curved into a slight smile.

I know exactly what she means. Sometimes it's annoying to witness the sweetness between Luke and Piper, but it's hard to begrudge them their happiness. The truth is, I want what they have. At the thought, Linc's face pops into my mind and I think back to tonight at dinner with him and Ella. Not to mention afterwards when we'd talked. It had felt so natural, so right. What if there's something more there? I can't be too afraid to go after it. Right?

CHAPTER 16

Linc

I shove my hair back off my forehead, trying to remember where I put the level earlier. Harlow being here is such a distraction that I haven't been as meticulous about putting away my tools each time I finish using them. Not that I'm complaining, exactly. Harlow might be a distraction, but she's a damned sexy one. As far as distractions go, I could do a lot worse.

Now that I've realized I still have feelings for her, it's as if I can't stop thinking about her. And the thoughts I have aren't professional. Not that I need to be thinking of her that way. She's a friend, a client. I need to remember that this is strictly business. At the most, it's a friend helping another friend. So, no matter how sexy I think she is in a tight t-shirt and those short shorts, it doesn't matter. I'll just ignore it. At least, I'll try to. Ever since dinner the other night when I all but admitted I'd been stalking her for the last 2 decades, she's been acting differently around me. At least, I think she is. I'm too busy pretending to ignore her to know for sure.

But sometimes it almost seems like she's flirting with me. Which is ridiculous. Right? But she's been touching me more today. Brief touches to my arm seem to linger longer than necessary. And earlier, she'd stood close enough to me that I could feel her tits brushing my arm. I did my best to ignore it, but each time I moved to subtly put more space between us, she closed the gap. Am I imagining things? I must be, right?

My hair falls over my eyes again and I push it aside with the back of my hand. I spot the level near the far wall and walk over to pick it up. I don't even remember setting it down over here. I'm losing my mind these days. When I turn back, I find Harlow standing a few feet away, eyeing me. I go still, wondering at her expression. I look down at my shirt, wondering if I spilled something on it at lunch.

"What?" I ask when she doesn't say anything.

She looks torn for a moment, as if she isn't sure if she wants to say whatever is on her mind. Finally, she gives me a hint of a smile that affects me far more than it should and says, "When was the last time you had someone cut your hair?"

I huff out a laugh. That's not what I was expecting her to ask. Reaching up, I run a hand through my, admittedly too long hair. I shrug, thinking back. "Maybe a year or two? I've been pretty busy. I usually just trim it myself."

The look of abject horror on her face would be hilarious if it weren't directed at me. "You cut your own hair?"

I nod, enjoying the way I seem to have ruffled her. She looks like she wants to say more, but all she does is point to the empty chair and say, "Sit."

I shake my head with a grin. "Nah, I'm good."

"You are not," Harlow insists, her tone turning to that bossy one I like so much. "You've pushed your hair out of your eyes 13 times in the last 22 minutes."

I narrow my eyes at her. "Those numbers seem oddly specific," I say with a grin. "Have you been watching me?"

To my shock, the teasing tone makes Harlow's cheeks go pink. "A blind man could see that you need a haircut," she mutters, ignoring my question. She points at the chair again. "Sit."

Sighing, I make my way over to the chair and sit. "You sure about this?" I ask. "I thought you only styled women's hair?"

She rolls her eyes with a grin as she spreads a black cape over me and snaps it around my neck. Her fingers brush the skin at the back of my neck. Is it my imagination, or do they linger for longer than needed?

"That's a common misconception," she says. "I learned to cut and style all types of hair. It just so happens that most of my clients are women. But I style plenty of men as well."

That last sentence annoys me for some reason. I know I'm not jealous of her cutting some other man's hair, am I? That's just ridiculous. Especially considering she and I are just friends. I shake off the notion and watch her in the mirror as she moves around the space, gathering the things she needs to work. It's interesting to watch the change settle over her now that she's got a task to do. It's as if all the restless energy that normally has her flitting all over the place is now directed at me. She's calm and focused on her task, moving gracefully around the space with sure hands that know just where everything is.

"It started when Ella was little," I say, wanting to fill the sudden silence. "Me cutting my own hair," I clarify. "Back then it was about money, time, and convenience. I had a baby to take care of and not a lot of time or money for things like going to a shop for a haircut."

She nods as she runs a comb through my hair. She was right, I realize as I watch her in the mirror. I do need a haircut. I hadn't realized how long it had gotten. I try not to think about how incredible it feels to have her hands in my hair. My mind goes to other scenarios where she might have her hands in my hair. If my face were buried between her legs, for instance.

"Lots of people skip the salon to save money," she says, pulling me back to our conversation and chasing away my inappropriate fantasy. "It's one of the first things to go when times are lean." She shakes her head. "Which means that people like me are some of the hardest hit when the economy is bad. Along with restaurant workers, I guess." She sighs. "Hard to wrap your head around being expendable."

She'd said it like it was a joke, something to laugh off. But there had been a note of sadness in her voice.

"You know better," I say. "No one would ever call you expendable."

I expect her to say something teasing in response, but she just smiles and reaches for the spray bottle on the little table beside her. Before she can start to wet my hair, I reach out and grab her wrist to still her. Startled, she meets my gaze in the mirror, a question in her eyes.

"Harlow, you're the opposite of expendable," I say. "You're incredible."

The silence hangs in the air between us. I can feel her rapid pulse under my fingers. I want to linger there, stroking the soft skin of her wrist with my calloused fingers. I want to use my grip on her to pull her closer, tumble her into my lap and bury my face in her neck. I want to inhale the soft, floral and citrus smell of her skin. Then I want to let my lips follow and—

Harlow gives her head a tiny shake, breaking whatever spell had us transfixed for that moment. She smiles at me.

"Thanks," she says, tugging her wrist free of my hand.

We're both quiet for several minutes as she turns her attention back to my hair. She sprays my hair down and combs it until it's damp.

"I'm just going to take a little of the length off," she says. "And give it a little texture. That should help keep it off your face."

I nod, having no understanding of what she's talking about. But she's touching me. And she's standing closer than she ever has before as she runs her fingers though my hair. Occasionally, she leans in close enough that I catch a hint of her perfume. I let my mind wander as she works, focusing on the relaxing feel of her hands in my hair and the quiet snip of the scissors. I watch her in the mirror, noting the graceful movement of her hands as she works. Her gaze is intense and focused. Something about having that intensity directed at me has my dick twitching in my pants. I try to ignore her closeness and the smell of her, but it's no use.

I'm half hard by the time she finishes my haircut. When she insists on washing it next, I want to refuse. This is dangerous. I've spent the last 20 minutes fantasizing about the things I'd do to her if I had the chance. I've already pictured at least five different ways I could take her in this chair. I could pull her down into my lap so she's straddling me, her tits in my face, my cock stretching and filling her. Or she could sit in my lap with her back to me, facing the mirror, watching while I thrust into her from behind. I could bend her over the chair and pound into her, my fingers digging into those full hips. I could—

"Linc?" Harlow's questioning voice cuts into my fantasy and I meet her eyes in the mirror. She gestures toward the sink in the back. "Time for a wash."

The last thing I need is for her to lean over me as she washes my hair, those full breasts threatening to spill out of that low-cut shirt of hers. But I don't argue. I'm afraid if I speak it will be to beg her to let me touch her, to kiss her, anything. Instead, I remain silent and let her lead me over to the bowl. As I follow her, I try to discreetly adjust my cock which seems to have developed a mind of its own this afternoon and is now standing at full attention. Luckily the flowing cape covers me so she can't see the tent that has sprung up in my pants. She waits while I sit in the chair and lean my head back over the bowl.

Harlow runs her fingers through my hair as the water warms up, pushing it back away from my forehead. I try not to focus on her nearness and her scent invading my senses. She directs the spray of warm water over my hair and scalp, wetting my hair.

"How's that feel?" she asks, her voice soft.

"Huh?" I speak without thinking, unsure what she's asking. Having her hands in my hair along with the warm water feels incredible.

Harlow laughs. "The water. Is it too hot?"

"Oh," I say, shaking my head. "It's fine."

She nods and runs her fingers through my hair some more as she directs the spray. I watch her for a few seconds, but eventually my eyes drift closed as I settle into the relaxing feel of someone else washing my hair. I can't remember the last time I had this kind of treatment. It's been years, I know. Harlow lathers my hair with shampoo that I realize smells familiar a split second before I realize why. It smells like her. It's that combination of flowers and citrus that I always smell when she's nearby. Inhaling deeply, I can't quite hide the smile on my face.

"Sorry," she says. "You're stuck smelling girly until you wash it again."

I crack one eye open to look at her. "You're going to ruin my manly reputation."

She grins. "If some shampoo is enough to do that, you haven't been trying hard enough."

I laugh as she rinses the suds from my hair, her fingers combing through the strands. "You're probably right."

"Besides," she says, reaching over me for the conditioner. "I think it smells pretty good."

I watch the way her shirt stretches tight across her chest with her movement, wishing my body didn't have such an immediate reaction to the sight. I clear my throat before speaking.

"I guess it's not so bad," I say, my voice rough.

By the time Harlow finishes washing my hair, I feel like I'm seconds away from exploding in my pants. Since when is a haircut supposed to be sexual? It's not. I'm just such a horny bastard that I can't seem to help myself when it comes to Harlow. I can only pray she doesn't notice. I sit up as she wraps a small towel around my hair, gently squeezing out the excess water.

"Come on," she says, motioning me back toward the chair in front of the mirror.

I take a seat, knowing that I should stop this and get back to work. I'll just let her brush my hair and then I'll put an end to it. Harlow removes the towel from my hair and tosses it into the hamper under the counter. Then she takes a comb and gently works it through my hair, removing all the tangles. I can already see the difference when I look in the mirror. My hair still reaches nearly to my shoulders, but it looks neater now, lighter. When she reaches for the hair dryer, I shake my head.

"You don't have to dry it."

She smiles at me, giving my shoulder a little squeeze. "I want to."

There's something about the way she says those three words that has me glued to my seat. I couldn't leave now if I wanted to. I keep my eyes on the mirror, watching Harlow as she dries my hair, brushing it out. I don't know that I've ever had a woman dry my hair like this. Before I started cutting my own hair, I used to go to the local barber shop. This is a far cry from the retired Army medic who told war stories to everyone who would listen and only knew three types of cuts, one of them involving a bowl. I nearly laugh at the memory and Harlow flicks off the hair dryer to study me.

"What's funny?" she asks.

I shake my head. "Nothing. I was just thinking of my last hairdresser."

"Stylist," she corrects.

I narrow my eyes. "I'm not sure that term applies to him, but is that the term you prefer?"

She lifts one shoulder in a shrug. "It's what the industry prefers. I've gotten used to using it. Not that it really matters in the end. Being called a hair stylist instead of a hairdresser doesn't make people assume I'm more of an expert in my field or anything. I just think it sounds better, but that's just my preference."

"I'm sorry," I say, smiling at her in the mirror. "Hair stylist, then."

She nods. "Back to the funny story?"

"Right. I was just thinking how much of an improvement this experience is over that one."

"How so?"

"Well, for starters," I say. "My hair isn't bowl-shaped right now. And no one nearly lost an ear to a set of ancient clippers."

She looks amused and horrified. "Who was your last stylist?" Then she closes her eyes and holds up her hand. "Never mind. Don't tell me. I don't want to know. I'm just glad you're safe now."

I laugh. "You and me, both."

She looks down at me for a second, her gaze thoughtful. "I like your laugh," she says softly.

She holds my gaze for another long second before she blinks and begins brushing my hair again. "No bowls here," she says. "Besides, it would be a crime to chop off all this gorgeous hair."

"You think I'm gorgeous?" The words are out before I can think them through; before I can reign in the flirty tone. I wait, wondering if I just made things weird. But Harlow doesn't seem bothered.

She just scoffs. "I'm not here to feed your ego, sir. I'm speaking from a purely professional standpoint. This is just about the hair."

I ignore the way her calling me 'sir' makes my dick sit up and pay attention. Now isn't the time to think about that. Instead, I keep my tone light and teasing to match hers.

"If you say so," I say.

She just shakes her head and turns the hair dryer back on, blasting me in the face with a quick burst of warm air before directing it back to my hair. Conversation is impossible over the noise of the dryer, so I content myself with watching Harlow in the mirror as she works. If my gaze strays to her legs peeking out from the bottom hem of those denim shorts, I can't be blamed.

CHAPTER 17

Harlow

"I'm telling you, Piper," I say. "He was totally flirting back."

I hold the phone between my ear and my shoulder as I search through my closet for something to wear for our girl's night out.

"Do you think he's picking up on you flirting with him?" Piper asks.

"I'm not sure," I say, tossing aside the black tank top I usually wear on our outings. I can't say why, but I feel like dressing up a little tonight. "It's hard to flirt while you're installing a sink, you know?"

She laughs. "I wouldn't know, actually."

Aha! My eyes settle on a white, flowy halter dress that hits my mid-thigh. I think I've worn this dress twice in the year since I bought it. It's simple, but cute. Not too fancy for a place like Peach Fuzz on a Friday night. I hold it out in front of me, considering.

"Piper, what are you wearing tonight?"

She hesitates before saying, "I don't know. I haven't thought about it. Why?"

"You know that cute, white halter dress I never wear?"

"The one that looks sexy as hell on you?"

"That's the one," I say, standing before the full-length mirror in my bedroom, the dress held up in front of me.

"Hell yes, girl!" Piper shouts. Then she says in a low voice, "Do you want me to make sure Luke shows up with Linc?"

I want to say yes, but it feels too calculated. Am I really trying to lure a man out to a bar on a Friday night when I've spent nearly every evening with him for the last week? Am I that desperate to be around him? I sigh, tossing the dress onto my bed. Yes. Yes, I am that desperate.

"Am I pathetic?" I ask.

"What the fuck? No. You aren't pathetic. You know what you want and you're going after it. That's called ambition."

I laugh. "Yeah, if you're a man. If you're a woman, it's called conniving."

"Pfft. Who cares what anyone else thinks. It's not like you're tricking him into something. You're just showing him what he could have if he wants to reach out and take it."

I nod, considering Piper's words. "You're right," I say.

"So, should I talk to Luke?" she asks.

"Yeah," I say. "And I'm wearing the dress."

"That's the spirit!" she shouts. "Okay, I need to go," she says in a lower voice. "People are giving me weird looks."

"That's what you get for not taking the call in your office," I say. "You know I'm not the best person for phone calls in public."

She laughs. "I'll see you tonight."

"Bye."

I end the call, considering Piper's words. She's right, I know. I'm not doing anything wrong. I'm just going to hang out with my two girlfriends and have a couple of drinks on a Friday night. There's no harm in that. And if a certain hot contractor happens to show up, that's just a coincidence.

I'm all nerves when I walk into Peach Fuzz a few hours later. I don't know why. There's no guarantee Linc will even show up tonight. He's already spent plenty of time with me over the last couple of weeks. Time he could have spent at home with Ella. I'm sure he'd rather be at home with his daughter than out at his brother's bar on a Friday night. He's probably sick of me by now.

I spot Piper and Layna sitting at our usual table and head in their direction. I do my best to put Linc out of my mind so I can focus on just having a good time with my friends. That's the whole point of girl's night.

"Holy shit, you look hot," Layna says when she sees me approach.

Grinning, I do a little twirl to show off the way the dress dips low in the back, showing off a lot of skin.

"Whew!" Piper says. "Linc won't know what hit him."

"Shh!" I whisper as I slide into the booth beside her. "Not so loud."

She rolls her eyes. "We're in a bar. There's music playing. Everyone is drinking. No one is paying any attention to our conversation."

"Besides," Layna says. "If anyone looks our way, they're going to be too distracted by how fuckable you look in that dress."

I laugh at her comment as my face heats. "Stop it."

"She's right," Piper says, raising her glass for a toast.

I lift the glass in front of me, pleased to notice that Piper ordered my favorite drink for me.

"To girl's night," Piper says.

"Chicks over dicks!" Layna shouts, making the couple behind us turn around and gape at her.

I laugh as we clink glasses and we all sip. The Old Fashioned is smooth going down with just a hint of a burn from the bourbon.

"So?" Layna says, looking at me.

"So, what?" I ask, confused.

She rolls her eyes. "How's the flirting? Are you making any progress?"

I sigh. "I don't know. Sometimes I think he's flirting, but then I think maybe he's just being nice and he's totally oblivious."

"Tell her about the haircut," Piper says.

Layna's eyes widen in horror. "Please tell me you didn't cut off that man's delicious hair!"

I shake my head, laughing. "Just a trim, I swear."

She sighs in relief. "Thank the gods. I didn't know I liked long hair on guys until I met Linc. That man is fine."

"Watch it," I say, making them both laugh.

Layna just shrugs. "I'm only speaking the truth. Besides, I know girl code. He's hot, but not really my type. Too brooding."

Piper laughs. "Please, your type is the buttoned-up CEO with a stick up his ass."

"Not anymore," Layna argues. "I'm looking for someone a little more fun these days."

Piper's eyes narrow as she looks at her sister. "Hmm."

Layna turns to me. "Back to the haircut. What happened?"

I groan. "Absolutely nothing. I cut his stupid, sexy hair and it was somehow super fucking hot. Which is weird, because haircuts are just my job, you know? They're not supposed to be sexy. But being able to touch him and run my fingers through his hair?" I close my eyes, reliving the scene in my salon. "It definitely made me want to do more than just touch his hair."

"Is it as soft as it looks?" Piper asks, making me laugh.

Nodding, I take a sip of my drink. "Yep."

"How long before you give in and tell him you want to fuck him?"

I choke on my drink, coughing and sputtering as Layna fights her laughter.

Piper hands me a napkin and shoots her sister an odd look. "Since when do you talk that way? You're usually so..." she trails off, searching for the right word.

"Uptight?" Layna finishes for her.

"I wasn't going to say that," Piper argues, but she can't quite meet Layna's eyes.

I have no idea what's going on between the two sisters, but it's true that Layna hasn't been herself tonight. She's been much more vocal, using more profanity than I'm used to hearing from her.

Layna shrugs. "I'm trying something new. It's called fun. You should try it, too." She grabs my hand as she stands, pulling me to my feet. "Let's dance."

Part of me wants to object, but the glass of bourbon I just drank combined with my frustration over Linc has me giving in. I let her pull me out onto the dance floor with her as the opening beat to Nelly's *Yeah* starts playing. As we start to move to the music, Layna pulls me in close enough to speak into my ear.

"Guess who just walked in."

A prickle of awareness rushes over me and I know she's talking about Linc. He's here. I don't dare look around for him. Instead, I meet Layna's gaze and she shoots me a wink. My heart pounds in my chest and I feel that familiar thrill shoot through me that happens anytime Linc's around.

"Show him what he's missing," Layna says before spinning around and working her hips in a rhythm I can only dream of replicating.

I smile, letting the music flow through me as I begin to move. I forget about the rest of the people in the bar. I forget that Linc is somewhere among them, possibly watching me. Instead, I focus on what Layna said before we left the table and do my best to have fun for the 3 minutes or so that we're on the dance floor. By the time the song ends, I'm breathing hard, and I know my skin is flushed because I'm hot and a fine sheen of sweat covers me. But I'm smiling as we leave the dance floor to head back to our table.

Piper is still sitting where we left her, but she's not alone. Luke is sitting next to her, his arm around her shoulder as he leans over the table to say something to Linc. Linc laughs in response, but I'm not close enough to make out what was so funny. Still, the sight of Linc's smile does something to my insides and part of me wants to turn around and return to the dance floor. Maybe I can dance until he leaves. I realize immediately how stupid I sound, even inside my own head. I'm the one who told Piper to make Luke bring him here tonight. So, why am I thinking of running away now?

Because you didn't really think this through, I think. *Put on your big girl panties and go talk to the man.* I've spent the last two weeks alone with him at my shop for hours at a time. So, what's the big deal now? *Nothing. Get your shit together.* I take a deep breath and let it out as I approach the table. I can do this. It's nothing I haven't done plenty of times before.

"Holy shit!" Layna grabs the glass from Piper's hand and downs its contents in three swallows. All eyes go to her, watching as she lowers the glass to the table. With a smile, she says, "Dancing always makes me thirsty.

Piper narrows her eyes at her sister. "You're buying the next round."

Layna shrugs and takes a seat beside Piper on the bench. "Fine by me," she says. "As soon as the server comes back, I'm buying shots."

The collective groans from the table dissolve into half-hearted objections. I risk a glance over at Linc only to catch him looking at me. I expect him to quickly look away or to smile in greeting, but he does neither. Instead, he holds my gaze for a long moment before slowly letting his eyes travel down the length of my body and back up to my face. The expression on his face is one I haven't seen there before. His eyes are dark and hungry in the low light, and I feel a thrill shoot through me. The expression lasts for only a second before it shifts back to his normal expression of neutrality.

"Hey, Linc," I say, giving him a little smile.

He dips his head in a single nod. "Harlow."

I wait for him to say something else, but he doesn't. Instead, he takes a sip of his beer, turning back to his conversation with Luke. Piper glances my way, giving me an apologetic shrug. I smile, trying my best to ignore how Linc's dismissal makes me feel. It's not like we're a couple. We're just friends. Yes, we've spent more time together lately than usual, but it's clear that I'm still just another client in his eyes. Which is totally fine. He doesn't owe me anything. And it's not as if I did something stupid like get my hopes up after Luke told me about Linc's high school crush on me. That would be a massive mistake.

This is for the best. Getting involved with Luke's best friend would be too messy, especially if things didn't work out. It would be impossible to avoid him without also avoiding my only friend in this town. No, thank you. It's better this way. All this runs through my head in the time it takes for Layna to order a round of shots. I didn't want a shot, but once it's in front of me, I don't turn it down.

The chilled peach whiskey still brings a burn to my throat and warms my belly pleasantly. I chase it with a sip of water, trying to keep myself hydrated. I don't want to end up shit faced by the end of the night and feeling like hot garbage tomorrow. I let the conversation flow around me, chiming in when it suits me. I'm hyper aware of Linc sitting next to me, even though he's barely spoken since I sat down. His jean-clad leg is inches away from my bare leg below the hem of my dress. His hand is resting on his thigh, and I can't help but picture him sliding it over and resting it on mine. My imagination serves up the images of that large, calloused hand sliding higher, pushing my skirt up until his fingers brush against the seam of my pussy. I'd spread my legs, giving him more room to touch me—a clear invitation to take what he wants. My breath falters, pulling me back to the present and the reality that Linc doesn't want me that way. He's never said or done anything to indicate his interest. I need to stop fantasizing about something that will never happen.

Without warning, Piper stands and holds out her hand to Luke. "Dance with me," she says. It's not so much an invitation as it is a command.

Luke grins up at her before taking her hand and rising to his feet. "I love it when she's bossy," he says, winking at the rest of the table.

Cole laughs before holding out a hand to Layna. "What do you say?" he asks.

Layna eyes him for a moment before shrugging. "Why not?"

I watch the four of them head toward the dance floor, leaving me and Linc in silence. I try not to feel awkward sitting next to him. If I were bolder, I could ask him to dance with me. But I'm not. The truth is, I'm only superficially bold. I can dye my hair wild colors and wear shirts with funny sayings that shock the senior citizens and pearl-clutching folks in town. But when it comes to anything important to me, I freeze. And anything having to do with Linc has been shown to make me consistently freeze for the past two decades. At least there's something I can count on.

"It would be a shame to waste that dress."

It takes me a second to realize that the words I just heard came from Linc. I look over at him, confused. He smiles and gestures to my dress.

"That dress deserves to be shown off," he says before gesturing toward the dance floor. "May I have this dance?"

For a full second, I just sit there staring at Linc. I'd imagined this moment so many times back in junior high school and high school. I'd dreamed of being noticed by Lincoln Prescott; having him ask me to dance with him at one of the school dances. But it never happened. Now, here he is, asking me to dance with him. And I'm just sitting here like a dumbstruck idiot. I force myself to nod.

"I'd love to," I manage to whisper.

Linc's smile is instant. He moves to stand, reaching out a hand for mine. I can barely breathe as I place my hand in his and his fingers close around mine. He doesn't let go of my hand as we walk toward the dance floor. I keep having to remind myself that this is really happening. I'm going to dance with Linc. When his large hand lands on my lower back, a thrill shoots through me. Thanks to the open back design of the halter dress, there's nothing between his hand and my skin and I savor the contact. I bring my free hand up to rest on his shoulder, trying to resist the urge to squeeze the hard muscles I feel under his shirt.

"You look amazing, tonight," Linc says. When I meet his gaze, he smiles. "In case no one's told you."

I return the smile, a warm feeling spreading through me at the compliment. "Thank you."

This version of Linc is one I'm not used to, but one that I know I could grow to like. He seems confident and charming. Not that he's not always attractive, but there's something about him tonight that makes me want him even more. It's almost like he's trying to impress me or charm me. It's not his normal behavior, but I'm not complaining. Especially since it means I'm in his arms on the dance floor rather than sitting in awkward silence at the empty table.

"How was your day?" he asks, breaking the silence between us.

I almost want to laugh. It seems like a question you'd hear between an old married couple. But his face is serious. He's not joking. He really wants to know how my day went. This is the first time in two weeks that Linc hasn't come by to work at the salon after his normal work day. We both decided to take the evening off to relax and unwind. I'd assumed he'd be spending his time with Ella, but I'm not upset that I was wrong and he's here tonight.

"Not bad," I finally say. "I finished my last client at around four. And since the new faucet had arrived, I decided to try my hand at installing it myself. It took me longer than I thought it would, but I managed."

I'm all set to tell him how good it all looks now that it's all together, but I realize he's frowning down at me.

"What?"

"Why didn't you wait for me to help?" He asks, surprising me.

I lean back far enough to really look at him. "Because I wanted to see if I could do it myself. Are you mad that I didn't wait for you?"

It's ridiculous for him to be upset at me for doing things in my own salon without him. And I plan to tell him exactly what I think of that. I open my mouth to speak, but he beats me to it.

"No, Harlow. I'm not mad that you did it alone," he says. "I'm proud of you. But you didn't have to. You don't always have to do things the hard way, you know?"

I shrug, ignoring the little thrill that shot through me when he'd said he was proud of me. "It's not the hard way if it's the only way," I mutter.

"Not anymore," he says. "It doesn't have to be. You have me now."

I ignore the way those words seem to wrap themselves around my heart and squeeze. I don't have Linc. Not really. I never have and I doubt I ever will.

I give a little laugh to disguise the hurt I feel at that thought. "Linc, I can't just call you every time I break something and can't fix it."

He grins down at me. "Why not? I'm happy to help."

"For starters, you have a life. You have a daughter and a business." I keep my gaze focused on a spot just beyond his shoulder, rather than meeting his gaze.

"Besides," I say, trying to keep my voice light. "Someday you'll have a girlfriend, or a wife and I doubt she'll appreciate it if you drop everything to run to my aid every time I need help with something."

Linc doesn't reply and my words hang in the air for a long moment. When I risk a glance at him, I see that he's watching me, his gaze intense.

"Anyone who gets upset about me helping a friend isn't someone I want to be with," he says, his voice hard.

I ignore the way the word 'friend' stings. Of course, we're friends. That's all we've ever been. That's all we'll ever be. Linc has never said or done anything to make me think otherwise. This dance tonight is just an illusion. It's only my traitorous brain that keeps wondering what it would be like to kiss him. I'm the only one in this 'friendship' whose mind is in the gutter. I force a smile and ignore the way his eyes on me are sending flutters straight to my lady bits.

"That's what you say now," I say.

We're both quiet for a few moments as we sway to the music. Linc tightens his hold slightly, pulling me closer to him as we dance. I want to lean into him, press my body to his and rest my head on his chest. I want to spend what's left of this song enjoying the feel of his arms around me, his body close to mine. But that feels like crossing a line. Would he welcome that? Would he read something into it? Like the truth?

"You're a good dancer," he murmurs, breaking the silence.

I look up at him and smile. "You're not so bad yourself." I keep my tone light and playful when all I want to do is kiss him and beg him to do unspeakable things to my body.

"I should have asked you to the prom," he says, his grin widening. "My date didn't dance with me once the whole night."

I know he doesn't mean anything by bringing up high school, but it feels like someone just dumped a bucket of cold water over me. He can't realize how much his casual comment bothers me. Back then, I would have given anything to be noticed by him. Instead, I went to prom alone. My mom made my corsage, and I wore a second-hand dress that took me months to save up for. All in the hopes that he would finally see me. Instead, he'd opted to take Hillary Mitchell as his date. She'd been one of the cheerleaders and he was the football star. They were a walking cliché, especially when they won Prom King and Queen, to absolutely no one's surprise.

I'd left before the perfect couple could make it onto the stage to accept their crowns. Instead of going home where I knew my mom would question why I left so early and want a full recap of the night, I drove to the beach and spent an hour walking along the sand until I was sure I was finished crying. I'd been so stupid to think someone like Lincoln Prescott would notice a shy band nerd who was nowhere near his social standing. Eventually, I tamped down my hurt and dried my tears. I finally drove home after I was sure it was so late my mom would already be asleep.

I've spent years blocking out the memory of that night, trying to forget the feelings of embarrassment and disappointment that seemed to be a running theme of my teen years. I thought I was past those feelings. I've done so much to move on and become a better version of that awkward girl. But Linc just brought it all back with one thoughtless comment. Not that he even realizes it. I manage to smile at him, but I don't say anything as the song ends and we walk back to the table.

I spend the next hour pretending with my friends that everything is the same as it was before my dance with Linc. But really, I'm counting down the minutes until I can break away and go home to mope in my pajamas. A dull headache is forming behind my eyes, and I don't think anyone but Piper notices when I quietly switch to drinking water. Whatever alcohol buzz I had at the start of the night is long gone.

By the time I finally excuse myself to go home, it's barely 9:30 and I'm completely sober. It's a good thing, though. I have appointments with clients tomorrow and I should probably go home and get some rest. At least that's the excuse I use when I tell the others I'm leaving. Piper puts up a token argument, but I can tell she senses something is bothering me and she doesn't press me to stay. Besides, I'm pretty sure she's ready to take Luke home. Those two haven't stopped touching each other all night. It would be cute if it weren't so annoying.

After a chorus of goodbyes and a hug from Piper, I'm finally out the door and on my way home. Luckily, I live close enough to Peach Fuzz that I can walk there in just a few minutes. I let myself into the salon and don't bother turning on the lights. I'm already imagining how good it's going to feel to take off this dress and put on a baggy shirt and crawl into bed. After locking up, I turn toward the stairs. I only make it three steps before I hear someone knocking at the front door. My heart jumps into my throat when I turn to see who's standing there.

Linc.

CHAPTER 18

Harlow

Linc is here. Why is he here? Did something happen? I walk over to unlock the door.

"What is it?" I ask.

Instead of answering, Linc squeezes past me into the darkened salon.

"Is everything okay?" I ask, suddenly nervous.

He nods. "Everything is fine."

"Did you forget something yesterday? Something you need for work?" I'm trying to figure out why he showed up here unannounced when I left him less than 10 minutes ago.

"What?" he asks. "Oh, no. That's not why I'm here."

"Then what are you doing here, Linc?" I ask, letting him hear the exhaustion in my voice.

"I wanted to make sure you made it home okay," he says, still not meeting my gaze.

A small laugh escapes me. "Seriously? From Peach Fuzz? It's like a 3-minute walk."

He lifts one shoulder in a shrug. "It's late. Anything could happen."

Confused, I just look at him. "It's not even 10pm. And this is Peach Tree we're talking about. The biggest crime in this town is jaywalking."

He sighs, running a hand through his hair in frustration. "Can't I just be concerned for a friend?"

There's that word again. 'Friend.' It would make me laugh if I wasn't already so angry and hurt from our little dance earlier.

"Sure, you can," I say. Using one hand, I gesture at myself. "Well, as you can see, I'm home safe. Your *friend* duties are finished for the night." I hear the emphasis I put on the word 'friend' and hate myself for it. I can only hope he didn't hear it too.

"Harlow, why are you mad at me?"

"I'm not," I say automatically. But I can't meet his gaze.

"Yes, you are," he insists. "You've been acting weird since we danced. I want to know why."

When I don't answer him, he says, "I've been wracking my brain trying to figure out what I said or did. Things were going fine until they weren't. So, what did I say?"

My frustration bubbles up to the surface and I let the words spill out.

"Prom," I say. "You brought up the stupid prom."

His brows lower in confusion. "What's wrong with prom?"

"Because you just throw things like that out there like it's some big joke. 'Oh I should have asked the dorky band nerd to the dance.' It's nothing to you. But you don't know what it was like. Do you really not remember high school? You were a football god, and I was just the band nerd with the hand-me-down clothes and a mom who worked too much to even come to see me play in competitions. You didn't even know I existed. But it's so funny to crack jokes about taking me to prom, right? Screw you, Linc."

I shoot him a glare, only to see confusion on his face.

His voice is careful. "What do you mean?"

"You don't get it," I say with a humorless laugh. I wave a hand in his direction. "You were the popular kid. You got everything you wanted. You don't know what it's like to want something and know you'll never get it."

I cut myself off abruptly, heart pounding. What the hell? Did I just almost confess to wanting him since high school? Maybe he didn't pick up on it.

Linc is looking at me with an expression I don't recognize. He looks like he's working on a difficult math problem in his head. Only he's staring at me while he does it. What is he thinking? I don't think I want to know.

"What are you saying, Harlow?" His voice is low, careful.

I feel my face heat and I turn away from Linc and take a few steps to put some distance between us. "Nothing. It doesn't matter."

"Look at me." His voice is nearly a whisper now, coming from directly behind me.

I go still, but I don't turn around. If I look at Linc right now, I'm afraid I might do something stupid, like kiss him. Or kick him for being so oblivious for all these years. Before I can gather my thoughts, I feel his hand on my shoulder. His touch is gentle, but insistent as he turns me around to face him. I keep my gaze on the floor at our feet, ignoring how his nearness makes my heart pound and my breathing shallow. I expect him to insist I meet his gaze, but he surprises me when he speaks.

"Are you saying you would have gone with me if I'd asked?"

Yes.

Absolutely.

In a heartbeat.

But I don't say any of those things. Instead, I keep my tone light and dismissive.

"It doesn't matter," I say with a shrug. "That was a long time ago."

"Stop saying that," Linc says, his voice hard now. "It does matter. The past matters, Harlow."

His grip on my shoulders tightens slightly. Not enough to be painful, but enough that I risk a glance up at his face. Immediately, I realize I've made a mistake. The intensity in Linc's eyes steals my breath. My heart hammers in my chest as we stand there, looking at one another. I wish I knew what he's thinking. I wish he'd say something. I wish—

"I'm such an idiot," he whispers.

I open my mouth to say something; I'm not sure if I planned to argue his statement or agree with it, but it doesn't matter. I don't get the chance to speak, because Linc's mouth is on mine. A startled sound escapes me at the feel of his lips. My confusion only lasts for a second before I melt against him.

His hands tighten on my shoulders, holding me still for the onslaught of his mouth. His lips move over mine in gentle, but insistent caresses. I can feel hard ridges of muscle under my hands, and I realize that my palms are flat against Linc's chest. When had I reached up to touch him? I don't remember doing it, but it doesn't matter now. I don't know what made him kiss me, and I don't care. All I know is how good his lips feel on mine. When his mouth opens and his tongue brushes mine, I stop thinking altogether and give in to sensation. All my feeble imaginings have been nothing compared to the reality of kissing Linc. Every nerve ending in my body feels alive right now.

The kiss deepens as Linc's arms come around me, pulling me against him. I go willingly, sliding my hands up and around his neck. I feel like I can't get close enough to him. After nearly 20 years of wondering what it would be like to have his arms around me and his lips on mine, I find that I don't ever want it to end.

When Linc's mouth leaves mine to trail over my jaw and down to my neck, a startled gasp escapes me. But I don't pull away. I bury my fingers in the soft strands of his hair, holding him in place. A delicious shiver runs down my body, gathering between my legs. Shit. Am I really getting wet from one kiss? Linc's hand slides lower, gripping my hip, fingers curling into the soft flesh of my ass and pulling me hard against him. His mouth comes back to mine as he walks me backward until my back touches the counter. Now, I'm trapped between his large body and the waist-high counter behind me as his mouth devours mine.

I strain to get closer to him, molding my body to his. He grips my leg, pulling it up around his waist. All at once I feel the hard press of his erection against my lower belly. Our height difference means it's not hitting anywhere near where I want it to. But it's so fucking hot to know Linc's as turned on as I am right now.

"Fuck," he whispers against my neck.

His hand trails up my side, sending a shiver of awareness through me. When I feel his thumb brush against the underside of my breast, I gasp and strain toward his touch. I want this man's hands on me. I want his touch everywhere.

His mouth moves lower, over my collar bone. He peppers kisses over the exposed skin there, nearly bending in half to reach. All at once, he lets out a growl of frustration and moves back from me. Disappointment floods through me, and I open my mouth to ask him what's wrong. Before I can speak, he reaches down and grips both my hips in his large hands. As if I weigh nothing, Linc lifts me up and sits me on the counter at my back. He looks at me, his mouth quirking up into a sexy grin.

"That's better," he says, stepping forward into the space between my legs.

This position means our height difference no longer matters. That becomes even more clear when Linc's body presses against mine and I finally feel the press of his incredibly hard cock right where I want it. I gasp at the sensation as I wrap my legs around his back. The thin cotton of my dress does nothing to mask the feel of him between my legs.

He cups my face with one hand, holding me still for his mouth. His kiss has ratcheted up in intensity, driving my own hunger for him even higher. I hear someone moan and I'm shocked to realize it was me. I want nothing more than for this man to keep touching me. I want his hands everywhere on me, inside me. My thoughts scatter and there's no room for anything in my mind except need.

When Linc reaches for the tie at my neck, I don't hesitate. Reaching up, I pull the end of the tie, feeling the material loosen over my chest an instant before Linc tugs it down the rest of the way, exposing my bare breasts to his gaze.

"You're so fucking beautiful," he murmurs before lowering his head to plant kisses on the swell of my breast. "I should have told you that months ago. Years ago."

I'm stunned by his words, but too caught up in what we're doing to respond right now. I tangle my fingers in his hair, holding him to me as my hips strain against his erection. I'm rubbing myself shamelessly against him, but I don't care. Every brush of his cock against my clit pushes me higher and higher. I think I could come from this alone, even with the barrier of clothes between us.

Linc cups my breast in his hand, lifting it as he lowers his head. I feel his tongue against my nipple, licking gently before sucking it greedily into his mouth. The sharp pleasure-pain makes me cry out, my hips rolling forward to rub against his cock again. The combination of his erection pressing against my clit and his mouth on my nipple sends a fresh wave of moisture to my pussy and wrings another cry from me.

Linc slides the dress down lower, leaving it to pool around my waist and expose more of me to his gaze. He moves to my other breast to lavish it with the same attention. All the while, I keep sliding my pussy against him, moving closer and closer to the peak. I know I'll feel embarrassed later, but right now all I can think about is how good this man feels against me, how amazing his mouth feels on my flesh and how much I want to come.

Linc's hips are moving now too, matching my frenzied movements, rubbing and sliding between my legs. His hands reach behind me and grip my ass, grinding me even harder against his cock as he sucks my nipple into his mouth again. The strangled moan that escapes me is one I know I've never heard myself utter before. I can feel the tell-tale pulsing begin low between my legs as Linc thrusts against me again, timing his movements with the suction of his mouth on my nipple. I can't believe I'm about to come without anyone even taking their pants off.

"Fuck," I moan. "Yes!"

Linc's hips move faster, his fingers digging into my ass as his cock slides over my pussy again and again, pushing me closer and closer to the edge. My fingers tighten in his hair as my pussy clamps down on nothing. His teeth close over my nipple and the sharp sting is enough to send me flying. I cry out as waves of pleasure course through me, my body shaking with the force of the orgasm. Linc keeps thrusting against me, driving my orgasm on and on. His fingers tighten on my ass, and he groans against my breast. A shiver goes through him, and he finally stills against me.

Neither of us moves for several seconds, our harsh breathing the only sound in the room. As my breathing begins to slow to normal, I register a few things. One of which is that I just had one of the best orgasms of my life without taking my panties off, all while sitting on the counter in my salon. The second is that things feel a little messier between my legs than they should after an orgasm. It takes me a second to understand the implications.

"Um," I say, not sure how to phrase my question. "Is that—"

Linc keeps his head lowered, not meeting my gaze. "I should go."

He pulls away from me, turning away quickly, but not before I see that he's got a significant wet spot on the front of his pants. That's not all from me, I know. Yes, I was shamelessly grinding myself against him. I also know how wet I was while doing it. Wow.

"Wait," I say, scrambling off the counter. "Don't leave."

"I'm sorry," he says, running a hand through his hair, looking everywhere but at me.

"I'm not," I say, making him stop and look at me.

"What?" he asks, clearly rattled.

I reach for my dress before it can fall completely off me. I can't help but notice the way Linc's eyes stray to my tits as he looks at me. I pull my dress up to cover myself as I step closer to him.

"I'm not sorry," I say, reaching out to touch his arm. He still can't quite meet my gaze. "I've wanted to kiss you for a long time. And that was the hottest first kiss in the history of first kisses."

He lets out a strangled laugh before shaking his head. "It's also a little embarrassing," he mutters.

I shrug. "Why? Because you came in your pants? Newsflash: so, did I. Should I be embarrassed?"

That finally makes him look up to meet my gaze. "You're not wearing pants," he says. "And you definitely shouldn't be embarrassed. That was sexy as fuck."

I smile up at him. "Yeah, it was," I whisper, leaning up to kiss his cheek. "Knowing that I can make you come like that, is so fucking hot."

Something else occurs to me and I hate myself for asking, but I need to know before things can go any further.

"Do you regret it?" I ask, feeling my heart in my throat.

He laughs. "The only thing I regret is not doing it sooner. Knowing that I've been missing out on that for all these years is going to be hard to live down."

I smile, a giddy feeling bubbling up inside me. Linc kissed me. He kissed me and he made me come and he doesn't regret it. One more question pops into my head.

"And you're not drunk, right?"

He rolls his eyes. "If I were drunk, I would have lasted a lot longer. I only had one beer." He looks down at the floor. "I feel like some idiot virgin who's never touched a woman," he mumbles. "I promise that's not my usual performance."

"I think I have to see that for myself to be an accurate judge," I tease. I link my fingers with his, feeling the calluses and the strength in those big hands. "Care to show me?" I whisper, pulling him toward the stairs.

CHAPTER 19

Linc

After my embarrassing performance in the salon where I came in my pants like a teenaged boy who's just seen his first pair of tits, I'm ready to crawl under a rock for the next decade. I finally got to kiss Harlow, to touch her, and I explode in my pants before I can even see her naked. What the fuck?

In my defense, watching her come apart in my arms and feeling her pulse against me had been more than I'd counted for when I kissed her. Who expects their first kiss with someone to end in orgasms for both parties? Not me, that's for sure. I'm nearly 30 years old, for god's sake. I should have a better handle on my dick than that.

But this is Harlow. The girl I've fantasized about for years. The reality of having her in my arms, willing and pliant, grinding against my cock had been too much for me to handle, I guess. But as embarrassing as it had been, I can feel myself growing hard at the idea of touching her again. So, I let her lead me upstairs to her apartment. I take my shoes off near the front door and follow her into the bathroom where she turns the shower on.

She doesn't say anything. She just reaches for my pants, unbuttoning them with a quick tug. I take over, quickly stripping out of my cum-soaked pants and boxers, kicking them off to the side. Harlow reaches for my shirt and tries to push it up over my head. She's too short to manage it, though. Grinning, I pull the garment up and over my head and drop it to the floor. I stand there, totally naked as her eyes roam over my body, lingering on my now-hard dick. When she finally meets my gaze again, I raise a brow at her.

"Damn," she whispers.

"Should I feel violated?"

She grins. "Only if you want to."

Then she strips out of her dress and underwear faster than I would have thought possible, leaving me standing there staring now. I'd seen her tits downstairs. I'd even had those pretty pink nipples in my mouth. They're fucking perfect. But seeing her standing here totally naked in front of me? Damn. She's beautiful. I take in her full breasts, those plump hips, and gorgeous thighs that were made to wrap around my face and I thank whatever lucky stars are shining down on me tonight.

"You're gorgeous," I say, letting my eyes roam over every inch of her.

Harlow blushes as she reaches for my hand and pulls me toward the shower. I follow because I'd have to be dead not to. Even then, I think I'd find a way. She pulls me under the warm spray with her, her hands sliding over my chest and abs. I'm rock-hard again, but that's not surprising. I've been in a perpetual state of hardness whenever I'm around her for weeks now. No wonder I blew my load so quickly earlier. It's been building up for weeks. Hell, for years if I'm being honest with myself. I hate that it took me so long to get here. I barely worked up the nerve to ask her to dance after spending the entire night trying not to stare at her in that fucking dress.

Now that I'm here, naked with her, I can't believe I wasted so many years being too scared to act on my attraction to her. When I followed her home earlier, I never dreamed it would lead to this. I just wanted to talk to her. To find out why she seemed upset. To smooth things over. But then she made that comment about high school and I lost it. Kissing her had felt inevitable. Like I might die if I didn't. And now I can't believe I waited all these years to do it. I don't know what this means for us. I don't know if this is a one-time thing, or if she wants more from me. Whatever it is, I know I'll take whatever she wants to give me. I've wanted this woman for so long. I know we need to talk about it. Eventually. Now that I have her naked in my arms, I'll do whatever I can to keep her there.

"Hey." Harlow's soft voice pulls me from my thoughts as her hand comes up to rest on my cheek. "Where'd you go?"

I shake my head and smile down at her. "Just wondering how I got so lucky."

She presses the full length of her naked, wet body against mine. "You haven't gotten lucky yet, sir. But just you wait."

A little thrill runs through me at hearing her call me sir, but I let it go. It's the second time she's called me that and the second time it's sent a signal straight to my cock. But I don't think she's ready for me to show her that side of me. So, I ignore that for now. Instead, I slide my hands down to cup her round ass, giving it a squeeze. Harlow sucks in a breath when the action presses her more firmly against my hard length. I bend down to kiss her, savoring the feel of her lips on mine, her tongue, her taste. I don't think I'll ever get enough of kissing Harlow. Now that I know, how can I ever go back?

She finally pulls away enough to reach for the shower gel. "Hope you don't mind smelling like me," she teases.

"Hell no," I say. "You always smell incredible. I might be walking around with a perpetual hard-on from smelling you all day, though."

She just smiles and lathers up a pink shower pouf before bringing it up to my chest. She rubs it over me in slow circles, not missing an inch of skin. When she reaches my cock, she forgoes the pouf altogether, using her soapy, slippery hands to wash me. She strokes my shaft up and down in long, lazy strokes, her eyes never leaving mine as she does. It's the most delicious kind of torture. She tightens her grip and gives my head a little twist on each upstroke, making me suck in a breath. I let it go on for as long as I dare before grabbing her wrist to stop her movements.

"If you want to get any real use out of it," I say, "you better stop now."

She grins. "I can't help it. I like touching you."

"My turn," I say, reaching for the discarded shower pouf.

I take my time washing her body, lingering over her breasts, and teasing her with my fingers until she's gasping. By the time I'm finished, the water is starting to turn cold, but neither of us cares. We're both so fucking turned on, it wouldn't matter if the water turned to ice. Harlow turns off the water and I reach for a towel as we step out of the shower. I pull her to me, wrapping the towel around us both. It doesn't quite reach, so my ass is uncovered in the cool air, but I don't care.

I ignore my wet body in favor of drying hers, gently rubbing the fluffy towel over her damp skin. I take my time, not willing to rush this. I've spent years waiting for my chance with Harlow. Now that she's here in my arms, I want to take my time and cherish her. I move around behind her to dry her back. Unable to stop myself, I bend down to plant a kiss on her bare shoulder. She shivers a little and I hear her take a shaky breath. Bending lower, I follow the path of the towel with my mouth, kissing down her spine to the dip just above her gorgeous ass. I linger there, spending a little more time kissing that patch of skin before moving back around to her front. Dropping to my knees, I rub the towel down the length of one leg to her foot, then do the same to the other.

I look at Harlow. Her eyes are on me, watching, waiting to see what I'll do next. My face is directly in front of her waiting pussy. I can't really be blamed for what I do next. It's what any sane man would do, right? Leaning forward slightly, I kiss her mound before giving her slit a long, slow lick. Fuck, she tastes good. I knew she would. I let out a low groan and lick her again, savoring the taste of her on my tongue.

"Linc," she gasps, her hands going to my hair.

I grin against her flesh, loving the way she grips me. Reaching out, I lift one of her legs, draping it over my shoulder and opening her to my gaze. Harlow leans back against the wall to steady herself, but she doesn't shy away from my gaze or my touch. She wants this just as much as I do, I realize. That only further solidifies my need to make this good for her. Especially after my embarrassing performance downstairs. I need to wipe that memory from both our minds.

Reaching up, I slide my fingers over her slickness, coating them in her wetness before dipping inside. Her mouth drops open in a silent gasp. With two fingers barely inside her, I lean forward and lick her pussy again. I feel her quiver around my fingers just a bit with that brush of my tongue on her clit. She's so responsive, even from that small touch. It makes my dick grow even harder.

I slide my tongue over her again, teasing her clit on each upstroke. Each time I do, she sucks in a breath and a little shiver runs over her. I push my fingers deeper inside her, loving the way she presses back against me, seeking more. Slowly, I pump my fingers in and out, in and out, fucking her with my hand. It's a tease, I know. For both of us. But I want to take my time with her. I want to push her as far as possible before she goes over the edge. I want to watch her unravel. I want to taste it on my tongue.

My tongue moves in lazy circles, teasing her clit each time but not enough to make her come. Not yet. I can hear her breathing growing shallow. Her hips push against my hand with each thrust inside her. I move my tongue in ever-smaller circles, paying more attention to her clit with each one.

"Linc," she gasps. "Please."

I know what she wants. I'm tempted to give in and grant her a quick release, but I'm having too much fun. I swirl my tongue over her clit just long enough to make her squirm before returning to my previous slow torture. She lets out a little huff of frustration that makes me smile against her sweet pussy. I pump my fingers in and out faster now, curling them slightly as I do. The moan Harlow rewards me with has my cock aching.

I lean back just enough to watch her face. Fuck, she's beautiful. Naked, eyes closed, head thrown back as she lets me fuck her with my fingers. She's panting now, little whimpers escaping her each time I push into her. I feel my own excitement rise as I watch her. I want to see her come apart. I need it. I lean in and capture her clit between my lips, flicking my tongue against it rapidly.

"Oh!" she cries, her fingers tightening almost painfully in my hair.

I keep going, feeling her clench around my fingers as her hips buck against my face. I tighten my grip around her waist, holding her still for my assault on her pussy. Her body goes rigid, and I feel her spasm around my fingers as a cry is ripped from her throat. I don't let up, pushing her to the edge and beyond it. I keep pumping my fingers in and out as I lick her clit, lapping up every drop of her release. I could happily keep doing this for the rest of the night if she'd let me, but it seems Harlow has other ideas.

"Stop, stop, stop," she whispers.

I freeze, looking up at her. "What's wrong?"

She shakes her head without opening her eyes. "Nothing." A smile spreads over her face. "I just need a second."

I grin up at her, even though she can't see it. Slowly, I slide my fingers out of her, loving the little whimper of protest she makes as I do. Turning my head, I kiss her hip, lingering there for a moment. "You've got five seconds before I'm burying my head between your legs again."

She laughs and finally opens her eyes to look at me. "I think I'd like something else between my legs."

She shocks me by dropping to her knees and straddling me. My hard length is pressed against her wet pussy now, a new kind of delicious torture for us both. My hands grip her hips as she rocks against me, sliding against me. I can tell when the head of my cock brushes her sensitive clit because she sucks in a gasp. When she rises up far enough for me to tease at her opening, it takes everything in me not to drag her down onto me and impale her on my shaft.

"Condom," I manage.

"Hurry," she says, still rocking and sliding against me.

I manage to reach for my pants and dig a condom from the pocket without releasing my hold on her. My cock is painfully hard by the time I get the condom on. We're both panting as she reaches down and grips my shaft, guiding it into her as she sinks down onto me.

"Fuck," I groan. "You feel so fucking good, baby."

Harlow sinks all the way down, taking all of me in one thrust. She stills for a moment, letting her body adjust to the feel of me inside her. I grip her ass, wanting to surge up into her. But I keep still, letting her set the pace. She grips my shoulders, using my body for leverage as she lifts herself up until only the head of my cock is still inside her. Then she sinks back down, fast and hard. Her mouth drops open and she looks down, watching this time when she rises up and back down again.

"You like that?" I rasp, my fingers tightening on her ass. "You like watching your body take me? Watching my cock disappear inside you?"

She nods, still watching the place where our bodies are joined.

"You take me so well, baby," I say as I pull her back down against me.

The extra force wrings a cry of pleasure from her, and I smile. "You want more?"

She nods again and this time I thrust my hips upward as I pull her down. Her cry is louder this time as I slam into her. I repeat the action three more times before I relent. Harlow makes a little sound of disappointment when she realizes I'm not moving anymore.

"What?" I ask. "You want more?"

She nods, leaning forward to kiss me. I take her mouth in a rough kiss before pulling back to look into her eyes.

"Tell me," I say, my voice rough. "Ask for what you want."

I want to hear her say it. I need the words. I can see the battle between need and embarrassment in her eyes and I can tell the moment the need wins out. "More," she whispers, closing her eyes. "Please."

"Look at me," I demand. "Eyes open."

Her blue eyes snap open and focus on mine.

"Do you want me to fuck you?"

She nods.

"Do you want it hard and rough?"

She sucks in a shaky breath, eyes glittering with excitement. "Yes."

That's all I need. A single whispered word. That's all it takes for me to let go. I pull her tight against me as I thrust upward, pounding into her from below. Harlow braces herself with her arms locked tight around my neck as the tight leash on my control snaps. I can hear her cries growing louder with every punishing thrust of my cock inside her. When I feel her begin to flutter around my length, I lower my mouth to her neck, kissing and biting the tender flesh until her body goes rigid and her nails dig into my back. I don't let up though, even as I feel her coming around my cock.

"Yes! Yes! Linc!"

Before she can fully come down from her orgasm, I pull her off my cock and flip her over onto her knees. She braces her hands on the edge of the tub as I push into her from behind. Her round ass slaps against me with every thrust. She pushes back against me, arching her back. Reaching forward, I grip her shoulder with one hand and use it as leverage to pull her against me as I fuck her. I grab her ass with my other hand, my fingers digging into the soft flesh.

I can feel my own orgasm looming, but I want to get her off once more before I finish.

"Play with your clit," I say, my voice hard and commanding. "Come on my cock again."

Harlow reaches down between her legs, and I can feel her fingers brush against my shaft as she strokes her clit. The image of her on her knees under me, taking my cock as I pound into her is one I know I won't ever forget.

"That's it, baby," I say. "You feel so fucking good."

My words combined with her own fingers on her clit are enough to send Harlow flying over the edge. Her pussy convulses around me, and she cries out.

"Oh, god! Linc! Yes!"

I keep going, pounding into her over and over as her pussy squeezes me. The pulsing of her wet heat around my shaft finally sends me over the edge.

"Fuck!" I shout as I begin to come. My words come out stilted as I grunt them with every thrust and every spurt of my release.

"Such. A. Good. Fucking. Girl."

I pull her ass tight against me as my cock twitches a few more times inside her. The bathroom is silent now except for our heavy breathing as we both come down from what has to be the best sex of my entire life. I ease gently from Harlow's body and dispose of the condom in the trashcan in the corner. She's leaning forward against the tub, her head resting on her forearms. I reach out and stroke a hand down her back and she lets out a tired sigh.

"Are you okay?" I ask, worried maybe I was too rough with her. It was our first time together, after all.

She surprises me by starting to shake with laughter. I smile, slightly confused by the reaction.

"Okay?" she asks. "I'm fucking outstanding."

She turns to face me. Her damp hair is a mess, hanging around her face in wild tangles. "That's what I've been missing all these years? Fuck. I should have made my move years ago."

I laugh, shaking my head. "So, I wasn't too rough with you?"

She looks at me like I'm crazy. "Hell no. That was amazing." She moves to stand, wincing. "Maybe next time we pick a softer surface than the bathroom floor, though. I don't think my knees will recover for a while."

I look down and see that her knees are red from kneeling on the tile floor while I just fucked her brains out. Remorse floods through me. "Shit, Harlow. I'm sorry."

She just shakes her head, still wearing a slightly dazed smile. "No. Don't ever apologize for what just happened. It was epic. I'll wear these bruises with pride."

I laugh before reaching out and scooping her up into my arms. Dipping my head down, I kiss her temple. "If it makes you feel better, I think I'll be sporting matching bruises."

She snuggles into my chest and nods. "It does, actually."

Chapter 20

Harlow

I can't believe Lincoln Prescott is in my bed right now. He carried me into my bedroom and laid me down before gently tucking the covers around me. Then, he'd climbed in beside me, pulled me against him and fallen asleep. I've tried to fall asleep too, but my brain won't shut off. I don't know what any of this means. I can't believe I just had insane, toe-curling, face-melting sex with Lincoln Prescott. I don't even know how we got here. One second, we were talking about high school and prom and then I'd gotten irritated with him for being so oblivious. Only this time, it seems he wasn't so oblivious. Then suddenly, his mouth was on mine.

I've pictured kissing Linc so many times over the years. I've imagined so many different scenarios where he'd finally realize how great we could be together. Then we'd kiss and everything would be perfect. I never imagined anything close to what just happened. I've never considered that Linc might be hiding a dominant side. This quiet, even-tempered man just totally fucked my brains out and made me come more times than any man ever has. Who knew he had such a filthy mouth? Not me. Remembering the things he said to me while he was thrusting into me is enough to make my pussy clench with need. I can't possibly be ready for more, right? I don't even know if he can get hard this soon after coming twice in the last hour. But I'd be willing to try for a third round if he is.

Linc's arm tightens around me in his sleep, and I snuggle closer to his side. I know we're going to need to talk about what just happened and where we go from here. But for now, I'm content to lie here with this man in my bed for a little while longer and ignore all those questions. Besides, I don't want to hear Linc tell me that this is a one-time thing. I don't think my heart could take that kind of rejection. Not after knowing how amazing things can be between us. These past two weeks, working alongside Linc has shown me how compatible we are. What happened today just verified what I've suspected all along. That if he and I ever came together, we could be amazing. I feel Linc stir beside me as he wakes. He lets out a sexy little groan as he stretches, and I smile.

"How long was I sleeping?" he asks, his voice husky from sleep.

"Not long," I say. "Maybe an hour."

"It's all your fault."

Leaning up on my elbow, I glare at him in the dark. "My fault? How?"

He grins. "You wore me out, woman."

I shrug. "Well, maybe you're out of practice."

His eyes narrow. "Is that so?" He leans forward until his mouth is inches from mine. "In that case, maybe I should get in some more practice. Just to make sure I'm all caught up."

"Maybe you should," I whisper just before his lips claim mine.

The kiss quickly takes on a life of its own as Linc buries his hands in my hair and shifts me so I'm under him on the bed. His big body covers mine, his chest brushing against my bare breasts, causing my nipples to rise to sharp points. I lose myself in his kiss, the feel of his arms around me, his body looming over mine. I feel like I could stay right here for hours, kissing him. It's that good. But Linc seems to have other ideas. He pulls away just far enough to see me clearly. His hand cups my cheek, the callouses on his thumb somehow comforting as it strokes my skin. The expression on his face is one I don't recognize as he gazes down at me. It's a mix of tenderness and wonder and makes my heart trip in my chest.

"What?" I ask, suddenly uncomfortable under his scrutiny.

He smiles. "I just realized that I don't have to hide it anymore."

My brow furrows. "Hide what?"

"The fact that I think you're insanely sexy," he says, kissing my cheek. "I've had to stop myself from staring at you so many times over the past few months."

My shock must show on my face because Linc laughs. "It's true," he says. "Every time we'd run into each other at Peach Fuzz, and you'd have on some short skirt that showed those sexy thighs or some low-cut top that had me drooling over these gorgeous tits." He leans down and kisses the swell of my breast. "I'd have to hide the fact that I was rock-hard for you."

I shake my head. "You're not serious."

His eyes narrow as he looks up at me. "I'm always serious about erections and sexy women."

I laugh, still shaking my head. "So, why didn't you ever make a move?"

He shrugs. "For starters, you weren't always single."

"Don't remind me."

Grinning, he traces a finger over my breast and around my nipple, causing my skin to break out in gooseflesh. "But mostly, I was convinced you wouldn't be interested in me that way. We didn't know each other all that well. And you're so much cooler than I am."

I burst out laughing at that. "Me?" I gasp. "The band nerd? Cooler than Mister Football God? You're delusional."

He sighs. "I keep telling you, high school was a long time ago. Who we were then doesn't matter now. And for the record, you weren't a nerd. I thought you were adorable in that uniform."

My face goes red. I try to cover it with my hands, but Linc pulls them away easily.

"Don't hide from me, Harlow," he whispers. "I've already seen all of you, remember?"

His voice is low and sexy. I can feel him, hard and insistent pressing against my hip. The reminder of the scene in the bathroom earlier is enough to make me ache with wanting. I feel myself growing wet.

"Tasted all of you."

He leans in to kiss my lips.

"Touched all of you."

His hand trails lower, down over my belly and toward the junction of my thighs.

"Been inside you."

His fingers slide between my legs, lightly teasing my already wet flesh.

"Felt you come on my mouth and my dick."

I suck in a shaky breath as his fingers graze my clit. My hips move, seeking more of his touch. His words bring back the memory of what we did in the bathroom earlier. His dominating presence, his filthy words as he filled me with his hard cock. I feel myself grow wetter as a shiver of desire courses through me.

"Heard you scream my name."

His fingers slide into me with a quick thrust, pulling a gasp from me. He holds his hand still, keeping me impaled on those two fingers. I clench my inner muscles, knowing he can feel the movement. Linc grins down at me.

"You like that, don't you?" He growls.

I nod.

"You like when I'm rough with you. When I take what I want."

I nod again, though he wasn't asking me a question. His eyes are intense as he watches my face. His fingers are still deep inside me, unmoving.

"Do you want more?"

"Yes," I whisper, clenching around him again.

"Ask for it," he says in that commanding voice I love.

My heartbeat ratchets up a notch. "Please."

"Not good enough." He begins to ease his fingers out of me.

"No," I cry out, reaching for his hand to stop him.

"Ask for what you want, Harlow," he commands.

I feel a sudden burst of shyness that I try to tamp down. Linc was right. He's already seen all of me. He's had his face between my legs while I came all over him. Why am I holding back now? I take a deep breath.

"I want your fingers in me," I say. "Please."

He grins. "Good girl."

The pleasure I get from hearing him say those two words shocks me, but I don't stop to analyze it. I'm too distracted by his long, blunt-tipped fingers filling me once again. A sigh of pleasure escapes me as he slowly slides his fingers out and back in. He keeps up that slow pace, his eyes still locked on my face. Just when I'm on the verge of begging him to move faster, he adds a third finger. My mouth drops open and a whimper escapes me at the stretching sensation. I feel almost too full, but in the best way.

"Is that too much?" he asks, stilling his movements with his fingers deep inside me.

I shake my head. "It feels good," I whisper, pressing down against his hand.

He smiles. "Tell me if it's too much."

I nod.

His hand starts to move again, pushing in and out. In and out. It doesn't take my body long to adjust to the fullness and soon he's thrusting into me faster. Harder. I can feel something building inside me; my body rushing toward something bigger than I've ever felt before. Linc's fingers curl inside me, pushing up against a spot I've always thought was a myth. My mouth drops open in a silent gasp.

"That's it, baby. Just let go. I've got you." His voice is low and rough and makes me want to do whatever it takes to please him.

His dark eyes never leave mine as his fingers continue their assault. Now, my body is working in tandem with his hand, pushing back against him with every thrust. That strange feeling is growing inside me, threatening to burst. I want to shy away from the foreign sensation, but it feels so incredible. I can hear the wet sounds coming from my body as his fingers stroke in and out of me. Tiny moans escape me each time he pushes his fingers inside me. Linc's hand moves faster, pumping into me with more speed now, still hitting that incredible spot inside me. I'm racing toward some unknown cliff, and I can't stop.

"I'm right here," he whispers. "Let go."

Faster.

Closer.

Higher.

More.

There!

I scream with the force of my orgasm as pinpricks of light explode behind my eyes. My pussy clamps down on Linc's hand and a rush of moisture floods from me, shocking me even as waves of pleasure roll over me. My entire body is alive with sensation. Linc keeps pumping his fingers into me, stroking me through my orgasm. My back arches off the bed as I cry out again and again, still fucking Linc's hand.

"There it is," he murmurs. "You're so fucking sexy when you come for me. Give me all of it, baby. Don't hold back."

His words of encouragement send me on another, smaller spiral of pleasure. The keening cry that's pulled from my throat is one I don't recognize. I'm lost in a haze of sensation and need. The only thing I can focus on is what Linc is doing to my body. He draws out my pleasure with teasing strokes of his fingers inside me as his movements slow. I wish I could hold onto this feeling forever, staring into Linc's eyes as I fall apart.

When the aftershocks of my orgasm finally subside, I realize that I'm gripping Linc's forearm with all my strength. I force myself to relax my grip as I come down from the most intense orgasm of my life. I'll be shocked if he doesn't have bruises that match my handprint on his arm. He eases his fingers from my body before giving my clit a soft stroke. I shiver, my pussy hypersensitive after coming so hard.

I lie there, trying to remember how to breathe while my body comes down from whatever the hell that was. I know I should feel embarrassed, but I can't find it in me. That was too incredible for me to feel anything but bliss.

"What was that?" I ask, still panting.

"That was fucking hot," Linc says, still grinning. "You just came all over my hand."

"I know an orgasm when I have one," I say, leaning up onto my elbows to look at him. "That was an out of body experience."

He grins as he covers my body with his and leans down for a kiss.

"You've never had anyone find your g-spot before?" he asks, trailing kisses over my jaw and down to my neck.

Shocked, I lean back far enough that I can see his face in the dark. "Is that what that was?"

Linc studies me for a moment before speaking. "I don't know whether to be mad or grateful that I'm the first man to ever make you squirt."

He says it casually as if talking about squirting is a normal conversation you have with someone after the first time you have sex with them. I feel a wave of embarrassment wash over me and I want to hide my face, but Linc is looming over me and there's nowhere to hide.

"That's so embarrassing," I mutter, turning my face away from his.

"Like hell, it is," he says. "Look at me, Harlow."

There's a command in his voice. The same command I heard before, when he made me ask for what I wanted. I couldn't disobey if I wanted to. Heart pounding, I turn my head and meet his gaze.

"What happens between us is never embarrassing," he says in that same tone that brooks no argument. "Did you like what I just did?"

When I hesitate, he asks again. "Did you?"

I nod. "Yes." My voice is barely above a whisper.

"Good." His hand comes up to stroke my cheek. "Pleasure isn't something to be embarrassed about. If what we're doing is consensual and we both enjoy it, you will not feel shame or embarrassment. Do you understand?"

I nod.

"Say it," he commands.

"I understand," I whisper.

"Good girl."

I suck in a shaky breath at the words.

A slow smile spreads across his face. "You like that, don't you?" His hips move and I feel his cock slide against my pussy, slipping through the wetness there. "You like when I call you my good girl?"

I nod, unable to pretend otherwise. "Yes," I whisper.

He grins as he lowers his head to take my mouth in a searing kiss. His hips move again and I gasp against his mouth when his cock brushes my clit. After another, lighter kiss, Linc leans back far enough to look at me.

"If there's ever anything you don't like, or you truly don't want to do," he says, "you need to tell me. This is important. I'll never do anything that makes you uncomfortable. Just tell me to stop and I will. Immediately. Got it?"

I nod.

"Say it, Harlow."

Something about that command in his voice has me wanting to please him. To obey him. I've never felt an urge like this before. When I answer him, the words fall naturally from my lips.

"Yes, sir."

Linc gives a little hum of approval before leaning down to kiss me again. This time, he's not holding anything back. He takes my mouth with a fierceness that has me writhing under him, trying desperately to get closer to him. Part of me is still in shock that this is truly happening. Linc is here with me. In my bed. About to fuck me for the second time tonight. Just a few hours ago, I'd been convinced that this attraction was one-sided. I'd been ready to crawl into my empty bed alone and imagine what it would be like to have him there with me. Now, I don't need to imagine anything.

Not that my feeble imagination could have created anything remotely as good as the real thing.

I give myself over to sensation and instinct, letting my hands travel over Linc's body; letting my fingers comb through his long hair, holding him close as we kiss. I never want this night to end. When he finally thrusts into me, filling me, stretching me; he murmurs my name, and it sounds almost reverent.

CHAPTER 21

Linc

It's still dark when I wake up to a naked, warm Harlow draped across my chest, her hair tickling my face. I grin in the darkness. Harlow is a cuddler. It doesn't surprise me, but it does please me. I love the way she wraps herself around me, even in her sleep. I try not to think too hard about how happy just holding her makes me. Much as I'd like to stay here in this bed with her all day, ignoring my responsibilities, I know I need to get home before my mom brings Ella home. The last thing I want is to explain to my mother why I'm coming home in last night's clothes. And I definitely don't need my daughter to ask the kinds of questions that I'm sure she'd have if she knew I'd stayed out all night.

I try to slip out from under Harlow's sleeping form without disturbing her. The sleepy grumble of protest she makes when I pull away from her has me smiling. I don't know what last night means to her or where we go from here. We didn't talk about that. We didn't talk about much at all if I'm being honest. I know what I'd like last night to mean. But now isn't the time to discuss it. I don't want to wake her at this ungodly hour after I kept her awake most of the night. Instead, I quietly go about getting dressed in the clothes I wore last night, minus the underwear which have now turned into a hard, crusty mess after what happened downstairs. I'm still embarrassed about that. But Harlow hadn't seemed bothered. In fact, she'd seemed pleased by the fact that I came just from watching her come. The memory makes my dick twitch in my pants, even after everything we did last night.

Once I'm dressed, I weigh out whether I should let Harlow sleep or make sure she knows I'm not sneaking out or doing some walk of shame. She's only been asleep for a few hours. It feels wrong to wake her up right now. I finally decide to leave her a note. I find a notebook on the kitchen counter and take my time deciding how to word things. When I'm finally satisfied, I leave the note on the pillow on the empty side of her bed. Then I kiss her forehead and slip out without waking her.

I don't see anyone on my way home. It's too early for most people to be stirring in Peach Tree on a Saturday. When I get home, I park next to Cole's car in the driveway and quietly unlock the front door and slip inside. Cole isn't usually a light sleeper, but I don't want to face him just yet. I know he'll have questions after the way I left the bar last night. I'd like to savor this thing between me and Harlow for a little longer before my brother starts in on his teasing. And I know there's no way I'll be able to avoid that. My brother is nothing if not predictable.

"Well, well, well. Look who finally made it home."

Fuck.

I jump, startled by Cole's voice coming from the dark living room. Reaching over, I flick on the lamp causing him to blink at the sudden brightness in the room. He's sitting in a chair in the corner wearing what I think might be last night's clothes. I narrow my eyes at him.

"What are you doing up this early?"

Cole stands and holds up one finger. "First of all, this isn't about me. This is about where you've been all night. I've been worried sick. I didn't sleep a wink. I was up all night pacing the floors, worried about my big brother."

I roll my eyes as I brush past him, heading toward the kitchen for a glass of water. "You were not."

Of course, Cole follows me. "I absolutely was. No call? No text? Mom would not approve."

I turn and point a finger at him. "Don't say shit to Mom."

Cole just laughs. "I'm not stupid. So? You gonna tell me where you were all night?"

As I fill my glass with water from the refrigerator, I feel a smile tug at my lips. "A friend's place."

"Hmm," Cole says. "Is this friend female? Blonde? About 5 feet, 5 inches tall? Owns a salon?"

I down half the water in my glass before turning to look at him. "Stop being an idiot. You know who I was with."

Cole grins as if he's just won something. "Yeah, but I want to hear you say it."

I sigh. Time to get this over with. It's not as if he doesn't already know where I went when I left Peach Fuzz last night. I hadn't tried to hide the fact that I was following Harlow home to make sure she made it safely. I'd ignored the weird looks from my friends, not wanting to explain why I couldn't let her leave without making sure she was okay. No one had questioned me, but I'd caught the knowing looks on their faces. I'm sure our entire friend group was speculating on what happened between the two of us after I left.

"I was with Harlow," I say. "Happy now?"

Cole lets out a loud cheer. "It's about time! Holy shit. What's it been, like 15 years?"

I grit my teeth against the urge to smack him, trying to remember that our parents would be upset if I strangled my little brother.

"Shut up," I mutter. But he doesn't. Of course.

"Dude. I'm happy for you." He grips both my shoulders and gives me a little shake. "You and Harlow! It's finally happening."

Cole is right, even if he's annoying about it. I'm a little in shock myself that last night went the way it did. I'm also irritated that I'm here with my brother this morning, talking about it instead of back in Harlow's bed, waking her up with my face between her legs.

But I know my parents will be coming to drop Ella off soon before they start their Saturday morning routine of checking out every garage sale in the county so my dad can acquire more junk to add to his growing collection. Not that he sees it that way. Everything he buys at a garage sale is 'a damned good deal, son.' I've learned not to argue with him about whether or not he needs the things he buys. Regardless, it means they'll be here early to bring Ella home and I need to shower before that happens. Pushing pash Cole, I head for the stairs.

"Keep your big mouth shut for now," I say. "I don't want Mom or Dad—and especially not Ella—to find out about it and freak out."

Cole makes a locking motion with his hand on his lips. "Your secret is safe with me."

"It's not a secret," I say, suddenly defensive. The idea of keeping Harlow a secret never occurred to me. Hell, I want to shout it from the rooftops that I finally kissed her, and it was more amazing than I ever thought possible. But until I talk to her about it, I don't think she'd appreciate me telling the world about us. If there is an 'us', I mean.

"I just need to find out what this means for me and Harlow before telling the world, okay?"

He looks at me with raised brows. "You guys didn't talk about that before you left?"

"She was still sleeping."

Coles eyes go wide. "You snuck out while she was still sleeping? Are you stupid?"

"I didn't sneak. There was no sneaking. I just didn't want to wake her up this early. She didn't get much sleep last night."

Cole grins. "I'll bet she didn't."

I close my eyes and sigh, knowing I walked right into that one. "Don't be gross," I say.

"Are you really that out of practice?" Cole asks. "You hook up with the girl you've had a crush on since high school, and you leave before she wakes up the next morning? Are you trying to screw it up before it even starts?"

I open my mouth then close it again, unsure what to say. Cole might be right.

"I left a note," I say lamely.

"A note? What the fuck, dude?"

"Maybe I should call her," I say, reaching for my phone. Glancing at the time, I realize it's probably still too early to wake Harlow. Even if it is to reassure her that I didn't sneak out this morning. I also realize I've got about 15 minutes before my parents show up to drop off my daughter. And none of them need to see me in last night's clothes.

"I'm taking a shower before Ella gets home," I tell Cole. "After Mom and Dad leave, I'll call Harlow."

CHAPTER 22

Harlow

When I wake up and find the bed empty beside me, my first thought is that I dreamed it all. Last night didn't really happen. Linc and I didn't really have the most amazing sex of my life. He didn't pull me into bed and finger me until I squirted, then fuck me until I screamed his name and fell into a post-coital coma. That had been some kind of lucid dream, right?

When I sit up in bed and feel the slight soreness between my legs, I realize that it was incredibly real after all. Linc and I had sex last night. And he'd left before I woke up. I try not to let that bother me, but the truth is that I'm a little hurt that he's not here right now. Then again, he has a daughter who has far more reasons to expect to see him in the morning than I do. That thought helps me put things into perspective and I shake off the hurt. It takes me a second to notice the white sheet of paper lying on the pillow beside me. It's folded in half with my name written in big letters. Linc left a note. I smile as I reach for the paper.

Harlow,

I'm so sorry I had to leave before you woke up. I needed to get home before Ella gets there and I didn't want to wake you.

Last night was one of the best nights of my life. Please let me make up for this morning by taking you out on a proper date. Dinner tonight? I can pick you up at 6.

Yours,

Linc

I read over the letter two more times and let out a little squeal of excitement. I have a date. With Linc. Tonight. This definitely feels like a dream. I can't believe I'm going on a date with the guy I've crushed on since I was 10. I wonder where he's taking me. What should I wear? My phone buzzes, pulling me out of my thoughts. I reach for it and see a ton of missed texts from Piper and Layna. Apparently, the two of them started a group text this morning. And I've been the subject of their discussion.

Piper: Harlow, tell me why Linc's truck is still parked outside of Peach Fuzz this morning.

Layna: Oh, shit. Somebody got LAID!

Piper: OMG, did you?!

Layna: It was the dancing, right? I told you it would drive him crazy.

Piper: We want details, woman!

Layna: Seriously, stop holding out. Especially after I was such a great wing-woman.

Piper: She's really not going to tell us?

Layna: Maybe his dick put her into a coma?

Piper: I've had dick that good before.

Layna: Please. Stop. I don't want to hear about you and my future brother-in-law.

Piper: Your loss.

Layna: You forget I'm staying with you guys right now. I've heard.

Piper: Shut up! You're not supposed to tell me that.

Layna: I'm not supposed to hear it, either. But here we are.

Piper: Enough about my sex life. Let's focus on Harlow.

Layna: Agreed.

Piper: EARTH TO HARLOW!

Layna: Blink twice if you're being held against your will.

Piper: Blink once if it's not against your will. [winking face emoji]

I scroll though all the texts, laughing and shaking my head. Finally, I type out a reply.

Me: You guys are ridiculous.
Piper: She lives!
Layna: How was it?
Me: I'm not giving you two details of my sex life.
Layna: Why the hell not? We're invested.
Piper: Rude.
Me: I'll just say that yes, Linc stayed the night here last night and yes, there was a coma afterwards. And nothing was against my will. [winking face emoji]
Layna: Fuck yeah!
Piper: It's about time!
Layna: I want details.
Me: NO! No details. That's all you get, you freak.
Layna: You're no fun.
Piper: I can respect it. Besides, I'll get you drunk one night, and you'll tell me everything.
Me: Shut up. Drunk me talks too much.
Layna: Drunk you is fun.
Me: He's taking me on a date tonight.
Piper: Aw!
Layna: Wear something slutty.
Me: You're awful.

My phone rings in my hand, startling me. I see Linc's name on the screen and smile, even as the butterflies in my stomach swarm. I swallow and take a breath before answering.

"Hello."

"Good morning, beautiful," Linc says, making me smile even wider.

"Mm," I say. "Compliments right after I wake up. I like it."

"I didn't wake you, did I?" he asks, a hint of concern in his voice.

"Actually, no. I was awake and responding to the 92 text messages from Layna and Piper."

"I'm guessing they know?"

I lay back on my pillow, still clutching his note. "Yep. Piper saw your truck still parked at Peach Fuzz when she went to open the shop this morning."

"Whoops," he says. "I guess the secret's out."

"Were you planning on keeping me a secret?" I tease.

"Absolutely not," he answers immediately. "Did you get my note? I want to take you out tonight. What do you say?"

I sigh. "I don't know. You did sneak out this morning without a word."

"Hey! I left a note. And why does everyone keep accusing me of sneaking?"

I laugh. "Who else accused you of sneaking?"

"Cole. He said I was stupid for leaving you this morning without waking you up. He said I was going to screw things up before they even got started."

I smile. "Is that why you called?"

"It's partly why," he admits. "I wanted to make sure I didn't screw things up already."

"You didn't," I say. "I answered the phone, didn't I?"

"A fact I am forever grateful for," he says.

"I'd love to go on a date with you," I say. "Just tell me one thing."

"Name it."

"You said the reason you called was partly to make sure you didn't screw things up with me. What was the other part?"

I can hear the smile in his voice when he answers. "To hear your voice, of course."

I can't help but smile at that. "Okay, that was charming."

"Charming enough to get you to kiss me later?"

"We'll see."

"I'll see you at 6, Harlow," he says, his voice low and sexy.

"See you then."

I end the call and let out another loud squeal as I kick the bed with both feet. I can't believe this is finally happening.

CHAPTER 23

Harlow

I'm not sure how I make it through the day's work. I barely remember a single client by the time I close the doors at 4pm and flip the sign to say 'closed'. As long as no one was unhappy with the work I did, I'm happy. I have 2 hours to get ready for my date with Linc and I still don't know what I'm wearing. He didn't tell me where he's taking me, but I assume it's not somewhere in Peach Tree. There aren't a lot of dining options in town and the most popular one is owned by his brother. Surely, he won't take me to Peach Fuzz. Right?

I can't focus too much on that since I need all the time I have to get myself ready. After I shower, shave and wash my hair, I go to the closet in the spare bedroom and start pulling dresses out and tossing them onto the bed. Some of these are dresses I've never worn before. It's not like I had a lot of opportunities for high fashion in Peach Tree. But tonight feels like the right night to pull out all the stops.

I settle on a black, slinky cocktail dress that hugs my curves and has a slit that shows off a good bit of my right thigh. It's definitely too fancy for a night out in Peach Tree, but for my first date with Linc, it feels perfect.

I dry my hair in soft waves down my back and spend far too long applying my makeup. By the time I finish, it's nearly time for Linc to pick me up. Part of me wishes I'd taken every last second to get ready. It might make me feel rushed, but at least I wouldn't have time to overthink everything before he gets here. What if he's taking me somewhere more casual? What if I'm totally overdressed? What if the date goes horribly wrong and we find out that there's nothing between us beyond the physical? That thought bothers me the most. I don't want to finally have a date with Linc, only to discover we can't hold a conversation.

I tamp that thought down immediately. We've spent hours alone together for the past few weeks. I would have noticed if we had no chemistry. Besides, there's no way two people can have sex like we had last night and have no real chemistry. Right?

I'm a walking ball of nerves by the time Linc shows up for our date. I rest a hand on my abdomen and take in a few deep breaths to steady myself before I make my way to the door. When I see Linc standing there, the breath leaves me in a rush, taking the nerves with it. He looks so good.

His dark hair is pulled back off his face into a low ponytail. He's trimmed his beard so it's not so unruly. He's wearing a dark, button-down shirt tucked into charcoal slacks. His eyes travel down the length of my body before coming back to rest on my face.

"Hi," I say, smiling.

"You're beautiful," he says, in lieu of a greeting.

I huff out a laugh. "Thanks. You look great."

He smiles, shaking his head. "No one's going to be looking at me."

I feel my face heat and close my eyes. "Aren't you charming?"

He leans in, still smiling. "If I'd known how much you like hearing it, I would have been telling you every day how gorgeous you are."

"You sure it's not just the dress?" I whisper.

He's so close his nose is brushing mine when he shakes his head. "You're always gorgeous. In this dress or in a t-shirt and cutoff jean shorts." He kisses me lightly. "Even in those llama pajamas."

I narrow my eyes at him. "You're never going to let that go, are you?"

"Nope."

Grinning, he holds out a hand to me. I place mine in it and he pulls me outside into the warm spring evening. He waits for me to lock up, then takes my hand again as we walk to his truck. I revel in the feel of his big hand enveloping mine. This casual affection isn't something I expected from Linc, but I can't deny that I love it. He seems lighter tonight; somehow more at ease with me than he's ever been. Maybe, after what happened last night, he realizes there's no reason to hold back with me.

A delicious shiver runs through me at that thought. He certainly hadn't held back last night. I suck in a shaky breath as I feel my panties grow damp at the mere memory of what happened last night. I can't believe Linc kept that dominant side of himself hidden for all these years. Not that I ever had a reason to know or suspect it before last night. Linc opens the truck door for me and waits for me to climb inside. I use the few seconds it takes for him to walk around to the driver's side to pull myself together and banish all the filthy thoughts from my mind. This date isn't about sex. It's about seeing if we're compatible outside of the bedroom.

"Ready?" Linc asks with a smile as he buckles his seatbelt.

"Definitely," I say with a nod.

He pulls away from the curb and I watch him for a few seconds as he drives. As if sensing my scrutiny, he glances at me quickly before turning his attention back to the road.

"What?" he asks.

I shrug. "Nothing."

"Then why are you staring at me?"

I smile. "Just admiring the view. I feel like after last night, I should get unlimited ogling privileges."

He grins and I can see that he wasn't expecting the compliment since his cheeks go pink. "Does that mean I get the same privileges?"

"When you're not driving, absolutely," I say.

He gives me a brief glance before looking ahead again. "Too bad I'm driving, then."

"Too bad," I say.

I make a show of adjusting my skirt where it slid higher on my thighs. I watch his eyes as they dart to my legs and back to the road. His grip tightens on the wheel.

"Harlow," he warns in a low growl.

"Hmm?"

"Don't make me pull over."

Something dark in his tone has my breath quickening and my pulse hammering in my chest. Before last night I would never have imagined Linc as the type of man to pull over on the side of the road for a quickie. After last night, I have no doubts that he'd take me right here in this truck if I gave the slightest indication I was into it. That thought brings a whole host of images to the forefront of my brain, none of which help settle my newly awakened libido. Why does Linc have to be so sexy?

"Harlow." This time my name sounds like even more of a warning. "Stop looking at me like you want me to fuck you."

Holy shit, why do those words coming from his mouth make me so hot? Is it just because it's him? I don't know. But it doesn't matter.

"What if I do?" I whisper.

His jaw clenches and I watch him grip the steering wheel so tightly his knuckles turn white. "Much as I'd love nothing more than to pull off into some field, pull you into my lap, push that dress up around your hips and sink balls-deep into you, I promised you a date. You didn't get all dressed up for me not to take you somewhere and show you off. So, stop eye-fucking me. You're making it hard for me to be a gentleman right now."

My eyes go wide, and I stare at him for a few more seconds, half wishing he'd do what we both want. But I know he put a lot of effort into this date tonight. If he wants to take me out somewhere and show me off, I can behave for a few more hours. Maybe later I can talk him into being less of a gentleman.

"I'll behave," I say, turning back to face the road instead of Linc.

He huffs out a little laugh. "Good girl," he says in a low voice.

I close my eyes as the last time he said those words to me flits through my mind, making me even more turned on than before. When I glance over at Linc, I can see a hint of amusement on his face. He knows exactly what he's doing.

"Ass," I mutter, making him laugh.

Linc drives us into Savannah, and we park in a lot in the riverside district. The sun is beginning to set, bathing the river and the cobbled street in gold-tipped shadows. I've always loved this city, especially the old riverfront. I smile at Linc as he walks around to open my door for me. He takes my hand to help me down, but he doesn't let go once I'm standing on solid ground.

"I love this city," he says. "I usually only get to come here for business or appointments. Never for fun."

We walk toward a multi-story, red brick building. When I see the sign, I narrow my eyes at Linc.

"Are you taking me to a hotel?"

He laughs and points beyond the hotel to another building. This one looks like a warehouse, and I can see two smokestacks in the distance.

"That's where we're going," he says. "Unless you'd rather check into a hotel?"

I just smile. "Let's save it for dessert. I'm starving."

"As you wish."

Linc leads the way into the building, and we make our way up to the roof where a hostess seats us at a small table overlooking the river. The weather is warm, but not humid. It's a perfect late spring evening for a rooftop dinner. The railings are wrapped in white string lights that add a magical glow to the area. Linc waits until I'm seated before taking the chair across from me.

"I hope this is okay," he says. "I've heard good things about this place."

I smile, looking around at the elegantly appointed rooftop restaurant. "It's perfect."

CHAPTER 24

Harlow

Dinner really is perfect. The restaurant, the ambiance and the food are everything I could think to ask for on a first date. Having Linc seated across from me makes it even more perfect. I keep having to remind myself that I'm not dreaming this. I'm really on a date with Linc. And he's charming and funny and he keeps touching my hand where it rests on the white linen tablecloth. Linc smiles at me as I sip my wine.

"What?" I ask.

He shakes his head, still smiling. "Nothing. I'm just happy you said yes to this date."

A laugh escapes me. "After last night, did you have doubts?"

His eyes grow dark and his gaze drops to my mouth, making me blush.

"Not exactly," he says. "But I'd be lying if I said I wasn't nervous about tonight."

"Nervous? Why?"

He grins. "I worried that maybe you regretted what we did. That you might want it to be a one-time thing."

I laugh aloud this time before leaning over the table toward him. "I don't think it's a shock to you that I had an amazing time last night. Was I expecting that? No. Do I regret anything about it? Absolutely not." His fingers play over mine and I watch, remembering the feel of those fingers inside my body last night. Sucking in a shaky breath, I try to focus on the conversation before I beg him to fuck me right here on the table in front of all these people.

"To be honest," I say, "I was worried you'd realize halfway through this date that I'm boring and that you made a mistake following me home last night."

Linc's gaze on me is piercing. "Not a chance," he says. "You're anything but boring."

I smile, feeling my face heat again.

"I'm not just saying that because you let me fuck your brains out last night," he says, his voice pitched low enough that only I can hear him.

The low timbre of his voice combined with his filthy words sends a signal straight to my lady bits. How did we go from barely speaking a month ago to being seated at a fancy restaurant with him saying all these naughty things to me? Has it really only been a couple of weeks since my pipe burst and he showed up to help me save my business? So much has happened in that time. What changed?

"Why did you follow me home last night?" I ask. It's been on my mind since he appeared at my door last night and I don't buy the line about just wanting to make sure I made it home okay.

Linc looks down at our joined hands, his face a careful mask. He takes so long to speak that I begin to worry that whatever he's going to say will be awful.

"I didn't follow you thinking we were going to sleep together," he says. "I didn't even think to wish for a kiss. Though I can't deny I've thought about kissing you for a long time."

I'm shocked to hear him say that. He's never let on that he's interested in me. He's so unreadable. So silent most of the time. Even though we've spent weeks working together, tonight is probably the most we've ever spoken. He's different tonight. Easier. More open. It's as though he's finally letting his guard down and letting me see the real Linc. If I thought I liked him before, it's nothing compared to what I'm feeling tonight. He shakes his head with a rueful laugh.

"I've never been great in big groups," he says. "It's why I tend to stay quiet. I don't know what to say. I feel awkward. So, I observe. And I keep quiet. And that feeling gets worse when you're around. It always has." He meets my gaze. "You stun me, Harlow. You always have."

I blink at him, confused by his admission.

"It's why I've never been able to talk to you. Or even talk much at all when you're around. But these past few weeks, I've gotten more comfortable with you. Gotten to know you. I've seen you with my daughter. I've grown used to seeing you every day. It's one of the best parts of my day; knowing I'm going to see you. I was getting sad that it's almost over. I was going to tell you all this last night while we were dancing. I was going to ask you on a date."

What?! He was going to ask me out even before we slept together? My heart squeezes almost painfully in my chest.

"But I blew it when I mentioned the prom. And you shut down. I didn't know why, but I knew it was my fault. I hated seeing that light in your eyes dim."

He meets my gaze. "I needed to fix it. I needed to know I didn't screw everything up. That's why I followed you last night. Because I couldn't stand the idea of you being angry with me. And I damned sure didn't want to be the one responsible for hurting you."

My throat goes tight and I swallow against the lump there. I've seen Linc when he's kind. I've seen Linc when he's sweet with his daughter. I've even seen the version of Linc that's dominant in the bedroom. But this vulnerable side of him is one I didn't know I needed to see. I can feel the ground slipping out from under me just a little more; feel myself falling just a little harder for this man. Leaning across the table, I motion for him to meet me halfway. He does, leaning in far enough so I can kiss his lips lightly.

"You didn't screw anything up," I whisper.

He grins. "I'm glad."

When we lean back, he still doesn't let go of my hand. I find that I don't mind in the least. I've never been the overly affectionate type, but I love that Linc seems to want to touch me all the time. It's sweet and slightly possessive. Which is another thing I didn't think I'd be into. That brings me back to thoughts of last night and Linc's dominant tendencies in the bedroom. It feels like something we should talk about if we're going to keep seeing each other. Last night might just be the tip of the iceberg where his domination is concerned. Is that something I can be comfortable with? I'm not sure. It depends on how far he wants to take things.

"Where'd you go, Harlow?" Linc asks, pulling me from my spiraling thoughts.

I feel my face heat. "I'm not sure how to ask," I say.

Linc smiles knowingly. "Is this about last night?"

I nod. "Yes."

"Did it make you uncomfortable?"

I shake my head immediately. "No." Just thinking about it is turning me on.

"But you want to know how far I want to take things?"

I nod, wondering how he seems to be reading my mind.

"The thought crossed my mind," I say softly.

He smiles and dips his head in a quick nod. "It's not an easy question to answer," he says. "I've never fully explored how far I'd like to go with that side of me. I've never had a partner that was into it. So, I just didn't try."

Part of me wonders what kind of boring sex he's had in the past, but I squash that thought quickly. I don't want to think about Linc with other women. Instead, I think back over the events of last night, considering whether I'm willing to test my boundaries. I think about his commanding presence, his domineering tone and the almost rough way he took my body, wringing every ounce of pleasure from me. It was intense, but just thinking about it makes me wet. Do I want more of that? I'd need to be dead not to. Looking away from our joined hands, I meet Linc's gaze.

"What if it's something I'm interested in exploring? With you?" I ask.

Linc sucks in a breath and his eyes turn hungry. But I'm surprised when he speaks. "I don't want to pressure you into anything, Harlow. That's the last thing I want."

I shake my head, my grip tightening on his hand. "That's not what this is," I say. "Last night was new for me, but I loved it. More than I thought possible. I felt safe and—I don't know—almost worshipped." I laugh. "I know that sounds weird."

He shakes his head. "Not weird. I told you last night. As long as it's consensual and brings pleasure, there's nothing weird or wrong about what we do. I want you to feel safe with me. And worshipped. But I need you to be sure you're okay with this."

Something occurs to me and I have another question. "You're not into torture or pain, right? Not that I'm kink-shaming. I just don't think it's for me."

He looks amused. "No, Harlow. I'm not into anything that would cause either of us pain." He takes a deep breath before looking at me. "But there are some things that might be uncomfortable." His voice is dark and full of promise.

"Like what?" I whisper.

He leans closer. "Edging, forced orgasm, light spanking, being tied up."

I feel my heart speed up and a sliver of excitement courses through me at the thought of Linc spanking my ass or tying me up. I'm a little shocked by how turned on that makes me, but I've decided not to question that right now. Right now, I'm just interested in learning as much as I can about Lincoln Prescott's secret sexual preferences. If I'm going to pursue this thing with him—and let's be real, I totally am—then I need to know what I'm getting into. Nothing I've learned so far has scared me away or grossed me out. It's actually had the opposite effect. I think I'm more turned on than I've ever been.

"Of course, I wouldn't do anything without your consent," he says. "Whatever happens going forward, we'll talk about it first. That's the most important part of this. Communication."

Part of me is still in shock that this is the same quiet, shy Linc I've known since 4th grade. He's sitting across from me casually discussing light bondage while we sip wine in a nice restaurant. Two months ago, he could barely make eye contact with me. But then I remember how he buried his face between my legs and licked me until I came all over his beard. I like this hidden side of him.

"Okay," I say. "Let's see where this goes."

Linc's smile is bright in the dim light making my breath catch as I look at him.

CHAPTER 25

Harlow

By the time the server asks us if we'd like dessert, darkness has settled fully over the city. We pass on dessert, and instead take a walk along the riverfront. It's a perfect night with a slight breeze coming off the water. I feel another little burst of pleasure as I look around the city. It really is gorgeous here.

"I have a confession to make," I say, reaching for Linc's hand as we walk along the cobblestone street.

"What's that?" he asks, threading his fingers through mine.

I take a deep breath and let it out. "I've been thinking impure thoughts about you since the appetizers came out."

He laughs, making my heart squeeze. "Just the appetizers? I've had them since I first saw you in that dress at your place."

I use my free hand to gesture to the dress. "This old thing?"

Linc looks me over and I can see the naked lust in his eyes for a moment before he deliberately masks it. We keep walking at our slow, leisurely pace.

"I think it's only fair that I admit something to you now," he says, using our joined hands to pull me closer to his side.

"Oh? What's that?"

He stops walking and grins down at me, but I can see a hint of nerves in his expression. "I had a crush on you all through senior year," he finally says.

Even though Luke already told me that, I'm still shocked to hear Linc say it aloud. I still can't quite believe that someone as popular as Linc had been in high school would have even noticed me. But I can't deny the little thrill that goes through me at his admission. I feel a blush creep up my cheeks as I smile up at him.

I can't help but ask. "Why?"

He grins, turning to look out over the river. "You were so above it all. All the popular bullshit. You were so cool. Meanwhile, I was struggling to fit in and hoping no one noticed how much I was pretending."

When I laugh, Linc turns a questioning look on me. "I'm sorry," I say. "It's just that I can't believe you thought that about me when I spent all of high school pretending!"

His brows draw low in confusion. "What were you pretending?"

I shrug. "I don't know. Everything. I was pretending I knew what I was doing. Pretending my family wasn't poor. Pretending I didn't want to *be* one of the popular kids. Pretending I wasn't envious of them. At least a little, anyway." I pause to consider my words. "I think most people go through life pretending," I say, my voice softer than before. "No one wants to admit they feel lost."

"Do you still feel lost?" Linc asks, turning to look at me.

I smile at him. "Sometimes. Less so, these days."

"What about tonight?"

"If I'm lost right now, I'm happy to stay that way for a little while longer."

"Me too," he says before leaning down to kiss me lightly on the lips.

I want the kiss to last longer. I want to wrap my arms around him and never let him go now that I have him. *Whoa. Slow down.* Where did that thought come from? It's our first date, for crying out loud. I can't think in those terms right now. I don't even know where we stand. I break the kiss and put a little space between us, taking his hand again as I start walking. I'm not sure if Linc senses that I'm trying to slow things down or not, but he doesn't seem bothered by it. Instead, he keeps the conversation going, asking me about my time after high school. I tell him how I'd opted to go to school for cosmetology after a semester at college showed me all the things I didn't want to do.

"I got a paid internship at a big fashion magazine based in Atlanta. Granted, it didn't pay great. But it was enough to afford a meager lifestyle filled with all the Top Ramen I could eat."

He laughs, as I'd hoped.

"I got to do hair and makeup for a lot of glamorous models. It was stressful, but a lot of fun. Looking back, I don't know how I didn't get an ulcer from all the stress." I laugh. "I had plans to be some super model's

personal stylist, move to New York and be ultra glam."
I smile at the silly notions my younger self once had.
"That obviously didn't work out. I did score a lot of great
clothes, though."

Linc looks at me, full of curiosity. Even though I
know what he's going to ask next, part of me wishes
he wouldn't. I don't want to spoil this amazing night by
talking about the dark times in my life. But I won't hide
it from him either. So, I take a fortifying breath and wait.

As I'd predicted, he asks, "What made you move
back?"

I clear my throat and say the words. "My mom got
sick." I can hear the shift in my tone immediately. I know
he can, too. This is the version of me that sticks to
the facts and uses dark humor to deflect from the real
feelings. I hate it, but I can't seem to stop doing it.

"In true Maggie fashion," I say, "she waited until the
bitter end to admit to anyone that she needed help. She
didn't even tell me she was sick until her second round
of chemo." I shake my head and suck in a ragged breath.

"I so wanted to be pissed at her," I whisper, my voice
threatening to break despite my best efforts. "But I came
home, and I could see how sick she was. How bad things
were."

We stop walking. I can feel Linc's hand tighten on my
own, but I don't dare look at him. I can't. I've told this
story to only a few people over the years and it never
gets easier. I don't know why I'm telling it now; except I
don't want to hide things from him. Even the dark things.

"But I couldn't be mad at her. There was no use. It
wouldn't change anything. So, I just got to work. On the
house. The bills. Taking care of her. Whatever needed

doing. But it was too late by then. For my mom and for the house. She'd taken out an extra mortgage to pay for her medical bills. But when she couldn't work anymore, that money went fast. So, it was either sell the house or sell my body."

I laugh, hoping he'll join in, but he stays silent. I risk a glance up at him and see the sadness in his eyes. I shake my head immediately.

"Don't," I say. "I've cried enough over that part of my life. I won't have you make me cry tonight. Not when this date has been so perfect."

When he doesn't smile, I glare at him. "I'm serious. Smile. Or else."

Linc finally gives me a small smile that doesn't quite reach his eyes. Then he reaches over and tucks a wayward strand of hair behind my ear.

"Only because you said so." He doesn't sound quite like his normal self, but I don't comment on it.

Despite the smile he just gave me, I still feel dangerously close to tears. I grip the front of his shirt and lean forward to rest my forehead on his muscled chest. Linc doesn't say anything. He just brings his hands up to my shoulders and holds me against him, his thumbs stroking my upper arms gently and his chin resting on my head. It takes me several shaky breaths before I can trust myself enough to look up at him without tears in my eyes.

"Thank you," I whisper, grateful that he seems to understand what I need without me even knowing.

When Linc smiles at me this time, it reaches his eyes. "When are you going to realize I'd do anything to see you smile?"

My heart squeezes almost painfully in my chest and I have to fight the urge to throw my arms around him. Instead, I smile up at him just before he leans in to kiss me. It's a sweet kiss, gentle. It's the kind of kiss you might expect for a first date. In other words, perfect. When the kiss ends, we turn silently and make our way back to Linc's truck, his hand still holding mine.

We're both quiet as Linc turns the truck back toward Peach Tree. The silence isn't an uncomfortable one, though. I'm thinking over the events of the night and how amazing everything was, even with the way it ended. Normally if things get too quiet on a date, I rush to fill the silence, worried that his lack of conversation means he isn't interested. But it's not like that with Linc. He's a silent sort of guy. Except in the bedroom. My face warms as memories of last night flow through my mind again.

Linc reaches over and takes my hand in his, threading his fingers through mine as he drives with one hand. I smile at the sight of our joined hands resting on the center console. I love how big he is compared to me. He's taller than me. Stronger. Larger in every way. And yet, I know he'd never hurt me. I've never felt safer than I did last night in his arms. I can't explain why; not even in my own head. But it doesn't matter.

"What are you thinking?" he asks, pulling me out of my thoughts.

I smile over at him, not quite ready to delve into the truth of my feelings with him right now.

"I was thinking about last night," I say, letting my eyes roam over him.

"Harlow." His voice is a warning, as it had been earlier before dinner.

"Lincoln," I say, mimicking his tone.

"If you make me pull over, there will be consequences," he says.

A dark, delicious thrill runs through me at the thought of what consequences Linc might have for me. I'm not afraid though. I know he'd never do anything to hurt me. I take a deep breath.

"Maybe that's what I want," I say, pulling my hand from his to reach across the center console and touch his thigh.

He sighs, tightening his grip on the steering wheel. I feel a shiver of desire course through me, and I squeeze my thighs together to ease the ache between them. It doesn't work, though. All I can do is think about his warning from earlier and what he'd love to do to me in this truck.

"I thought you wanted to fuck me in this truck?" I say, sliding my hand up toward his crotch.

"Be careful what you wish for," he says.

I slide my hand over the hard bulge in his pants. "All I want is this inside me."

I can see the internal struggle in his eyes and the moment he makes a decision.

"This is a bad idea," he mutters before slowing the truck and turning onto an unmarked dirt road.

I feel a shiver of excitement at the idea that he's going to make good on his threat. Anticipation courses through me, making my skin feel hot and prickly. There's just the tiniest hint of worry about the consequences he mentioned, but that's overshadowed by lust. The truck rattles over the rough dirt road as Linc drives until he spots an opening in the trees to the left. He turns into it and I can see what used to be an old house, but now it's mostly just the foundation and a few walls with weeds growing throughout. Linc pulls the truck in far enough so it's hidden from the road and shuts off the headlights. When he turns to look at me, my breath catches at the naked hunger in his gaze barely visible in the glow of the lights from the instrument panel.

"Take off your underwear, Harlow," he commands. "Now."

Immediately, I move my hands from his cock and reach under my dress to pull the scrap of lace down my legs. Kicking off my shoes, I pull them all the way off and show him. Linc holds out a hand.

"Give them to me."

Again, I don't hesitate. I hand Linc my damp panties without a second thought.

"Good girl," he says, closing his fingers around the lace.

Reaching under the seat, he finds the lever to move his seat back as far as it will go before reaching for his belt. I watch as he unfastens the belt and unbuttons his pants.

"I told you what would happen if you kept eye-fucking me, didn't I?"

I nod. "Yes."

He unzips his pants and slides them down until his hard cock springs upward. He reaches down and gives it a slow stroke with his hand, making me suck in a breath at the sight.

"Get over here," he commands. "Now."

I scramble over the center console to straddle him. Linc's mouth is on mine before I'm even seated on his lap. His hands grip my hips, holding me in place. When he breaks the kiss, his dark eyes are locked on mine.

"Are you wet already?" he asks.

I nod.

"Show me."

I reach for the hem of my dress, pulling it up to expose my dripping pussy. But Linc shakes his head.

"Not like that," he says. "Touch yourself. Spread all that wetness all over your fingers."

I suck in a breath at the filthy command, but I do as Linc says. I'm beginning to wonder if I can refuse this man anything. Reaching down between my legs, I slide my fingers down over my clit and lower, to my opening, then back up again. A bolt of pleasure moves through me and I gasp.

"That's good, baby," he rasps. "Just like that."

His encouragement makes me want to please him even more. I keep going, rubbing my wet pussy over and over. My breath is coming faster as I play with my clit, the little jolts of pleasure rocketing up from between my legs.

"Push two fingers inside," Linc says roughly.

My mouth drops open, but I nod. It feels so wicked to be doing this, to be touching myself at his command, to have him watch me as I do. But it's undeniably sexy and I can feel myself growing even wetter with each order he gives me. So, I do as he says and slip two fingers inside me, pumping them in and out a few times before bringing them back up to my clit to play with it. I swirl my fingers faster, gasping at the sensation. I'm already close to coming and he's only kissed me so far.

"Stop."

The command in Linc's voice has me freezing immediately. His gaze is locked on mine.

"Let me taste you," he says.

Holy fucking shit, that's hot.

I nearly whimper as I bring my hand up and he leans forward, sucking my fingers into his mouth. I feel his tongue flick over my fingers as he tastes me.

"Mmm," he groans as he releases my hand. "Delicious."

"Linc," I moan, not sure what I'm asking.

"Again," he says, his eyes darting downward. "Touch yourself, Harlow."

I reach between my legs again, my fingers slipping over my wet pussy.

"Three fingers," he says.

With a whimper, I work three fingers inside. It's awkward and I can only push them in halfway, but I do as Linc says, not wanting to disappoint him.

"I warned you there would be consequences," he says. "Didn't I?"

I nod as I work my fingers in and out before swirling them over my clit. Each brush of my fingers against my clit pulls a gasp from me.

"Yes," I whisper.

"Faster," he says, and I obey.

I work quick circles over my clit, the way I know will get me off the fastest. Linc's hands are on my hips, his hard cock standing at attention between my legs. I want him inside me so badly, but I can't help but do as he says.

"Are you close?" he asks. "Are you going to come, Harlow?"

I nod, my mouth dropping open.

"Do you want to come?" he asks.

I nod again, my hand moving faster. My breaths are coming in pants now. I'm so close that I can feel the little shivers wracking my lower body.

"I'll bet you do," he says. "You want that sweet release."

I'm so wet now that I can hear the sounds my fingers are making against my flesh. I can't find it in me to feel embarrassed. I just want to come. I'm so close. A whimper escapes me and I press harder on my clit.

"Stop." He's not loud, but the single word carries the weight of an order. My hand freezes and a cry of disappointment escapes me.

"Take your hand off your pussy, Harlow," he says in that same voice. "You will not make yourself come. Do you understand me?"

I suck in a shaky breath, but I nod.

"Do you understand me?" he asks again.

"Yes, sir," I whisper.

"Good. From now on, all your orgasms are mine. Understand?"

The feminist in me wants to argue, wants to ask him who he thinks he is to tell me what to do. But the rest of me doesn't care about feminism right now. I nod.

"Yes, sir."

"Good." He hands me something in the dark and I take it, realizing right away what it is. A condom.

"Put it on my cock, Harlow," he says. "Be quick about it."

I fumble in my attempt to open the foil packet. I want Linc inside me so badly I'm almost shaking. When I finally get the condom out of the wrapper, I reach down and grip his thick erection, loving the feel of him in my hand. Hot, hard, ready for me. I give his length a long, slow stroke and Linc sucks in his breath. But he doesn't rush me. Instead, his gaze drops to his lap and he watches as I stroke him once more. That's all the teasing I can stand, though. Much as I'd like to draw this out until we're both a mess of need, I want him too badly for that. I quickly roll the condom down his length and look back up to his face.

"Good girl," he says.

Then he lifts me up and lowers me down onto his hard cock. I'm so wet that he slides in with little resistance. I'm still a little sore from last night, but it's a good kind of sore. The feeling of being filled and stretched by Linc's cock is worth any soreness I may have tomorrow. My breath leaves me in a sigh of pleasure as I sink down, taking Linc fully.

"Now, ride me until I come," he says.

Immediately, I begin to move, riding him slowly.

"You feel so good," I whisper, rolling my hips on every downstroke.

His fingers dig into my hips, gripping me tightly—almost painfully. But I love it. I love his strength and his power and the control he's using to let me take the lead. I pull him to me for a kiss without breaking my rhythm. Linc's kiss is hard, his beard rough against my lips. I love it just as much as the tender kisses he gave me last night in my bed.

I keep going, riding him faster and harder until my thighs are burning. Linc slides one hand down between my legs and finds my clit with his thumb. My pace falters as I gasp at the new pleasure. Linc smiles wickedly, but he doesn't stop. My legs are shaking with the effort to keep going. Little spasms of pleasure radiate out from my clit up to the rest of my body. I know it won't be long before I fall apart in his lap.

"You're close, aren't you?" Linc says, as if he's reading my mind.

I nod and my mouth opens on a silent gasp as I rock up and down on his dick.

Linc grins, his thumb moving faster on my clit.

"You want it, don't you?"

I nod again, ready to beg if necessary.

"You need it. Don't you?"

"Mm," I nod. My thighs are shaking now.

"Who do your orgasm belong to?" Linc asks.

"You," I pant.

"Who does this pussy belong to?" His fingers swirl faster over my clit, driving me closer to the edge as I ride him even faster.

"You."

"That's right," he says. "And who's going to let you come tonight?"

"Oh, God," I moan, balancing on the edge.

"Not God," Linc says, increasing the pressure on my clit. "Just me."

I moan again, my hips rocking faster against him. I'm beyond words at this point. I'm balanced on a knife's edge of lust and need. The pleasure is so intense it's almost too much. It keeps building past the point where it should have detonated by now. Linc releases my hip to squeeze my breast. He pinches my nipple through the layers of my clothes, and I cry out. That's all it takes and I'm flying over the edge into oblivion.

I keep moving, riding him faster now. Each pulse of pleasure wrings a cry from me. All the while, Linc keeps swirling his thumb over my clit, pushing me higher and higher. His hips surge upward, thrusting into me from below, intensifying my movements. In seconds, he lets out a guttural groan and I can feel him pulsing inside me with his own release.

"Fuck," he pants, kissing my neck.

His hands are resting on my splayed thighs. I'm still straddling him and his half-hard cock is still inside me. I'm too exhausted to move just yet, so I hope he doesn't plan on making me. I lean forward, resting my head on his chest.

"I don't think my legs are going to work after this."

He huffs out a laugh and his hands begin to knead my thighs. "Maybe after a nice massage, I can coax them into working properly."

"Mmm," I say, leaning in to kiss him again. "That sounds nice."

When I lean back, Linc is looking at me intently, his gaze serious.

"What?" I ask, a stab of worry hitting me.

He shakes his head. "I can't believe how stupid I've been all these years. We could have been doing this for the last 10 years."

I smile at him, simultaneously touched and saddened by his words. "Maybe this is the way it was supposed to be, Linc. Besides, we might not be the people we are today if we'd been together all this time."

He nods. "Maybe you're right." Then he grins. "I guess we'll just have to make up for lost time then."

CHAPTER 26

Linc

"Thank you guys for coming with me today," Luke says. "It really means a lot."

"Of course, man," I say. "That's what the best man is for, right? You know I'm here for you, no matter what."

"Hey!" Cole says. "The head groomsman is important too."

Luke and I laugh.

"I told you," Luke says. "You're first alternate. If something terrible befalls your brother, you get to step into the role of best man."

Cole narrows his eyes at me. "So, if he were to—I don't know—die in his sleep, between now and the wedding, the job is mine?"

"No, dumbass," I say. "You'd be in prison because you suck at deception. There's no way you'd get away with something like that."

Cole makes a face at me, but then shrugs. He knows I'm right. He's never been able to lie or keep a secret.

Besides, I know he's not actually envious of my best man status. If Luke could have 2 best men, I know he would. But he and Piper are planning on a simple affair with a small wedding party. Only 2 attendants for each of them. Today Cole and I went with Luke to try on tuxedos. The big day isn't for a few more months, but the preparations are already well underway.

"Regardless," Luke says. "I still appreciate it. I know you've been busy lately."

Cole points at me. "He's certainly been busy these days. With a girl."

He says the last part in a sing-song voice that makes me wish I could punch him in public without causing a scene. But since we're seated at the bar in Peach Fuzz, surrounded by a bunch of employees who are loyal to him, I decide against it. I settle on glaring at him. He really is terrible at keeping secrets. Not that Harlow and I are a secret. It's still new, is all. It's only been a few days since our first date.

Remembering the way that date ended brings a smile to my face. Since that night, I've worked at her salon every evening. It's been hell trying to keep my hands off her and focus on finishing the job. Not that either of us are complaining. We're too busy enjoying ourselves. Just yesterday, I bent her over the counter in the back and fucked her until she screamed. Needless to say, the second faucet didn't get installed yesterday. I guess that means I'll need to come back another day and finish the job.

"Oh, yeah," Luke says. "How was the date?"

My gaze shoots to his and I almost worry he can see my dirty thoughts on my face. "How do you know about that?"

He rolls his eyes. "First thing you need to learn about being part of a couple is that there are no secrets. If Harlow tells Piper, chances are good that Piper is going to tell me. Apparently, there's a group text with them and Layna. I caught Piper laughing and squealing at her phone the other morning. When I asked to see the funny video I assumed she was watching she told me what happened."

I narrow my eyes at my best friend. "Just how much did she tell you?"

Luke laughs. "Just that you stayed the night and that you were taking Harlow on a date. No dirty details. Thankfully."

He takes a deep swig of his beer before smiling at me. "I'm happy for you, man. Harlow's great. You could do a lot worse."

"That's what I keep telling him," Cole mutters.

"Gee, thanks," I say making them both laugh.

"Seriously, though," Luke says. "What the hell took you so long? Didn't you have a crush on her like 10 years ago?"

I open my mouth to reply, but I don't have a real answer. Finally, I sigh. "The truth is, I was too caught up in my own life to worry about dating. Ella and work kept me busy. Plus, Harlow and I didn't exactly hang out back then. We only started hanging out at all because of you and Piper. I don't know how long it would have taken me to figure out how great she is if it hadn't been for you and that fake dating disaster."

Luke grins. "I wouldn't call it a disaster. It landed me a fiancé, didn't it?"

"True," I say.

"He just sucks at wooing," Cole says. "I've tried to help him, but he won't listen to me."

I roll my eyes. "You and that word again. Why don't you find your own girl to woo and stay out of my love life?"

Cole just grins, unbothered by my words. He lifts his beer to his lips. "Maybe I will."

"So, what's the plan with you two?" Luke asks. "Is it serious?"

I consider his question. It's been three days since my first date with Harlow. That's too soon to decide if it's serious, right? What's the protocol on things like this? I suddenly realize that I have no idea. I haven't been in a serious relationship since Ella's mom. I'm not even sure I'd call that serious if I'm being honest. Maybe Cole is right, and I really don't know how to woo a woman. Shit.

Looking up, I catch sight of blonde hair shot through with hot pink and everything goes still. My thoughts settle. The noise of the restaurant fades into the background. All I can see is her. Harlow. I don't know why she's here right now, but I don't care. I'm just happy to see her. She looks incredible, in a casual sleeveless dress that shows off her legs and a smile that I know she only gives to me. From the corner of my eye, I notice Luke staring at me. When he follows my gaze, he laughs.

"I guess that answers my question."

"He's a goner," Cole chimes in.

I ignore them, keeping my eyes on Harlow, watching as she walks toward the bar where I'm seated. It takes me a second to notice that Piper and Layna are with her.

"I hope you guys don't mind," Luke says. "Piper and I planned to meet for dinner after the fitting. But when I told her we were all hanging out, she asked the girls to come along."

I smile at Harlow as she approaches. "I don't mind at all."

"Hey," Harlow says, looking a little unsure about how to greet me.

Standing, I close the distance between us, lean down and kiss her cheek. "Hello, gorgeous," I whisper before straightening to my full height.

When I turn back to the others, I find four sets of eyes staring at me and Harlow, who's now blushing at the attention. Cole is the first to move. He gives one, loud clap and grins.

"That's what I'm talking about, Linc," he says. "Woo."

Luke laughs as Layna and Piper just look confused.

"What's he talking about?" Harlow says in a voice low enough that only I can hear it.

"I'll tell you later," I whisper, taking her hand in mine.

I may not know the answer to whether Harlow and I are serious. But I do know one thing. I like being with her. And I'm going to do whatever it takes to keep being with her. Including wooing her. Whatever the hell that means.

"It's about time you two figured your shit out," Layna says. "Can we get a table? I'm starving."

Cole leans in toward her. "I may know someone who can get you into a booth."

Layna rolls her eyes, but she's smiling. "The hostess could get me a booth."

Cole laughs as he stands. "Come on. I had them save us one in the back."

We make our way to the booth Cole reserved for us and Harlow slides in next to me. I keep her hand in mine, resting it on my leg. I can't help but marvel over the differences between now and the last time we were all here. For the first time, I don't have to try to keep my eyes off Harlow. I can stare all I want. I can kiss her and show her casual affection and no one cares. Our friends are not only okay with us being together; they seem thrilled by it. Nothing about the night feels awkward or forced. It feels like the most natural thing in the world. Because it is.

It all feels normal. It feels like this is what we should have been all along. I feel another pang of regret for all the time we wasted not being together. But Harlow was right the other night. We might not be the people we are today if we'd been together back then. Things happened the way they did for a reason. Nothing good comes from dwelling on the past. It's time to focus on the present, and right now I'm having a great night out with my friends and the woman I'm starting to care an awful lot about.

When the server appears with a round of drinks, I lean close to Harlow so only she can hear me.

"Go to the bathroom and take off your panties," I say. "Slip them into your purse. I want to see them when you get back."

I try to put as much command into my soft words as possible without the others hearing. She turns to me, eyes wide and I hear her suck in a breath. But there's a hint of excitement in her gaze as well. I raise a brow in challenge.

Leaning close to her ear, I whisper, "Do it quickly and I'll let you come tonight."

I can feel her practically vibrating with excitement. Her head dips in the slightest of nods and I feel my cock swell in my pants. I don't know what made me give her the order. She'd just been sitting next to me in that dress looking so pretty, and I couldn't help but wonder what she had on underneath it. I wondered if my nearness was affecting her the way hers was affecting me. So, I gave in to my curiosity.

"Good girl," I whisper, my lips grazing her ear.

She shivers delicately before sitting up straight. While we had our little conversation, the others had been distributing the drinks around the table. No one is paying us any attention. But when Harlow moves to stand, Piper notices.

"Where are you going?"

Harlow smiles. "Bathroom."

Layna slides to her feet. "I'll go with you."

"Me, too," Piper chimes in.

Harlow's eyes dart to me and I have to fight off a smile at the hint of panic in her blue eyes. I raise my brows in challenge.

She turns back to the other two ladies and smiles. "Let's go."

Then she turns and walks toward the back of the restaurant where the bathrooms are located, Piper and Layna following behind. I feel a coil of anticipation tighten low in my belly. Harlow will do it. For one thing, she doesn't back down from a challenge. For another, she enjoys following my commands. I think she likes the freedom that comes with giving in and letting someone else call the shots. She's spent so much of her life alone and figuring everything out on her own. She's never had someone willing to take control. Or maybe she's never had someone she trusted to take control before. Maybe it's a little of both. Either way, I'm not going to waste a second with her.

When the ladies return, I see a slight flush to Harlow's cheeks that makes my erection grow that much harder. When she slides into the booth next to me, she leaves no distance between us, leaning her head on my shoulder. Her purse is in her lap and my eyes follow the movement of her hands as she opens it just enough for me to see a bright pink scrap of satin the exact color of the streaks in her hair. Satisfaction surges through me at her willingness to obey me. It's immediately followed by a bolt of lust so strong that I have to fight the urge to drag her off to the nearest private room and fuck her until neither of us can walk. But I know I can't do anything to reward her until we leave later. The anticipation of what's to come is enough to drive me crazy.

We spend the next hour laughing and talking with the others. I join in as much as I can, but I'm so distracted by Harlow's nearness and the knowledge that her pussy is bare under the thin material of her dress. I want to know if she's wet for me, too. I want to drop to my knees under the table and bury my face between her legs. But Peach Fuzz is crowded with patrons and there are four other people at the table who would absolutely notice if I disappeared under the table right now. Damn it. Patience is usually something I pride myself on, but tonight it's being sorely tested. Is it too early to leave? I'm about to lean in and whisper to Harlow that we should go when Luke pulls Piper out onto the dance floor for a dance.

"How about it, Layna?" Cole says, turning to Layna with a playful wink. "You know you want to."

Layna rolls her eyes, but she's smiling. "Fine," she says. "But I get to lead."

He laughs. "Yes, ma'am."

Layna stands and heads toward the dance floor with Cole following behind her like a puppy.

Harlow looks at me with a smile. "You wanna dance?"

I drop the mask I've been wearing since she returned to the table with her panties in her purse and let her see the burning lust in my gaze. Harlow's eyes widen and she sucks in a shaky breath.

"I've got a better idea," I say, taking her hand and pulling her to her feet. "Follow me."

The thing about being the brother of the owner and the person in charge of the building's remodel is that I know where every single room is in this place. I know about every office and supply room and pantry. And I have a master key to all of them. I walk purposefully and confidently toward the back of the restaurant, avoiding the busy kitchen in favor of a side hallway that I know leads back to Cole's rarely-used office. He prefers to work among his employees and only uses the office if someone has a private issue they need to discuss with him. Which makes it perfect for my needs. I unlock the door and pull Harlow inside without turning on the light. I close and lock the door before turning back to face her.

Her chest is rising and falling rapidly with her breathing and I can see hot anticipation in her eyes, even in the dim light from the desk lamp.

"Linc," she says. "We can't."

I reach for her, pulling her into my arms. "Shh," I whisper. "Do you trust me?"

She nods. "Yes."

I run my hands down over her ass, pulling her hard against my erection. She sucks in a startled breath and her eyes fall closed. I could fuck her right now. We both know it. We both want it. But this isn't about me. I need to reward her for doing as I asked. I slide her dress higher until I encounter the bare skin of her ass. I squeeze the soft flesh.

"You followed my orders," I say. "Such a good girl."

She nods.

"Good girls get rewarded."

"How?"

I smile before leaning down to kiss her. The kiss is hungry and full of promise, but I break it off sooner than I'd like and spin her around so her back is against my front. I wrap my arms around her waist and walk her forward until she's in front of the desk.

"You have to be silent," I whisper. "No moaning or everyone will know what we're doing in here. You don't want them all to know, do you?"

Harlow shakes her head.

"Put your hands on the desk."

She complies immediately, making me smile. "So obedient," I muse.

"You're going to come for me, Harlow," I say, my tone making it clear it's a command. "And you're going to do it silently. Understand?"

She nods. "Yes, sir." I can hear the slight shake in her voice that tells me just how turned on she is right now.

My dick is impossibly hard now and straining against the confines of my pants. But this isn't about me. This is Harlow's reward. Later, when we're alone, I'll take my time with her. But right now, I want to feel her come apart in my arms.

I reach down and pull up her dress, exposing her bare ass to my view. Putting a hand between her shoulder blades, I push gently until she bends forward, bracing herself on the desk with her hands. I nudge her foot with one of mine and she widens her stance a bit. The movement causes her back to arch slightly, pushing her ass up into the air. I stand there, admiring her for a moment. She looks so fucking gorgeous like this, bent over with her ass on display, waiting for me to reward her.

"So pretty," I whisper, sliding my hands over her ass and down to her thighs. "You should see yourself right now. Bent over and waiting for your reward, your pretty pussy on display for me." I tease my fingers closer to her pussy, loving the way she sucks in a breath at the movement.

Before I can get carried away and bury my cock in her tight pussy the way I'd like to, I drop to my knees behind her and lean in to lick her from behind. Harlow gasps and I pull back.

"Silence," I say. "Or you won't get your reward."

She nods. "Sorry."

I grin, loving the way she's so eager to please me. This time, when I lean in to lick her, it's not such a shock for her. I hear her sharp intake of breath and her body gives a little shiver, but she doesn't make a sound. I keep going, licking and sucking at her pussy, driving her wild. I love the taste of her. I don't think I'll ever get enough of it. I push two fingers into her, watching as they plunge in and out of her wet pussy. With my other hand, I reach around and stroke her clit in fast, firm circles that I know will get her off in seconds. I'd love for this to last longer, but I also know that if we're gone too long the others will wonder where we are and it won't take them long to figure out what we're up to. Harlow's gasping now, her hips bucking back against my fingers. She's close, I know. But I know one thing that will help push her over the edge.

"I love the way you take me, baby," I whisper. "My cock. My fingers. All of me."

She shivers against my hands.

"Look at you. So needy. So fucking perfect. Bent over and getting ready to come all over my hands."

"Linc," she whispers.

I increase my pace, pumping my fingers in and out faster now. I can hear the wet sounds of her pussy as I finger her and it takes all the willpower I possess not to replace my fingers with my aching cock. When I feel the first flutter of her pussy that signal her impending orgasm, I smile wickedly in the dark.

"That's it, baby. Take your reward. You earned this orgasm. Come all over my hands. Let me feel it."

Her body is shaking now as her pussy clamps down on my fingers and she lets out a whispered curse. I keep fucking her with my fingers and stroking her clit, staying with her until her orgasm tapers and I can no longer feel the rhythmic squeezing of her inner muscles around my fingers. Slowly, I ease my fingers out of her pussy.

"Turn around," I say.

Harlow's breathing is loud in the small office, but she's otherwise silent. The fact that she was able to remain quiet while coming on my hands is a testament to how much she wants to please me. She turns on shaky legs to face me. Her dress falls to cover her as she straightens, hiding her from my view. I hold her gaze as I lick my fingers clean. She sucks in a shaky breath.

"Later, I want you to scream as loud as you want when you come on my cock, baby."

"Yes, sir"

CHAPTER 27

Linc

"Are you sure I should be going to this thing?" Harlow asks for what feels like the millionth time. "I'm not exactly family."

I smile at her obvious nerves. Reaching over the console, I take her hand in mine and shift to face her.

"Yes," I say. "I'm sure. Besides, Ella wants you here. She'll be heartbroken if you're not."

I feel a little guilty using Ella this way, but it's true that she wants Harlow to be here tonight. She's been going on about her art presentation for the last two weeks and she practically begged Harlow to come and see her work.

Every year, her school has a gallery night where they showcase the best art submissions for each grade and Ella's drawing was chosen as one of the finalists. She's always loved to draw, paint and color and I've always encouraged her interest in art, even if I don't know where that talent came from. I've always believed she was talented, but I didn't know if that was due to fatherly bias. Having her art teacher agree with my assessment has made Ella's year, I think.

When she brought home the letter from her art teacher, I was so proud that I wanted to frame it and hang it on the wall. But Ella had argued against it. I didn't display the letter, but I did tuck it into a box for one of those days when she's doubting herself. Now, it's gallery night and Harlow and I are sitting in my truck in the school's parking lot while I try to convince her that she doesn't have any reason to be nervous.

"It's just an elementary school art night," I say. "There will be a bunch of kids and their parents."

She gives me a skeptical look. "You mean half our graduating class and their kids? Not to mention some of the same teachers I had when I went to this school?"

I shrug. "So, it's just like a trip to Walmart."

That makes her smile. Rolling her eyes, she says, "Fine. But I'm doing this for Ella. I don't want her to wonder why I'm not here."

"Good," I say. "She's going to be thrilled to see you."

Harlow points a finger at me. "And no PDA in the school, mister."

"I don't think you can get detention for holding hands if you don't attend the school anymore," I say.

"But you can become gossip for the bored housewives of Peach Tree," she argues. "No, thank you."

I sigh. "Fine. You win. I'll do my best to keep my hands to myself."

She narrows her eyes at me. "And try not to look at me with those fuck me eyes."

"I don't know what you mean," I say, dropping my gaze to her lips.

She shakes her head. "Oh, no you don't. That's what I mean. Stop looking at me like you're picturing me naked."

I laugh as I reach for the door handle. "I'm always picturing you naked," I mutter.

I don't hear her response as she climbs out of the truck, but I can guess it's something along the lines of, 'I know.'

It's been almost a month since our first date, and I haven't gone a single day without seeing her in some way. She comes to dinner at my place most nights. Sometimes I convince her to stay the night after. If she can't make it for dinner, I make an excuse to stop by her salon during the day to drop off flowers or her favorite latte from Piper's shop. The truth is, I can't get enough of her. I don't know why I waited so long to act on my attraction, but I'm glad I finally did. Part of me worries I'm falling too hard, too fast. I'm letting Ella get too attached to a woman when it might not work out between us. But I can't help myself.

We haven't jumped into talk of feelings yet, but I know I've never felt anything like this for another woman. I know she makes me happy and the idea of not being with her is so abhorrent I refuse to picture it. Is that love? I don't know. Right now, I don't care. I'm just happy to be with her. I've also had the best sex of my life in the last month. Just thinking about it can make me instantly hard. Harlow wasn't wrong when she admonished me not to give her 'fuck me eyes', as she calls them. I know I'm guilty of doing it without even realizing it. How can

I help it when I know what it's like to be with her that way?

I've never had another woman welcome my dominant side in the bedroom. In the past, they've all been caught by surprise when I told them how I like to take charge during sex. Most of them were shocked by my dirty talk, saying that they thought they were getting a quiet, sweet family man. I don't know why I can't be both of those things. Apparently, the contradiction was too much for them.

But Harlow loves that side of me just as much as she loves the quiet, reserved side of me that everyone else sees. I don't have to hold anything back with her. She loves it when I'm rough with her and when I tell her all the filthy things I want to do to her. She loves it when I'm in control and command her to do wicked things. I've never felt that sort of freedom in a relationship. It's just another thing about her that convinces me I don't want to be without her. I glance over at her as we walk toward the school.

"Stop that," she mutters without looking at me.

"Stop what?"

"Thinking dirty thoughts about me."

I grin. "I'd have to be dead."

I'm not sure how I manage to follow Harlow's rules of no PDA and no lingering gazes; but somehow, I behave myself for two whole hours. We walk through the school gymnasium which has been turned into something that's meant to mimic a real art gallery. The kids are all standing near their displayed art, waiting to answer questions and receive compliments. Ella had worn her favorite dress for the occasion and asked Harlow to style her hair.

When she sees us approaching her display, her face lights up. I expect her to run over to greet us, chattering a mile a minute, but she doesn't. She must have been instructed to stand there quietly while the gallery's 'patrons' admire the art, because that's exactly what she does. I can see how much it costs her to maintain her poise. She's practically bouncing on her feet.

"Beautiful work," Harlow says from beside me.

"Mm," I agree. "I especially love the artist's use of color."

A little giggle escapes Ella, but I don't look her way. I keep my gaze on her painting instead.

"I wonder what a beautiful piece like this must cost," I say.

"A small fortune, I'm sure," Harlow says. "Certainly, one can only dream of owning such a piece."

I sigh. "I'm sure you're right."

"Lincoln Prescott?"

A woman's shrill voice pierces the quiet air of the gallery and I automatically turn toward the source. I immediately regret it when I see the woman walking toward me. Her auburn hair is pin-straight and just reaches her shoulders. Her eyes are lined a little too heavily with dark eyeliner that makes her look much older than I know her to be. The overly large smile she directs at me makes me want to hide. From the corner of my eye, I see Harlow stiffen beside me and I know she's thinking the same thing I am. I manage to mask my expression and paste on a generic smile that I hope is convincing but not too inviting. After all, the last thing I want is to be trapped into a conversation with this woman.

"Hillary," I say, injecting just enough politeness into my tone to not be considered rude. "How are you?"

"I thought that was you!" she gushes as she closes the distance between us.

For a moment, I think she's going to try and hug me, but I reach out a hand at the last second. She hesitates, looking from my hand to my face and back again before reluctantly reaching out to shake my hand. I break the contact as soon as possible, sliding my hand into my pocket.

"It's me," I say. "I'm here to see my daughter's artwork for gallery night."

I gesture toward Ella's painting, trying to direct Hillary's attention away from me. She gives it the briefest of glances before turning back to me.

"Lincoln, it is so *good* to see you," she says. "It's been far too long."

I give her a smaller smile this time, but I don't respond in kind. The truth is that it's not good to see Hillary Mitchell. I dated her for about a month during our senior year of high school. That month was enough time for me to realize how vapid she was and how little we had in common. It was just long enough for her to convince me to take her to the prom. And after Harlow revealed to me that she'd wanted to be my prom date, the last thing

I want to do is make small talk with the girl I actually took to the prom. Seemingly oblivious to my lack of enthusiasm for the conversation or her presence, Hillary keeps talking.

"I was just talkin' to my momma the other day and she asked me how you were doin'." She leans toward me conspiratorially and I instinctively step back. Hillary doesn't seem to notice. "Between you and me, I think she still secretly wishes we'd stayed together for the long haul."

She laughs as if what she just said was hilarious. I do my best to look amused, but I'm not sure I pull it off.

"Say hi to your mom for me," I say, just to be polite.

"Oh, I will," she says, reaching a hand out and touching my arm. "She's going to be tickled pink when I tell her I ran into you."

My eyes stray to where her hand still rests on my arm. I risk a glance over at Harlow who's standing three feet away, not trying to hide the fact that she's watching our conversation play out. I can't tell if she's annoyed or angry. Her expression is carefully blank.

"We should have lunch one day," Hillary says, her voice full of sugary sweet and still just a touch too loud for the quiet gymnasium.

Harlow's jaw tightens, but she still doesn't say anything. Fuck politeness. I need to put a stop to this right now. Pulling my arm away from Hillary's grasping fingers, I move closer to Harlow and take her hand, lacing my fingers through hers. Thankfully, she doesn't pull away from me. Hopefully this doesn't violate her 'No PDA' rule.

"Actually, I don't think that's a good idea," I say, turning to Harlow and smiling. "All my lunches are booked up by Harlow these days." I raise our joined hands and kiss the back of hers. "Not that I'm complaining." I laugh and Harlow joins me, though I can tell she's caught off-guard by the cheesiness of this display.

"He's right, I'm afraid," she says, patting my chest. "I'm keeping him all to myself."

Hillary's smile slowly fades as she realizes what we're implying. Her gaze shoots back and forth between Harlow and me, surprise written on her face.

"Oh. I didn't realize you two were an item," she says.

I smile even wider. "I just hate that I didn't realize how amazing she is years ago," I say. "I was so blind back then."

It's not until Hillary stiffens and her eyes narrow just a bit that I realize how my words probably sounded to her—the person I dated back then. But I don't recall them. Let her think what she wants. I was an idiot to have dated her. She's always been conceited and self-absorbed. From everything I've seen, she still is. She married her first husband right out of high school. Supposedly it had been because of his successful real estate firm. Rumors are that she cheated on him with one of his junior salesmen and they divorced. Now, she's chasing after every single, successful businessman in the county, trying to land another wealthy husband. I want her to know she won't find what she's looking for with me.

Harlow smiles up at me adoringly. "I'm just happy you're seeing clearly these days, honey."

Honey? Since when does she call me that? She's laying it on thick. I wonder if she really is mad at me. I hope not. I'm doing my best to make it obvious to her and to Hillary that I only want her.

"Well," Hillary says, her voice more muted than before. "Good for you two."

"Thank you," Harlow gushes.

"I'm a lucky guy."

"Yes, well," Hillary says, clearly uncomfortable now. "I should be going. It was nice seeing both of you."

"Of course," I say.

"Bye!" Harlow all but sings the word, giving a little finger-wave as she does.

As soon as Hillary is gone, Harlow drops the fake smile and my hand. She crosses her arms over her chest and glares at Hillary's back.

"I really don't like that woman," she mutters.

"Me either," I say. Leaning closer to her, I whisper, "Sorry about the PDA. I know I broke the rules."

She turns to face me. "Are you kidding me? I was one second away from ripping her hand off your arm. If you hadn't done something, I would have been livid."

The vehemence in her voice catches me off-guard. "I didn't know you were the jealous type," I muse.

She rolls her eyes. "I'm not jealous. It's about manners. It's rude to walk up to a man who's clearly standing next to a woman and put your hands on him. And she didn't even attempt to acknowledge me until you brought me into the conversation. Even though I know she knows who I am."

I smile down at her and wink. "I think someone is just a little bit jealous."

"Hm. Think what you want. It's a free country."

"Does this make you my girlfriend now?" I tease.

"Shut up," she mutters, making me laugh.

After a second, she surprises me by leaning up on her toes to kiss my cheek before whispering, "Yeah."

My smile stretches wide, and I look at her for several seconds before my mouth drops open in shock.

"PDA!" I whisper, scandalized.

She laughs. "Ass."

"What about my ass?" I say, turning to look over my shoulder.

Harlow swats me with her hand. "Can we focus on the art, please?"

I do my best to behave after that, but the truth is that I'm ridiculously happy and having a hard time keeping the goofy grin off my face. I'm not happy that Harlow was jealous of Hillary. That would be stupid. Though I won't lie and say it wasn't a nice stroke to my ego to witness it. I'm happy because tonight was the first time either of us has put a label on what we are. I know we've been exclusive, but it's the first time either of us has used the word 'girlfriend'. At my age, I didn't think something like that would affect me so much, but I can't stop remembering the way she'd whispered that single word into my ear.

I'd love nothing more than to take her home immediately and drag her into my bed for the next few hours—or days. But Ella is with us and she's so excited about the gallery that I decide to take my two favorite girls out for ice cream afterward. By the time we finish our dessert, it's getting later, and Ella is visibly tired. She's had a big day and I know it's catching up to her. By the time we get home and she takes her bath, her eyelids are drooping.

"I'm proud of you, El," I say, watching as Harlow braids her hair into two pigtails.

"Thank you," she says through a massive yawn.

Harlow finishes Ella's hair and leans forward to kiss the top of her head. "I'm proud of you too," she whispers.

Something about the scene makes my heart melt just a little. It's not the first time Harlow has braided Ella's hair before bed. It's not even the first time she's casually shown her affection. It's that, for the first time since Ella was born, I feel like my heart doesn't belong solely to my daughter. Somehow, Harlow has come to occupy a large portion of it without me noticing when or how it happened. I know that should scare me, but somehow it grounds me instead. I feel like some part of my life was missing before but now it's not. I realize how ridiculous that thought is as soon as I have it. Sure, I've known Harlow since we were ten, but we've only been together for a month. It's crazy to think I might have fallen for her already. Isn't it?

"Come on, El," I say, reaching for her. "Time for bed."

I scoop her up and carry her to her room. She's getting heavier these days and I know it won't be much longer before I need to stop carrying her to bed at night. The realization that she's growing up faster than I thought sends a pang through me and I hug her for a few extra seconds before leaving her room. I watch as her eyes drift shut and her breathing evens out as she drifts off to sleep.

When I go back downstairs, Harlow isn't in the living room where I left her. Instead, I find her in the kitchen, sipping a glass of red wine. She smiles when she sees me and holds the glass out toward me. I take it from her and sip from it without taking my eyes off hers. She's wearing one of my t-shirts and a pair of baggy pajama pants with otters on them. Her feet are bare and her hair is loose down her back. She's never looked more beautiful. I set the glass on the counter and reach for her, pulling her into my arms.

"Alexa play *These Arms of Mine*," I say.

Harlow looks at me in confusion until I take her hands and place them on my shoulders. I wrap my own arms around her waist as the music starts to play through the small speaker on the kitchen counter.

"I realized how much I missed by not asking you to the prom ten years ago," I say. "I don't have a corsage, but maybe we can pretend I asked the right girl to the dance. Can I have a do-over?"

I know it's risky to bring up the prom. Last time I mentioned it while we were dancing, she'd gotten so pissed off she'd left the bar and gone home early. Granted, it had led to me following her home and kissing her until we both came. After our run-in with Hillary earlier and Harlow quietly proclaiming herself my girlfriend, I think maybe it's safe to mention it. When she leans into me and rests her head on my shoulder, I smile, relieved.

We sway slowly to the song, caught up in the moment. It's different from the last time we danced. This time there's only me and her. We're not surrounded by dozens of people at a bar. Our friends aren't here to watch us and wonder what's going on between us or tease us about how long it took us to figure it out. It just feels right.

"This is nice," she whispers.

"It is."

"I can almost imagine this is the way prom really went."

My arms tighten around her. "Let's pretend it did. Erase the memory of that other prom. That one wasn't real. This is."

She leans back to look up at me. "If you'd taken me to prom, would you have been a gentleman?"

I narrow my eyes at her. "I'm appalled that you would ask such a question. I'm always a gentleman."

She raises one brow. "Except when you're not."

The teasing quality to her voice has my dick jumping in my pants. I know she's talking about when we're having sex. It's the only time I'm not a gentleman with her. And I know it drives her wild.

"I thought you liked that side of me?" I tease.

"Oh, I do." She pulls me down toward her. "In fact, I think I'd like to see that side of you now."

Her lips meet mine in what starts as a soft, slow kiss. It morphs into something hot and sensual in seconds. Her fingers grip my hair as her tongue tangles with mine. My hands move lower to cup her ass, pulling her against me, letting her feel how hard I am for her.

"I want you," I say, my lips skimming her jaw.

She reaches for my pants, tugging at the button. "I know."

The button pops free under her hands and the zipper follows. The song comes to an end, making our ragged breaths sound harsh in the silence that follows. Harlow reaches into my pants and grips my cock, pulling a hiss from me. She knows just how I like to be touched, just how much pressure to use to drive me crazy. She pumps my length, squeezing the head just a little on each upstroke the way I taught her. I reach for the hem of her shirt to push it up, but she steps back just far enough so I can't. When I shoot her a questioning look, she grins.

"Tonight is about you," she says, reaching for my cock again.

I must still look confused because she gives me a wicked smile and lowers herself to her knees in front of me.

"Harlow, wait," I say, groaning as she strokes me harder this time. "You don't need to."

She raises one eyebrow in that sexy way I like. "I know. I want to. So, let me."

I smile down at her. "I thought I was the bossy one?"

"You can still be bossy," she says in a sweet voice. "Tell me how you want me to suck your cock. Sir."

Oh, fuck. I'm in trouble.

Hearing her say those words makes my dick grow even harder. It ignites something primal inside me that begs to take control. I've been careful with Harlow, not wanting to push beyond her boundaries or mine. The idea scares me a little. I never want to hurt her or do something that makes her afraid of me.

"Hey," she says softly. "Look at me."

When I do, she continues. "I trust you, Linc. I know you won't hurt me." She smiles. "Besides, I like it when you take control. It gives me permission to let go. To experience. To just feel and not think, for once. It's freeing. And really, really fucking hot." The last part is said as she strokes the length of my cock, making me catch my breath.

"Are you sure?" I rasp.

She nods, flicking out her tongue to taste me. "I'm sure."

"And you'll tell me if you want to stop? Or if I do something you don't like?"

She nods again. "As long as you do the same."

I nearly laugh. "Baby, I don't think you can do anything sexual that I wouldn't like."

She eyes me thoughtfully. "What about a finger in your ass?"

I almost laugh, but I'm not entirely sure she's joking. "It's not something I've tried, but we can revisit it another time if you want."

She smiles. "There's that adventurous spirit." Her face turns serious. "Now, are you going to tell me how you want your cock sucked or not?"

I swallow hard, my mouth suddenly dry. How did I ever get lucky enough to be here right now? Standing in my kitchen with my pants around my ankles and a beautiful woman on her knees begging to suck my cock? Not just any woman, either. It's Harlow. Amazing, fierce, kind, strong, and beautiful, Harlow. I don't know how it happened, and I don't care. I'm not going to waste this opportunity.

"Suck the head into your mouth," I say, using the commanding voice I know she loves.

Her mouth curves into a smile. "Yes, sir," she says sweetly before doing exactly that.

Her warm, wet mouth feels incredible. The suction is gentle, as if she's afraid to be too rough.

"Suck harder," I say, tangling my fingers in her hair.

My knees threaten to buckle when she complies. The pleasure shoots from the tip of my dick down to the base, pulling a groan from me.

"That's it. That's perfect."

She grips the base of my shaft with one hand while her mouth works on the head, sucking and bobbing lightly. She's just taking the head into her mouth for now, as I instructed. The sight of her mouth stretched around my cock nearly takes my breath.

"Flick your tongue on the underside."

Harlow immediately does as I say, her tongue flicking and swirling against the sensitive underside of my cock, just under the head. I groan at the new sensation. It feels incredible.

"Good girl," I manage to whisper.

I've got both hands in her hair now. My hips rock forward slightly, pushing more of me into her mouth. Her blue eyes come up to meet my gaze and I can see that she's loving this almost as much as I am.

"Can you take more?" I ask.

She gives me the barest of nods without releasing my cock from her mouth and I smile.

"Put your hands behind your back," I order her.

Without hesitation, Harlow releases her grip on my dick and reaches behind her to clasp her hands at the base of her spine. The sight of her kneeling before me, her hands behind her back and her mouth full of my cock is one I know I'll never forget.

"You look so good right now," I tell her. "So perfect. Swallowing my cock like a good girl."

Keeping my hands on her head, I hold her still for my shallow thrusts. I don't push too far. I don't want to hurt her. Her eyes close and she lets out a little hum that I feel vibrate down the length of my shaft.

"You like that?" I say through gritted teeth.

Harlow's eyes open and she looks up at me. "Mmhmm."

"You want more?"

"Mmhmm."

"Tap my leg if it's too much," I say.

Her tongue swirls around the tip of my cock once more. She gives me another tiny nod and I feel my heart swell at the trust she has in me. Holding her head still, I push my cock deeper before pulling out until just the tip is in her mouth. I repeat the action again and again, pushing deeper into her mouth each time until I can't go any further. I stop there, holding her still with her mouth full of my cock.

My heart is pounding so hard I can't believe it's not audible in the silent room. I look at Harlow's face, checking to make sure she's okay. She doesn't look upset or distressed. In fact, she looks like she's enjoying herself.

"Your mouth feels so fucking good, baby," I say, knowing she loves how vocal I am during sex.

I start moving again, pushing in and out of her hot mouth, fucking her slowly. Each time I bump against the back of her mouth, I hold there for a moment before pulling back again. It's the most erotic form of slow torture. I know I won't come like this, but I don't want to. I'm enjoying this too much.

"Do you want to try to take more?"

She nods, and my heart pounds harder in my chest.

"Good girl," I grit out. "I'll go slow."

This time, when I push my cock deep into her mouth, I can feel the moment she relaxes her throat and I'm able to thrust even deeper. I watch her to make sure she's okay, but she still looks calm and focused as she takes my cock down her throat.

"That's it," I rasp. "Damn, baby. You look so fucking good with my cock down your throat."

I ease back before thrusting down her throat again. She takes me with ease this time, letting me slide deep until nearly all of my cock disappears into her mouth. I grit my teeth against the urge to thrust hard and fast into her. Instead, I keep my pace slow and steady, never deviating in my thrusting.

"I wish you could see yourself right now. Fucking perfect."

I push down her throat again, holding myself still for a moment. When I feel Harlow swallow around my cock, I can't hold back a ragged groan. That one small movement on her part proves to be too much for me to handle. I pull out of her mouth and yank her to her feet in one fast motion. Shoving her pants down, I lift her in my arms. I walk forward until her back is against the wall, helping to support her.

"I need to be inside you now," I rasp, taking her lips in a rough kiss.

I reach between us to touch her, not surprised at all to find her wet and ready. Thank fuck for that. I don't know if I'd have the patience to get her ready. Not after what we just did. I slide my fingers over her slit, teasing her.

"Did sucking my cock make you this wet, baby?"

She nods. "You fucking my mouth was so hot."

God, this woman is perfect. I push two fingers roughly inside her, making her gasp against my mouth. I pump them in and out several times, making her moan.

"Linc! Please!"

"I know," I say, pulling my fingers out and moving my cock into position at her opening. I hesitate for a second before thrusting into her in one quick movement.

"Yes," she gasps.

Being buried to the hilt inside Harlow is the most incredible feeling ever. I can feel her squeezing every inch of me as I start to move. Then it hits me.

"Shit." I go still. "Condom."

She groans and I feel her pussy clench around my length. Fuck, that feels amazing. No wonder. I've never been with a woman without a condom. The sensation is heightened far beyond anything I've ever experienced.

"I have an IUD," she whispers. "And I'm clean."

I meet her gaze as I register what she's saying.

"I've always used protection," I say. "Always."

She reaches up to grip my neck with both hands and her blue eyes stare into mine. "Don't stop."

It's all the permission I need to keep going. Harlow pulls me down for a kiss as I begin to move again, thrusting inside her. The knowledge that there's no barrier between her body and mine shouldn't affect me as much as it does, but I can't help but think about it as I slide into her, over and over. Dipping my head, I kiss her neck, grazing the sensitive skin with my teeth the way I know she loves. I feel her stiffen in my arms as she gasps.

"Yes! Linc."

I move faster, wishing she weren't still wearing my shirt, but not willing to stop long enough to remove it. Instead, I manage to push it up high enough to expose one of her gorgeous tits. I squeeze it in my hand, pinching her nipple just hard enough to make her gasp.

"Touch your clit," I command.

Harlow immediately reaches down between us and begins rubbing herself in fast circles as I continue to fuck her hard and fast. I know I'm getting close to the edge, but I need her to go over it with me. I can feel the telltale tightening in my balls that signals my orgasm is close, but I force myself to hold on for a little longer.

"You feel so fucking good, baby," I say through gritted teeth. "I want to feel you come on my cock."

She moans, her fingers working faster on her clit.

"That's it, baby. I've got you. Come for me. Let me feel it."

Harlow's mouth drops open on a silent cry and at last, I feel her pussy clamp down on my cock as her orgasm hits. Her eyes close and I swallow her cries with a kiss as I feel her come undone around me. I don't stop, thrusting again and again into her tight pussy until I can't hold back my own orgasm any longer. My knees threaten to give out and a groan is ripped from my throat as I come, holding her tightly against me as I pour out my release.

I stand there, holding Harlow against me, my cock still deep inside her while we both catch our breath. I kiss her lips, lingering for a moment. I don't want this moment to end. I don't want to sever the connection with her. I don't want to let her go. Ever. I love being with her. I love having sex with her. I love just spending time with her. It hits me hard, like a punch to the gut. I love her. I'm in love with this woman I'm holding in my arms. It should scare me, but it doesn't. It fills me with a sense of peace. I love Harlow. Now that I understand that, everything else feels so simple.

I kiss her temple before lifting her off me and lowering her so she can stand. I want to tell her what I just realized, but I don't know if it's the right time. I don't know if it would scare her away. It's only been a month since we started dating. Hell, she only called herself my girlfriend tonight for the first time. It might be too soon to throw around words like love. Besides, I plan to be with Harlow for as long as she'll have me. I don't need to rush things now and risk screwing them up. We waited nearly 20 years for this. We can wait a bit longer.

Harlow sighs, leaning forward to rest her head against my chest.

"Wow," she whispers, making me smile.

Since I can't tell her I love her yet, I settle for telling her how amazing she is.

"You're incredible," I say, letting some of the wonder I feel creep into my voice.

We adjust our clothing and make our way up to my bathroom. I pull her into the shower with me and take my time helping her wash in between gentle kisses and soft touches. I can't get enough of her lips on mine, her soft skin against my fingertips. When we tumble into bed, Harlow reaches for me, wordlessly pulling my arms around her and snuggling into my chest. I hold her to me as she falls asleep, cherishing the feel of her in my arms. In my head, I repeat the words I can't say yet.

I love you.

I love you.
I love you.

CHAPTER 28

Linc

I'm in the middle of wiring an electrical outlet for a customer's new bathroom when my cellphone rings. Stopping what I'm doing, I pull the phone from my pocket to see that the call is from Peach Tree Elementary School. As always happens when Ella's school calls, I feel an immediate jolt of worry shoot through me. Is she sick? Is she hurt? Did something awful happen at the school? I swipe the screen to answer the call before all the possibilities can drive me insane.

"Hello?"

"May I please speak to Lincoln Prescott?" a friendly, woman's voice asks.

"This is Lincoln Prescott," I say.

"Mr. Prescott, I'm calling because Ella got into a fight at school today. Now, she's not hurt, but you're going to have to come pick her up and have a meeting with the principal."

The first thing that hits me is disbelief. Ella? In a fight? There's no way. She's never been in any kind of trouble at school, let alone for fighting. This has to be a mistake.

"Are you sure?" I ask. "Ella's never been a fighter."

"Yes, Mr. Prescott," comes the woman's voice. "We're sure. We can discuss the details when you get to the school. How long do you think you'll be?"

I blink. Well. I don't suppose I'm getting much information out of her.

"I'll be there in 20 minutes," I say.

"Thank you, Mr. Prescott. We'll see you then."

She ends the call without saying goodbye, which is just plain rude in any society. I stand there for several seconds trying to think of a reason Ella might have been fighting, but I can't think of anything that would cause her to be violent. She's just not like that. Something extreme must have happened to cause her to act in such a way. I need to talk to Ella to find out what it was.

I find my foreman and let him know I'm taking off for the rest of the day for a family emergency. He's competent and capable of running things without me there to babysit and he tells me just that when I ask him if the crew will be okay without me. I laugh as I leave him to it. I know my crew will be fine without me there to supervise them. They're hard workers and they strive for perfection—or close to it. It's why I handpicked each one of them for this job. I knew they wouldn't let me down.

I wrack my brain as I drive across town to Ella's school, trying to think of something that would draw her into a fight. I still can't come up with anything. I can't even picture Ella fighting. It's not like I'm one of those fathers who thinks their kid can do no wrong. If the school had called to tell me that Ella was in trouble for convincing her classmates to sneak lizards inside from the playground, I'd have believed it. But fighting just doesn't sound like her.

By the time I park my truck in front of the school, I'm almost convinced there's been a case of mistaken identity. Or someone got the story wrong. Maybe other kids were fighting, and Ella tried to break it up. Or maybe she was standing up to a bully who was picking on another kid. That, I can almost believe. When I walk into the front office and see my daughter sitting in one of the plastic chairs, arms crossed and an angry scowl on her face, I start to reconsider my stance. I don't think I've ever seen her look so angry.

When she sees me, her expression shifts to one that's slightly more nervous and less angry. But I can still see the anger simmering in her eyes. I don't see any signs of injury. She looks perfectly fine, aside from her obvious anger. That's when I notice another kid seated in a chair on the opposite side of the waiting area. He's holding a napkin to his nose that's spotted with red. Blood. I quickly fill in the gaps. Ella hit another kid.

I sigh. *Shit.*

I walk over to where she's sitting and peer down at her.

"You okay?" I ask in a low voice.

She nods but doesn't say anything.

"Mr. Prescott?"

I look up to see an older woman behind the counter. She's giving me an expectant look which I suppose means I need to walk over and talk to her instead of my daughter. *Double shit.* There have been a few times since I've become a father in which I've been reminded just how unqualified I am for the job. This feels like one of those times. I'm supposed to be mature enough to handle a talk with the principal? I'm not sure I'm ready for this. But I give the woman a small smile and approach the desk as if I know what I'm supposed to be doing.

"Hi, I'm Ella's dad," I say, trying for a friendly tone.

"I know who you are, Mr. Prescott," the woman replies without smiling. "Come with me."

I glance back to where Ella is still sitting. "What about her?"

"The principal would like to meet with each parent one-on-one before bringing the children in," she says, turning to walk down a hallway located behind the large counter. I turn back to Ella.

"I'll be right back," I say, trying to reassure her. I still don't know what happened today or why that other kid is bleeding, but Ella looks scared now, and I can't stand that look in her eyes.

"It's going to be okay," I tell her. She nods, but I can tell she's still worried.

I turn and follow the other woman down the hall to an office at the end. The door is open and seated inside is a man who I'd guess to be maybe 10 years older than me. He's seated behind a large, mahogany desk with a name placard on it that declares him to be Principal Ramirez. He gives me a brief smile when I enter.

"Mr. Prescott," he says, gesturing toward one of the empty seats. "Take a seat, please."

I nod and do as he says. I don't care how old I get or how far removed from school, there's something nerve-wracking about being sent to the principal's office. Principal Ramirez looks like a nice enough guy, but he still represents an authority figure that young me was always trying to avoid. It seems adult me isn't any more inclined to spend time with the principal.

"What happened?" I ask, unable to think of another way to phrase the question.

Mr. Ramirez sighs and folds his hands on the top of the desk. "Your daughter punched a boy in the nose during recess this morning."

He says it quickly and matter-of-factly, as though he's ripping off a band aid. My shock must show on my face because he nods before continuing.

"That's what I thought too," he says. "Mr. Prescott, I know every kid in my school. I know the ones who like to cause trouble and the ones who don't. Ella isn't a troublemaker. Which is why I wanted to try and get to the bottom of what might have caused her to act in a way that's clearly out of character for her."

I nod at his assessment of Ella, but I'm just as confused as he is by this behavior. "And you're sure it was Ella?"

He nods. "There were several dozen witnesses," he says. "And Ella isn't denying it. I even gave her ice for her hand, but I don't think she needed it. Girl can throw a punch."

I will not feel proud of that statement. I will not feel proud of that statement.

"Did she say why she hit the other kid?" I ask.

Mr. Ramirez looks a little uncomfortable now. "I think he was saying some things to her that she didn't like. Playground teasing. That sort of thing."

I blink, wondering what some boy could have been saying to cause Ella to lash out with her fist. "Are you sure that's all it was? Teasing?"

"How's Ella's home life?" Ramirez asks. "Have there been any major changes lately to her schedule? Kids sometimes act out due to other factors that have nothing to do with the actual bad behavior."

Now, I'm getting annoyed. "Mr. Ramirez, has Ella gotten into any other trouble before today?"

He shakes his head.

"And have her grades fluctuated at all?"

He shakes his head again.

"So, it's safe to say this seems like an isolated incident?"

Ramirez considers this before nodding. "Most likely. But I have to ask. It's my job."

I nod. "And I appreciate that, Mr. Ramirez. I do. But Ella's happy. She's doing great at home and until today I would have said she's doing great at school too. Like you, I want to figure out why she would act so out of character. Do we know what the other boy was saying to her?"

"Violence is never a proper response to harsh words!"

Ramirez and I both shift to look at the person who just spoke. As soon as I see the woman standing in the doorway, I feel my annoyance spike. Hillary Mitchell. What the hell is she doing here?

"Mrs. Thomas," Ramirez says with a small smile in Hillary's direction. "Please come in. We were just discussing today's incident."

Thomas. That's must be the name of Hillary's last husband. I thought we were each going to meet with the principal alone. Isn't that what the dragon-lady out front said? I bite back my words of protest, knowing they won't help. Hillary smiles over at Ramirez, all teeth and fake southern charm before taking the chair beside me, effectively blocking off my exit from the small office.

"If by 'incident', you mean the assault on my son," Hillary says, "I'm all ears." She turns to glare at me. "Care to tell me why your daughter has such a thirst for violence."

I can feel my blood pressure rising at her insinuation that Ella is somehow a horrible person based on whatever happened today. But I do my best to remain calm.

"Mrs. Thomas," Ramirez says, pulling her attention back to him. "We were just discussing the events leading up to the incident."

Hillary looks indignant. "It shouldn't matter why she hit him. Violence is never the answer."

Ramirez dips his head in acknowledgment. "I agree. Violence is never okay. But we need to make sure it's not going to happen again. When a student acts out of character, we like to get to the bottom of why it happened. That's why I called you both here today."

Hillary looks irritated, but she remains quiet as Ramirez speaks.

"Now, I've spoken with a few of the kids who saw the incident," Ramirez says. "And they all had a similar story. They all say that Ella was playing with a group of friends when Kyle and two of his friends approached her group. Kyle said some things to Ella that she didn't like. When she told him to leave her alone, he persisted and continued to say inappropriate things to her. After several minutes of this back and forth, Ella threatened to 'make him leave her alone' if he didn't stop. Kyle continued to antagonize her. Which is when she hit him. In Kyle's defense, he didn't retaliate against her physically. To be honest, I think he was too stunned. Ella's a good deal smaller than he is."

I let Ramirez's words play through my head again, but I can't get past one thing he said.

"What inappropriate things was Kyle saying to Ella?" I ask.

When they both turn to me—Hillary in outrage and Ramirez looking sheepish—I know it's probably not something I want to hear. The possibilities of what might constitute 'inappropriate' for eight year olds is probably nowhere near as bad as what I can conjure. But I can still feel my blood begin to boil at the thought of what this boy said to my daughter.

"Well," Ramirez says. "I'd rather not repeat it."

"It shouldn't matter what he said," Hillary sputters. "Kids say all sorts of things. It's no reason to become physically violent."

I hold up a hand. "While I agree with the sentiment, Hillary, I also don't think it's okay for anyone to pick on someone. Your son was asked several times to stop taunting her and he didn't. She was wrong to hit him, but your son started it."

"Now, now," Ramirez says. "There's no need for pointing fingers and assigning blame. Both students have been reprimanded and will face their punishment."

"Kyle is the victim—"

"I understand," I say, cutting off whatever Hillary was about to say. "Ella was wrong to hit Kyle and she will face her punishment for that act. But I need to know what was said to provoke her into hitting someone. That's not like her."

"I really don't see the point—" Hillary begins.

I hold up my hand to stop her. "I know you don't," I say. "But I don't care."

Her mouth drops open in outrage. I can't say I blame her. It's beyond rude for me to keep interrupting her. I know it as well as she does. But I need to get to the bottom of this.

Ramirez looks resigned. He sighs heavily. "From what the other kids told me, Kyle made fun of Ella's hair. When that didn't seem to bother her, he said something about how she shouldn't have let that—" He clears his throat and I can see how much he doesn't want to continue.

"Excuse me," he goes on. "He said that Ella shouldn't have let that whore of a hairdresser mess with it." He keeps his gaze on the desk, unable to meet my eyes. "That's when Ella hit him."

I clench my fist, seeing red. I can't understand why an eight-year-old boy would talk that way. Or why he'd even know that Harlow had been around Ella.

"Well, I don't believe that for a second," Hillary says. "Those kids are lying. Kyle wouldn't talk that way."

"I assure you, he did," Ramirez says, his hard tone making it clear he's losing patience with Hillary's innocent act.

I turn to glare at the woman. "Where would an eight-year-old learn words like that? And why would your son know or even care about who's styling my daughter's hair?"

Hillary's eyes go wide, and she sputters, unable to form a sentence.

"I have a pretty good theory," I say. "Unless you want everyone in this town to know what a jealous, petty, insecure person you are, you'll make sure neither you nor your son ever mentions Ella or Harlow again. Do you understand?"

If my voice conveys even half the anger I'm feeling right now, Hillary should have gotten the message. I don't wait for her response. Instead, I turn to Principal Ramirez.

"How long is she suspended?"

He looks surprised that I've asked him a question and it takes him a few seconds to formulate an answer.

"Three days," he says. "She can come back on Monday."

I nod. "Thank you. I'm sorry about this incident. I can assure you she won't do anything like this again."

Ramirez nods. "Thank you, Mr. Prescott."

Without another word, I turn to leave the office. When I reach the front waiting area, I don't say anything. I just look at Ella and point toward the door. She scrambles from her chair and follows me out the door and out to my truck. I open the door for her and she climbs inside, buckling her seatbelt. We ride in silence for a full ten minutes before I hear a loud sniff from the backseat. Ah, hell.

I turn the truck at the next right, pulling into the parking lot of Peach Tree's main grocery store. I park in an empty spot and shift in my seat to look at Ella who's doing her best to look like she's not crying as she stares out her window.

"Hey," I say, softly. "I'm not mad at you."

She sniffs again and swipes her hand over her face. "I can tell when you're mad," she says in a voice that sounds too small for her.

"I am angry," I admit. "But not at you. Hitting that boy wasn't the right thing to do. I know you know that. I've taught you better than that."

She nods as more tears fall down her cheeks and her lower lip begins to tremble.

"Ella, look at me, sweetheart." When she turns her big hazel eyes on me, I give her a small smile. "I'm not mad at you. Yes, you did something wrong. Yes, you're going to be in trouble for it. But I'm not mad at you. I'm mad at what happened. I'm mad at the mean things that boy said about you and about Harlow. It was wrong. But you don't need to cry, okay?"

She nods, sniffing again. "I'm sorry," she says.

"I know you are. You can't hit people who say mean things." I sigh. "I was hoping you had a few more years before I needed to teach you this, but the world is full of mean people who will say and do mean things. But it's full of good ones, too. Usually more good people than bad. It just doesn't always seem that way. People being mean to you says more about them than it does you. But how you react to it is what's important. You can't hit everyone who says mean things to you. No matter how badly you might want to."

I reach back and take her little hand in mine. "You've got to rise above the ugliness. I know it's hard. Believe me, I wanted to say a whole lot of mean things to Kyle's mom today, but I did my best not to."

That gets a smile out of her. But it only lasts a second before she turns her sad eyes on me.

"Don't tell Harlow," she says.

I blink. Of all the things I'd expected her to say, this wasn't it.

"Why not?"

"It'll make her sad," Ella says. "She'll feel bad. I don't want her to feel bad."

Ella's right, I know. Telling Harlow what that kid said to Ella and how she handled it will only make her feel guilty. She'll worry that it's her fault Ella got into trouble, and she'll blame herself for the teasing Ella had to endure. But I hate the idea of keeping this from her. She'll wonder why Ella is in trouble and why she's missing school. I don't want to lie to her either.

"I've got to tell her something, El," I say. "It's not okay to lie to her. Even if the truth might hurt her feelings."

Ella seems to deflate a little, but at least she's not crying anymore. She knows I'm right.

CHAPTER 29

Harlow

Today was a weird one. It started out normal enough. I kissed Linc goodbye and left before Ella woke up to get ready for school. It's not as if she doesn't know we're dating. She does. We talked to her about the situation weeks ago, and she was happy about it. But she doesn't know I'm sleeping over most nights. Linc wanted to tell her before, but I wanted to hold off a little longer. I'm not certain why. I just didn't want her to feel like we're making too many changes to her life at one time. I wanted her to grow accustomed to having me around more. I wanted to make sure she was truly okay with me being her dad's girlfriend. That's all.

Baby steps.

At least that's what I tell myself. Not that Ella seems bothered by my presence in her house in the least. In fact, she seems to love having me there as much as I love being there. I smile as I drive to work, thinking about how much that little girl has wiggled her way into my heart in such a short time. She's so smart and funny and kind. I love helping her with her hair and her homework, even though I'm better at the first one than the latter. I love hearing her giggles when Cole says something ridiculous to make her laugh. I know I should be worried about how much I've come to care for Ella and Cole, to say nothing of what I feel for Linc. But I can't manage to feel anything but happiness when I think of the last month. Things have been damned near perfect. Which scares me more than anything else could.

I keep waiting for something bad to happen to end things. I keep waiting for Linc to realize he can do better and that he needs someone more like him as a partner. Not that he's given me any indication he feels that way. In fact, he's the one who wants the whole world to know we're a couple, while I'm more reserved. It's not that I don't want everyone to know. I'm not trying to hide us. I guess I just have this insane notion that the more people know about us, the more it will hurt when it ends. Which is stupid, but I can't seem to stop the negative thoughts from intruding.

Soon, I tell myself. Soon, I'll get to a point where I'm not always waiting for the other shoe to drop. Not waiting for everything to fall apart. Just because it always has before doesn't mean it will this time. Right?

My day at work moves with agonizing slowness due to the mostly empty morning schedule. By the time Miss Dottie shows up for her usual cut and color, I'm beyond ready to get to work. Spending too much time alone with my thoughts isn't doing me any favors. As usual, Miss Dottie talks all through her hair color session.

She talks about the weather. "It's going to be a hot summer this year." As if it's not hot every summer in south Georgia. She talks about the changes I've made in the shop. "I didn't want to mention it, dear, but those old sinks were terribly uncomfortable. These new ones are much better."

I smile and nod as I work, the conversation not requiring much input from me. That is, until she says something I don't expect.

"Oh, I do hope Ella is alright after what happened yesterday," she says. "You tell Lincoln that no one thinks she was in the wrong. Especially after what that boy said."

She shivers dramatically. "I don't know how he was raised, but that sort of language deserved a punishment. Maybe not quite a punch to the nose." She laughs. "Though, time was, I'd have done the same to a boy who talked that way to me. I know it's hard to believe, but I used to be quite the hellion when I was younger."

I don't know what she's talking about, but I give her a confused smile. Clearly something happened to Ella yesterday. She punched a kid in the nose? For saying something mean to her. That doesn't sound like the Ella I know. She's never been violent. Ever. She sometimes gets frustrated. Sometimes she grumbles under her breath when she's frustrated. I've seen her stomp off to her room once when Linc told her it was time for bed and she claimed she wasn't tired. But she's never done anything like hitting someone.

Ella got into trouble at school yesterday and I'm hearing about it from Miss Dottie. Granted, I'm not Ella's mother. I don't have any right to get upset. Right? Except

I thought Linc and I were getting serious. I spend nearly every evening with him and Ella. I've grown close to her over these past few weeks. Why wouldn't he tell me about this last night when I was at his house with them?

I think back over the night before as I work on Miss Dottie's hair and she goes on about the hellion days of her youth. Linc and Ella were already home by the time I made it to their house. Ella seemed unusually quiet, but I attributed it to her being tired after a long day of school. She'd even gone to bed early. But I hadn't really thought anything of it. Linc hadn't acted out of the ordinary. Surely if Ella had punched a kid at school yesterday, he would have been upset or at least mentioned it to me. Maybe Dottie is mistaken? That seems unlikely. The woman is old, but her gossip is always spot-on. Maybe Linc just didn't want to worry me? It's ridiculous of me to feel hurt by this. Right?

By the time Miss Dottie leaves the salon—in better condition than she'd arrived in, this time—I've created a dozen different scenarios in my head for why Linc didn't tell me about Ella fighting at school. I know the smart thing to do would be to just ask him. Call him, tell him what Miss Dottie said and just ask him what happened. Then ask him why he didn't want to tell me. But that might seem like I'm trying to interfere with his parenting of his daughter. That's the last thing I want to do. Linc has done an amazing job raising Ella for all these years without my input. I'm sure he doesn't want or need it now.

So, like the coward I am, I opt to call Piper instead. If the gossip about Ella has made it to Miss Dottie, chances are she's heard about it by now. Thankfully, it's mid-afternoon so the rush should have died down at Piping Hot by now. She picks up after two rings.

"Hey, Harlow. What's up?"

"Oh, nothing. Just finished up with Miss Dottie's hair."

"Oh, no," she says, laughing. "I'm sure there's loads of hot gossip, right?"

I bite my thumbnail, trying to decide how to ask my friend if she heard anything about my boyfriend's daughter without sounding like I don't know what's going on with my boyfriend. Then I roll my eyes at my own ridiculousness. This is Piper. If there's anyone I can count on to be honest with me and not pass judgement, it's her.

"Have you heard anything about Ella punching some kid in the nose at school yesterday?" I ask.

There's a moment of silence before Piper speaks.

"Yeah, I wondered if it had made it to Miss Dottie yet," she says. "24 hours must be some kind of a record."

"What are you talking about?"

"Miss Dottie. That woman must have spies. I don't think she leaves her house except to go to your salon and my shop. I wonder who's feeding her intel."

"Piper!" I snap, pulling her out of her musings. "What happened with Ella?"

"You don't know? Linc didn't tell you?" Piper sounds shocked which makes me think I was right to be hurt by that fact.

"No," I say quietly. "Tell me, Piper."

"Shit," she mutters. "Hold on. Let me get somewhere private."

It takes her a couple of minutes to walk to a place where she can speak freely; my guess is she went to her rarely used office in the back of the coffee shop.

"Okay," she huffs. "What do you know?"

I repeat everything Miss Dottie told me this morning, trying not to leave anything out. When I finish, Piper is quiet.

"Well?" I say. "What am I missing?"

"I can't believe Linc wouldn't tell you," she says. "But I guess I understand why."

"Piper," I say. "Focus. What happened to Ella?"

She sighs. "Shit. I think you should talk to Linc."

"Piper. Damn it. I'm invoking girl code. Tell me right now."

"Fuck. Fine. But promise me you won't freak out about this," she says.

"I promise," I say quickly.

"Why don't I believe that? She mutters.

"I have no idea," I say, sweetly.

Piper sighs. "Ella was being teased by this kid at school yesterday. She kept telling him to leave her alone and he wouldn't. Eventually, she got sick of his shit and punched him in the nose. He started bleeding and crying, and they both ended up in the principal's office."

I feel that same shock I'd felt earlier when Miss Dottie had talked about Ella hitting someone. I can't understand why she would do something like that. And I really don't understand why Linc wouldn't tell me about it.

"That doesn't seem like her," I say.

"I was pretty shocked when Luke told me about it," Piper says.

"Luke told you?" So, Linc spoke to Luke about it, but not me. That makes sense, I guess. Luke is practically family to Linc. They talk about everything.

"Uh, yeah," Piper says. "I guess Linc talked to him yesterday. Sorry."

"Don't be," I say brightly. "Luke's his best friend. Of course, he'd tell him."

"I wonder what would make Ella so upset that she'd hit someone, though," I say, changing the subject.

When Piper is quiet, I press her. "You know, don't you." It's not a question, and she knows it.

She sighs. "I think it might also be why he didn't tell you," she says.

I feel dread wash over me as I wonder what could have been so awful to make a sweet, kind little girl turn to violence. Not to mention, bad enough that Linc wanted to keep it from me.

"Tell me. Please."

"He said some mean things about Ella's hair," Piper says. "And then called her dad's girlfriend a whore."

"What the fuck?" I say, shocked that an 8-year-old would use such language. "Who the hell is this kid?"

"Hillary Mitchell's son," Piper says, a hint of disgust in her tone.

I feel hot anger rise up in me as I remember the way Hillary had tried to weasel her way onto Linc's arm the other night.

"That bitch!" I say. "I guarantee you she said those things about me in front of her son. Which is just gross, by the way. And he just repeated them to Ella. Though I don't know why he would. I can't believe this. Kids don't deserve to be involved in adult drama."

"I agree," Piper says. "Which is why you're going to let this whole thing go, right?"

"Does Hillary not realize that high school is over? No one cares that she was the prom queen 10 years ago."

"She's a petty, jealous bitch," Piper says. "But you're not going to let this bother you, right?"

I know I can't control the actions of someone else's child. But the fact that someone went out of their way to hurt Ella—all because I'm dating her father—makes me feel awful.

"What happened to Ella?" I ask. "With school?"

"She's suspended for the rest of the week and has to write a letter of apology to the kid," Piper says.

"Shit," I say. "She was sticking up for me. And now she's in trouble at school."

"Harlow, wait," Piper says. "This isn't your fault."

I know she's technically right. I know that. But it doesn't stop the guilt I feel.

"Yeah," I say. "I know. Thanks for telling me, Piper. I have a client. Gotta go."

"Wait," she says.

"I'll text you later. Bye."

I end the call take a seat in one of the chairs, pulling my knees up to my chest as I think over everything I just learned. One glaring fact keeps repeating in my mind. Linc didn't tell me.

CHAPTER 30

Harlow

I'm quiet all through dinner, smiling and nodding when necessary but not saying much. When Linc asks me what's wrong, I tell him I'm just tired from my long day at work. He doesn't press for more from me, which is good. I can't tell him how I feel about Ella being bullied because he didn't talk to me about the issue. I obviously don't expect him to include me in issues of parenting his daughter. We've only been together for a month, after all. But she's being teased about our relationship. About Linc being with me. Am I wrong to feel like he should talk to me about it? That we should discuss it with Ella and make sure she's okay, together?

I'm not angry at him. Not really. I'm not exactly hurt either. I'm honestly not sure what I'm feeling right now. That's the hardest part of this whole thing. If anger was the right emotion, I could lash out or pick a fight. I could find some way to express what I'm feeling. But I'm not angry. I'm not hurt. I'm not anything. Except maybe sad.

I just know that for the first time since our first date I don't feel like we're in this together. And I hate the feeling. Even worse, I'm not totally surprised by it. That's the worst part of all of this. I've been telling myself that this thing with Linc is different. It doesn't feel like any other relationship I've had before. I'd started to hope that maybe this was the real thing. That thing I've been telling myself not to hope for. But now I wonder if I've only been imagining it. Maybe I'm the only one feeling this way. And if that's the case, I'm not sure I want to know. Not yet.

So, I keep quiet. And I don't pick a fight or force a conversation. I don't do anything that might push him to tell me he wants to end things. Because I want to keep him just a little longer. When we go to bed, I exaggerate my tiredness, rather than reach for him as I normally do. Instead, I turn my back to him in the bed and pretend to fall asleep. I'm not sure how long I lie there awake, wishing he'd wrap me in his arms and pull me back against his large body to hold me while we sleep. Instead, I listen to his even breathing while I feel my heart crack just a little.

The next morning, I manage to leave just after breakfast without Linc commenting on my odd behavior. I use the excuse of having an early client, but it's a lie. I don't have any clients until the afternoon. I'm stalling. I hate lying to him, even about something so trivial. But I hate the idea of asking him to define what we are even more. I don't want to hear him tell me he doesn't feel what I feel. What do I feel? I shy away from that thought too. Wow. I'm such a coward I can't even admit to myself how I feel about the man.

Rather than focus on the many ways I'm failing as a human, I decide to organize the stock room to keep my mind occupied. I spend an hour staring at bottles of toner and moving them around on the shelves without really accomplishing anything before I finally give up. I drop into one of the chairs in the back with a sigh. It's no use. I can't focus on work when I feel like my personal life is falling apart. It's strange. I've had my personal life fall apart more times than I can count. I've been dumped and cheated on and dumped guys before. But I've never felt this lost and confused about it. I've never been this upset over a man. And Linc and I haven't even broken up; we haven't even had an argument. I drop my head into my hands. What the hell is wrong with me?

The bell rings out front signaling the arrival of a guest. I check the time. It's too early for one of my appointments. Walk-ins are rare in Peach Tree, but not unheard of. Sitting up straight, I suck in a fortifying breath and paste what I hope is welcoming smile on my face before walking out to the front of the salon. When I see who's standing there, my breath snags in my chest and I feel my stomach clench nervously. I recover almost immediately, but I'm not sure it was quick enough to fool Linc.

"Hey," I say, walking toward him. "This is a surprise. Did you come for a trim?"

I try to make my voice sound flirty and light, but I can hear the strain in my words, and I think he can too. He gives me a smile that doesn't quite reach his eyes. Fuck. This is it. This is the conversation I'd tried to avoid.

Linc shakes his head. "I don't need a haircut," he says. "I came to talk to you."

I keep my smile in place, hoping I won't do something foolish like cry or beg him to stop talking before he ruins what we have. He steps closer to me, his expression shifting to one of confusion.

"Is everything okay?" he asks. "You seemed a little off when you left this morning."

I turn and busy myself with folding the small pile of towels I'd washed yesterday. I paste a smile on my face, but I can't meet his gaze.

"Fine," I say. "I was just in a hurry."

"For your early client," he says.

"Exactly." I nod.

"Harlow."

The way he says my name makes me pause in my folding.

"Look at me, please."

I feel my resolve crumble as I turn to look at Linc. "Why does it feel like you're putting distance between us? Things have been weird since yesterday. Will you tell me why? Or tell me I'm crazy. But tell me something."

I feel my throat tighten painfully. *Oh, no. Don't you dare cry right now.* I clear my throat and swallow hard. I can't lie to him. And clearly, I can't hide what I'm feeling behind a fake smile. Linc's too perceptive for that.

"I heard about Ella being bullied at school," I say.

Linc sighs and his shoulders drop. "Where did you hear about that?"

"Does it matter? It wasn't from you." I want to call the words back as soon as they're out. It's not fair of me, and we both know it.

"I'm sorry," I say. "That's not fair."

Linc shakes his head. "Don't be. You're right."

"No, I'm not," I say. "I have no right to ask you to include me on things like that. I'm not her mom. And we're not—"

"Don't." Linc's command is harsh and loud, cutting off whatever I'd been about to say. "Don't finish that sentence," he says. "I want to include you when it comes to Ella. I want to include you when it comes to every part of our lives. I'm sorry I didn't. I just didn't know how to deal with it myself. And since it was about—"

"Me and you?" I finish when he trails off.

He nods. "Yeah. I didn't want you to think our being together was somehow harming Ella. I should have told you. But she asked me not to. So, I kept it from you. And I shouldn't have."

"She asked you not to tell me?" Why? Does Ella not want me in her life?

He nods. "She said she didn't want you to feel bad. She knew you'd be upset and think it was your fault."

I close my eyes on a sigh. "She was trying to protect me?"

He nods. "I argued against it. I didn't want to keep anything from you. She convinced me to let her tell you herself. But then she chickened out. I talked to her again this morning. She's planning to talk to you later today. And if she didn't, I would have."

"Really?"

Sweet Ella was trying to protect me after she'd been bullied. That sounds like something she would do. I feel stupid for being so upset, but I can't help the doubts swirling around in my head. If Linc and I weren't together, Ella wouldn't have been bullied to the point that she just got suspended from school. I hate myself for asking, but I can't help it.

"Do you regret this thing between us?" I ask, asking the question I'm not sure I want the answer to. "Just the thought of someone being mean to Ella because of something I did breaks my heart. I can't imagine how you feel. I understand if you want to end things. It's only been a month, after all." My words come out fast and jumbled, panicky.

"Don't." Linc's voice is a low, harsh whisper. "Don't do that. Don't push me away."

"That's not what I'm doing," I say, picking up another towel. "I just think we need to think things over."

"I don't think we do," Linc says, reaching for me. His hands come up to grip my arms, halting my movements.

"Look at me, Harlow." I can't ignore the low command in his voice. My eyes go to his face, and I take in the determined expression there.

"If you don't want this, don't want me, tell me that. Tell me now, and I'll let you go."

I freeze, knowing I'll never be able to utter those words. Of course, I want him. I've always wanted him. If anything, I want him more than ever now that I know what it's like to be with him. But we're too different. We're in different places in our lives. Linc is a dad, and his focus needs to be on Ella. After what happened yesterday, I can see how much being with me has distracted him from that. I won't be the reason that little girl comes home crying from school. But I can't make myself say the words that will end this. Not yet. I'm too much of a coward for that.

"But if you're pushing me away because you think I'm going to leave or cheat on you or let you down, so you want to end it before that happens, don't. And don't try to hide behind Ella. She doesn't deserve that, and neither do I."

I open my mouth to argue. That's not what I'm doing. I'd never blame a child for adult problems.

Linc's fingers tighten slightly on my upper arms. "I can't tell you what the future holds, but I know I've never felt this way for anyone else. Never. I think you feel it too. And that's worth holding onto. That's worth fighting for. So, stay with me. Please."

Panic blooms inside me at his words. He's right, I know. I've never felt anything like this for another person. And it terrifies me. I've only ever seen relationships fail. I've only ever known the ones that don't work out. And none of them have ever broken me. But this? Loving Linc and then losing him? That would break me. My eyes prick with unshed tears and my vision blurs.

"Linc," I manage in a choked whisper.

"Answer one question, Harlow," he says, his voice somehow soothing me. "Answer it and then I'll go."

"What?" I ask, unable to stop the question from spilling out.

"Will you be happier if we go back to just being friends? If we end this and you and I go back to what we were before that first kiss, will you be happier than you were the other night, slow dancing with me in the kitchen after Ella went to bed?"

My brain automatically conjures the memory of his arms around me as we swayed slowly to Otis Redding that night. I've never felt such peace. I've never felt so at home as I did in his arms in that kitchen.

"If the answer is yes," Linc says, "I'll leave, and we can go back to the way things were."

The idea is so abhorrent that I want to immediately protest. I want to throw myself at him and beg him to forget that the last ten minutes ever happened. But I can't seem to say anything. I'm afraid that whatever I say will be the thing that ruins everything. So, I stand there frozen while Linc talks.

"You want to know what I thought while we were dancing? I thought, 'Wow. So, this is what Luke was talking about.'" My brows lower in confusion, but Linc just smiles.

"I asked him once how he knew that Piper was the one for him and that he loved her. How, with all the women in the world, could he be certain that she was it for him? He told me, 'I just knew.'" He looks at me, his eyes filled with something I don't recognize.

"And he was right," he says. "So, I'm going to go now. I'm going to give you time and space to decide what you really want. But just for now. I need you to know that I'm not giving up on you. On us. I'm not one of those other guys. I can see how amazing you are, and if you let me, I'll spend every day from now until forever showing you how amazing we are together."

Linc bends down and plants a gentle kiss on my forehead. I close my eyes as tears escape and fall down my cheeks. I stand there unmoving long after I hear the door open and close behind him. Even without that sound and without opening my eyes, I can tell he's gone.

The room feels colder and darker without Linc here to brighten it.

I stand there for several long seconds, thinking about everything he just said. I try to piece everything together, to make sense of it. But my mind keeps going back to one thing. Love. Did he say love? Does Linc love me? My heart pounds in my chest when I dare to let myself consider the idea of Linc loving me. *From now until forever.* That's what he said. Forever. With Linc by my side. With Ella. A future with someone who loves me and won't let me down. Do I really think I'm capable of that? I shy away from the answer to that question and consider the one he asked me.

Will I be happy if we go back to just being friends? I want to laugh at the absurdity of the thought. Of course, I won't be happy going back to being friends with Linc. I don't even know if that's possible after these past few weeks. The idea of going back to awkward greetings and stilted conversations after everything we've shared is ridiculous. But that's not what he'd asked me. He didn't ask if it's possible; he asked if it would make me happy. And I hadn't given him an answer. Like an idiot, I'd just stood there and let him walk out.

What the fuck is wrong with me?

CHAPTER 31

Linc

Walking away from Harlow is one of the hardest things I've ever done. I felt like I was leaving a piece of myself behind as soon as the door closed behind me. By the time I reach my truck, I feel like I might be sick. But I don't know what else to do. I might be head over heels in love with her, but she isn't there yet. I ignore the little voice in my head telling me that she may never get there. I refuse to consider that.

She just needs time to realize that we belong together. I thought I'd done enough to show her that she can trust me; that I'll be here for her, no matter what. But after today, I can see that it's not something that has a determined finish line. It's something I'll have to keep showing her, over and over again. For as long as it takes for her to realize I'm not going anywhere. I'm never going to give up on her. Or us.

So, I'd told her just that. And then, like an idiot, I left. What if she really does end it? I feel a pang in my chest at the thought before I push it away. I can't afford to think that way. I need to have some optimism. She just needs time to think things through. I know she cares for me. I can feel it each time she kisses me. I can see it in the way she looks at me. I just need to be patient. I can do that. I can wait as long as it takes for her to see that we belong together. I blow out a breath and tighten my grip on the steering wheel.

I need to put the truck in gear and drive, but I can't force myself to put more distance between us. Besides, I don't know where to go. I should go to work, but I know I won't be able to focus on the job. And that could put someone in danger. I could go home, but everything there reminds me of Harlow. Plus, with it being empty it will just depress me. I could go to Peach Fuzz. But Cole is there, and he'll ask questions I'm not ready to answer. I could go see Luke, but chances are he's with Piper. Like I need the reminder of what a happy, committed couple looks like when I might have just blown my last chance to be happy with the woman of my dreams. I mutter a curse and reach for the gear shifter, but a knock at my window has me jumping in my seat.

Heart pounding, I turn to see who's there. My heart stutters before racing into overdrive. Harlow is standing there, tears trailing down her cheeks. The sight of her crying is like a punch in the gut. She never cries. Unbuckling my seatbelt, I push open the door and climb out. Before I can say anything, Harlow is in my arms, her face buried in my chest. I wrap my arms around her and just hold her.

"Don't go." Her choked voice is like a knife in my chest.

"Oh, baby," I whisper. "I'm here. I'm not going anywhere."

"I'm sorry."

I shake my head. "Shh. Don't. You have nothing to be sorry for."

She sniffs loudly. "I'm an idiot."

I laugh. "It took me 20 years to figure out I'm in love with you," I say. "So, who's the real idiot?"

Harlow tips her face up to look at me, her blue eyes shining with tears and wonder. "You mean that?"

"That I'm an idiot?" I nod. "Absolutely."

She laughs, rolling her eyes. "Not that part. The other thing."

Smiling down at her, I wipe a tear from her cheek. "That I'm in love with you?"

She nods, more tears rolling down her cheeks.

"Yeah," I say. "I'm so in love with you. Madly, ridiculously, hopelessly in love with you, Harlow St. James. And I'm sorry it took me so long to figure it out."

Tears are streaming down her cheeks now.

"Don't cry, baby," I say. "Please. We don't have to figure anything out right now. It's enough for me just to be together."

She shakes her head, and a watery laugh escapes her. "They're not sad tears," she says.

I go still, eyeing her. "What kind of tears are they?"

She laughs again and sniffs loudly. "The happy ones. The kind you cry when you realize you have everything you ever wanted. When you realize the person you're in love with loves you back. That kind."

I swear, my heart stops. Just for a second before it pounds so hard in my chest that I'm surprised she doesn't hear it too. Harlow smiles up at me with damp eyes full of love and hope.

"I love you, Linc," she whispers.

She pulls me down for a kiss and I can't help but feel that I'm right where I'm supposed to be, right here, with her in my arms. Reaching down, I wrap my arms around her and lift her up. Harlow doesn't resist; she just wraps her legs around my waist, her mouth never leaving mine. Turning, I press her against the side of the truck and lose myself in the kiss. I feel myself growing hard against the soft press of her body, a fog of lust clouding my mind.

The loud honk of a car horn rips me out of my haze of longing. I pull my lips from Harlow's and turn to see a familiar vehicle has pulled up beside my truck. I hadn't even heard the car's engine; I'd been so caught up in kissing Harlow. Cole is behind the wheel, a bemused grin on his face. He leans toward the open window.

"Do you two want to get arrested for indecent exposure? Get a room!"

Harlow's body shakes with laughter against me, reminding me that I still have her pinned between my body and the truck. She does an admirable job of acting casual as I lower her until her feet touch the ground.

"Sorry about that," I say, smiling at my brother. "But she loves me."

Harlow points at me. "And he loves me." Her eyes are dry, and she's wiping away the last of her tears. Her smile is wide and bright as she looks up at me.

"No shit," Cole says. "Everyone already knew that. Took you two idiots long enough to figure it out."

I shoot him a glare. "Go away."

He just laughs. "I'm happy for you two," he says.

I pull Harlow closer to my side, unwilling to let her go now that I know she loves me. "Thanks. Now, leave."

He laughs again. "I'm going. But I was serious about indecent exposure. They'll arrest you for it in this town. Don't ask how I know."

He raises the window and drives away, leaving me standing there with the woman I love. Harlow turns and gives me a questioning look.

"I don't think we want to know," I say.

"You're probably right," she says. "Let's take his advice and get a room."

"Yeah?" I grin down at her.

She nods, gripping the front of my shirt and tugging me with her as she walks backward. "I know just the place."

"Is it close by?"

"Mmhmm." She nods as I follow her back toward her salon. "I've got two hours before my next appointment. Maybe we can find something to do?"

CHAPTER 32

Harlow

We're tearing at one another's clothes before we make it halfway up the stairs. I need Linc like I need air. I keep thinking about how I almost pushed him away. If he weren't so sure in his feelings for me, I might have been successful.

"I'm sorry," I say between kisses. "I wasn't thinking clearly." Kiss. "I should have just talked to you."

"No, I'm sorry," Linc says, yanking my shirt up over my head. "I should have told you sooner."

I reach for his belt, tugging at the leather. "It doesn't matter now."

He tangles his fingers in my hair, holding me still so he can look in my eyes. "Harlow, I love you. Whatever happens, we'll face it together."

I nod. "Together."

His mouth comes down to cover mine and I stop thinking altogether. I finally manage to get the belt undone and his pants unzipped. I shove them down past his hips, pushing his boxers down with them. Linc has managed to get my bra off and his hand is down the front of my leggings, sliding against my wetness, seeking my clit. As soon as his cock is free, I reach for it, stroking him firmly the way I know he likes. Linc lets out a little hiss at the sensation of my hand gripping him.

I push him forward until he has no choice but to fall back to sit on the couch behind him. I shove my leggings down and off until I'm standing before him completely bare. Linc looks me over and smiles, giving his hard length a stroke as he does.

"I'll never get over how gorgeous you are," he says.

I move forward to straddle his hips, my hands on his shoulders. He grips my hips with both hands, giving me a gentle squeeze.

"And all mine," he rasps.

"Yours," I whisper.

He leans forward and kisses me deeply before pulling away to look me in the eyes.

"Climb up here and ride my cock until we both come," he says in that commanding voice that never fails to drive me crazy.

"Yes, sir," I say.

Never taking my eyes off him, I raise my hips up until I feel him pressing against my center, hard and thick and insistent. Linc grips the base of his shaft while I lower myself onto him, sinking down until he's completely buried. I let out a little sigh at the feeling of fullness. Linc brings one hand up to my breast to tease my nipple as I start to move, rocking back and forth slowly at first, grinding against him.

"That's it, baby," he says. "Take what you want."

I love the way he talks to me when we're together like this. The tone of his voice changes to something only I ever get to hear. I've never had another man tell me how amazing I am the way he does. I've always held back some part of myself in the bedroom. I've never felt truly comfortable enough to let go and be myself. But with Linc, I can. I can show him all the parts of me I've always kept hidden and know that he's going to cherish them. Because he loves who I am rather than just who I can be for him.

Sliding my hands up to his neck, I pull him toward me for a kiss as I continue to rock harder against him. My fingers fumble in his hair until I can pull it free from the ponytail and let it fall loosely around his shoulders. I can tell he's holding back, letting me set the pace. I love him for that, but right now I want him to let go. To lose control and take me hard and fast. I need all of him.

"I need more," I whisper. "Please."

Linc doesn't hesitate. He wraps his arms around me and surges to his feet while still buried deep inside me. Turning, he lowers me back onto the couch so he's above me. When he thrusts into me this time, it's an entirely different angle that wrenches a cry of pleasure from me. Linc's hands go to my waist, holding me still as he thrusts into me again and again. I can already feel my orgasm building, like a dam threatening to burst. Linc knows my body so well. He knows what drives me wild and he uses that knowledge now. His hands move down to my legs, pushing them up toward my chest, deepening the angle even more. My eyes fall closed and I give myself over to sensation as the first faint flutters of my orgasm begin.

"Oh, god! Yes!"

"That's it, baby. Tell me. Are you going to come on my cock?"

I nod, unable to speak.

"Say it," Linc demands, still pounding into me so hard our bodies make wet, slapping sounds with every thrust.

"I'm coming," I manage as I feel myself begin to unravel.

My pussy spasms around his length as he keeps up the punishing pace. It's fast and rough and dirty, but it's exactly what I need. Linc always seems to know exactly what I need. I open my eyes to look at him and see that his dark gaze is on my face, watching me intently.

"I love to watch you come," he says, his pace slowing just a fraction.

"I love you," I gasp.

Linc's expression shifts from one of dark hunger to adoration in an instant. He releases my legs and bends forward to take my mouth in a deep kiss. He's still inside me and still rock-hard, but his movements have slowed dramatically. I wrap my legs around him, holding him against me as I kiss him back. When the kiss ends, Linc brings his hand up to cup my cheek.

"I love you so much," he says, making my heart do a complicated flip inside my chest.

Linc presses his forehead to mine as his large body moves over me, pushing his cock deeper into me. I wrap my arms around him and cross my feet behind his back. He moves slowly, filling me completely before easing out, only to repeat the action. It's a slow, sensual torture. Even now, I can feel another orgasm building inside me.

Something about the slow, powerful motions of Linc's large body between my legs drive me crazy.

"One more," he says. "Give me one more, baby."

Reaching down between us, Linc brushes his fingers over my clit the way he knows will get me off fast. His hand, combined with the deep, rhythmic thrusting of his cock inside me are enough to send me flying. I cry out as the first wave of euphoria hits me, gripping his arm tightly.

"Come with me," I whisper through my haze of pleasure.

I don't even know if he's close to coming. All I know is that I want Linc to feel at least a fraction of the ecstasy I'm feeling right now. I want us to experience it together. Linc sucks in a breath at my words and begins to move slightly faster. My pussy clenches over and over around his hard length as my orgasm goes on. I grip his arms, my fingers digging in as I gasp with each thrust.

"Yes! Yes, baby! Oh, god!" I cry.

Linc shudders above me and lets out a guttural groan. "Fuck," he grunts.

He thrusts deep into me and goes still as I feel him empty his warm release inside me. The lingering aftershocks of my own orgasm squeeze him as he pulses inside me.

"I love you," Linc says, reaching up to brush my hair off my face.

I give him a brilliant smile, still in slight disbelief that this is real.

"I love you," I whisper, pulling him down for a kiss.

CHAPTER 33

One Month Later...

Harlow

"I'm moving out," Cole announces as I'm pouring coffee into my mug.

Linc and I both freeze, turning to stare at Cole who's casually spreading butter on his toast.

Linc's brows lower and he wipes his mouth with his napkin before speaking. "What? Why?"

Cole shrugs. "It's time."

"Why now?" Linc asks. "Is this because of a woman? Are you seeing someone?"

For the first time since Linc and I started dating, I feel awkward in his house. I haven't technically moved in, but I'm here most nights. I help Ella with her hair in the mornings before school and I cook dinner with Linc almost every evening.

The last month has been amazing. I finally feel like I'm where I belong. Here, with Linc and Ella and even Cole.

I feel like I'm part of a family for the first time in my life, and I've never been happier. But now Cole says he's moving out. It's coming from out of nowhere. It's clear that Linc is just as shocked as I am about this. I can't help but wonder if it's because of me. Is my presence here making him feel like he needs to leave? I can't have that.

Cole rolls his eyes at Linc's question, but he's not looking at his brother as he answers. "No. There's no woman. But if I'm ever going to find one and settle down, I can't very well bring her back to my brother's house, can I? It's time for me to grow up a little."

"You own a successful business," Linc argues. "You're the world's best uncle. You're not exactly a kid these days. Having your own house doesn't change that."

"I know. But you and Harlow and Ella need time on your own to be a family. It's not like I'm leaving the country. I'm just looking for my own place in town."

"Is this because of me?" I ask. "Am I invading your space? I can—"

"No, Harlow," Cole interrupts, holding up a hand to stop me. "I'm happy you're here. You make my brother and my niece happy. And since they're two of my favorite people, that means you're number three on the list now. Please don't think this is about you. I've been thinking about this for the last six months or so. Before you two ever got together. I just think I need a change."

I nod, feeling somewhat comforted by the fact that I'm not chasing Linc's brother out of his house. Still, I can't help but feel like he wouldn't be doing this if it weren't for me being here.

"I have another idea," Linc says, suddenly. "Wait here."

He gets up and walks out of the room, leaving me and Cole sitting there in awkward silence. Luckily, he's only gone for a few seconds before returning with a large brown envelope in his hands.

"Don't move out," he says, looking at Cole. "You can stay here, and we'll move out."

Cole's face is a mask of confusion and I know mine matches his.

"What?" Cole asks.

"Technically I don't actually live here," I say. "I still have my apartment above the shop."

"Yeah, right," Cole laughs. "You're here more than you are there."

I open my mouth to object, but I know I don't really have an argument. Cole's right. I can't remember the last time I slept at my own place. Maybe 2 weeks ago? I do know that I was miserable and slept like shit the whole night, wishing Linc was there. The next morning, he'd texted me to tell me that he couldn't sleep without me in his bed and could I please never make him do it again. So far, I haven't made him. I look up to find Linc watching me, a serious expression on his face.

"I was waiting for the right time to bring this up," he says as he pulls a stack of papers out of the envelope in his hand. "I was hoping to make it more of a romantic thing."

He slides the stack of papers across the table toward me.

Cole makes a choking sound. "Bro, I'm not sure you know what romance is, if you think paperwork is going to cut it."

"Read it," Linc says, not taking his eyes off mine. His serious expression has my heart pounding in my chest. Whatever this paperwork means, it's clearly important to Linc.

I finally drag my gaze from his and down to the thick stack of papers in my hand. It takes my brain a full minute to comprehend.

"A house? You bought a house?"

"I bought *us* a house," Linc says softly. "I want you to come live in it with me and Ella. I want us to be a family."

I bring my hand up to cover my mouth as my eyes fill with tears, making it difficult for me to make out the words on the paper. But one thing stands out to me. The address of the house. I blink rapidly, trying to clear my eyes and look up at Linc.

"You bought my mom's house?" I whisper.

He nods. "I know how much it means to you. I know what losing her cost you. Not just her, but the house you grew up in. I've seen your face light up whenever we drive past it. It's the perfect house to raise a family in. You deserve to have it back."

I'm frozen in shock, wondering how I got so lucky that this man is mine. I don't have the words to tell him, so I just sit there staring at him in awe. I barely notice when Cole quietly sneaks out of the room, leaving us alone. Linc takes the papers from me and wraps my hands in both of his.

"Harlow, I love you. I hate that we wasted so many years not being together. I don't want to waste another second without you. So, I'm going to do what I should have been doing for all these years. I'm going to tell you exactly how I feel and what I want. And I'm going to hope you want it too."

I sniff loudly and nod, but I still can't speak.

"I want to wake up next to you every morning. I want to fall asleep with you in my arms every night. I want bed head and morning breath and dancing in the kitchen after Ella goes to sleep. I want all the good and the bad and everything in between. I want to build a life with you. I want you to be my last first kiss ever. Because you're it for me. So, let me be clear. I'm in love with you. Now, 10 years from now, 50 years from now. That's not changing. So, what do you say?"

I nod, a laugh escaping through my happy tears. "I say, yes."

"Yeah?" Linc asks, his face lighting up in a smile.

I nod again. "Yeah. I love you so much."

I wrap my arms around his neck and pull him to me for a kiss. As our lips meet, I'm hit by an overwhelming sense of rightness that settles over me like a warm blanket. This is where I belong. In Linc's arms. Now. Tomorrow. Forever. When the kiss ends, Linc rests his forehead against mine and we both go still, enjoying the moment.

"Geez, for a second there I thought you were going to propose." Cole says from the kitchen entryway, startling a laugh out of me.

"When I propose, it won't be at breakfast with my brother in the other room," Linc says. "Give me some credit, here."

My eyes shoot to his, wide with shock.

"When?" I squeak. "You said when, not if."

He nods as he tucks a piece of my hair behind my ear. "Does that scare you?"

I consider the question for less than a second before shaking my head. I feel a laugh bubbling up inside me. The idea of Linc proposing to me doesn't scare me in the least. It fills me with excitement and hope. I put my hand on his chest, right over his heart. I look into his hazel eyes, so full of love and happiness and I feel my own heart squeeze in my chest. How did I get so lucky?

"I'm not scared. I can't wait."

His smile spreads slowly as he lowers his lips to mine.

"Is this going to be a thing?" Cole asks, but I barely hear him. "You two making out at breakfast, I mean."

When we don't respond, Cole keeps talking.

"Because I could do with less of that. Just saying."

"It's a good thing Ella isn't here. This might scar her for life. Hell, I feel scarred."

"When are you guys moving out again?"

"Seriously? With the kissing?"

"You know people eat in this kitchen, right?"

"I'm just going to take my coffee to go, then."

Linc breaks the kiss, smiling at me. "Bye, Cole."

"Bye, Cole," I mimic, pulling Linc back down for another kiss.

I barely hear the door closing as Cole leaves. I'm too caught up in kissing the man I love.

End of Book Two

A WORD FROM ISLA

So, I tend to plan my books and plot them out before I write them. At least, I make a loose plot and I try to stick to it as closely as possible. Which is why this book caught me by surprise. I didn't know Linc was going to have a dominant side until I wrote it. I swear, it just came out. But damn, am I glad it did. I think I say this every time I write a new book, but he might be my favorite book boyfriend. (Of the ones I've written, anyway. I'm looking at you, JP Cane.)

I questioned some of the scenes, wondering if they felt believable for a small-town single dad. But then I thought more about it and realized that no one is any one thing. And it's wrong to think that a small-town, single dad might not enjoy a few dominant tendencies in the bedroom. Or some dirty talk. Or some edging. Whatever.

This book wasn't written as a how-to. It was written from the standpoint of a man who knows what he likes but hasn't been able to explore those desires with a partner until he connects with the girl that's been in front of him all along. They're both beginners to the world of BDSM. Which means they're learning together. I'd like to think they continue that sexual exploration together as the years pass. At least, those are the scenarios I dream up in my head...

The book's title was inspired by a song lyric, which is where I got the inspiration for Linc's speech when he says he wants Harlow to be his last first kiss. Harlow has been through a lot and has trouble trusting people to stick around. I relate a lot to that, which seems to be a running theme for my books. Her learning to trust him and to trust her own emotions is honestly the major conflict of the book. I felt that was more real than a miscommunication or some silly misunderstanding that might pull these two apart. In life, it's mostly our own insecurities and issues that keep us from believing we deserve happiness. Yeah, sometimes therapy looks a lot like a paperback book. Moving on.

I truly hope you all enjoyed reading this one and will stick around for Cole's story. He's a romantic at heart who's deep-down tired of being a player. It's not until the girl he secretly wants decides to enter the dating world that he realizes it's time to get his shit together. Hilarity will ensue. And there's a wedding. If you miss the King family, you'll want to read this one.

Made in the USA
Middletown, DE
30 September 2023

39421259R00201